D0396647

FRANK L. COLE

SHADOW
MOUNTAIN

For Michael—My brother and my hero.

© 2020 Frank L. Cole

Illustrations © 2020 Owen Richardson

All rights reserved. No part of this book may be reproduced in any form or by any means without permission in writing from the publisher, Shadow Mountain®, at permissions@shadowmountain.com. The views expressed herein are the responsibility of the author and do not necessarily represent the position of Shadow Mountain.

All characters in this book are fictitious, and any resemblance to actual persons, living or dead, is purely coincidental.

Visit us at shadowmountain.com

Library of Congress Cataloging-in-Publication Data

Names: Cole, Frank, 1977– author. | Cole, Frank, 1977–. Potion masters ; bk. 3.
Title: The seeking serum / Frank L. Cole.
Description: Salt Lake City, Utah : Shadow Mountain, [2020] | Series: Potion masters ; book 3 | As the fight intensifies between B.R.E.W and the Scourges, it falls to Gordy and his friends to unite the potion-making community and stop Mezzarix from plunging the world back into the Dark Ages.
Identifiers: LCCN 2019019683 | ISBN 9781629726069 (hardbound : alk. paper)
Subjects: | CYAC: Friendship—Fiction. | Magic—Fiction. | Magicians—Fiction. | Good and evil—Fiction. | Monsters—Fiction | LCGFT: Fantasy fiction. | Novels.
Classification: LCC PZ7.C673435 Se 2020 | DDC [Fic]—dc23
LC record available at https://lccn.loc.gov/2019019683

Printed in the United States of America
Lake Book Manufacturing, Inc., Melrose Park, IL

10 9 8 7 6 5 4 3 2 1

1

Rain pelted Gordy Stitser's umbrella as he dashed through the backyard toward the garden. Leaping over enormous, pulsating pumpkins, he barely avoided a nasty collision with one of Tobias McFarland's booby-trapped plants hiding beneath a patch of otherwise unassuming dirt. The forested land beyond the backyard was littered with McSwooshers, Boomclobbers, and, Tobias's personal favorites, Spikey McOuchies. The Irishman had drawn a map pinpointing their locations, but he couldn't remember where he had planted all of them, which made venturing too far from the house a risk. One false step might lead to a disastrous accident.

As Gordy knelt down, trying to spot any other hazards lurking in the shadows, something much larger than a common raindrop splatted against the taut fabric of his umbrella. He chanced a quick glance at the flock of seagulls circling overhead. Tobias's place was nuts! If the plants weren't threatening to tear off your limbs from below, the birds were dive-bombing you from above. And for what reason? Something about specialized fertilizer, but Gordy wasn't entirely certain.

After a few close calls with other suspicious vegetables along the path, Gordy arrived at the garden shed. Stepping under the awning, he retracted his umbrella and rapped softly on the metal door. Less than a minute later, Bolter's face appeared from inside the dimly lit building.

"You're late!" Bolter whispered, peering over Gordy's shoulder before ushering him into the room. "Thought you weren't coming." His button-down shirt had scorch marks along the hem, and he was wearing skinny jeans. But all jeans were skinny jeans when Bolter wore them.

"My mom is still awake," Gordy replied, wiping his boots on the bristly doormat and dropping his umbrella in the corner.

Bolter straightened to his full height, six and a half feet, though it was hard to tell. The man had horrible posture. "Well, then you must go back at once!" Bolter started for the door, but Gordy grabbed his elbow.

"It's okay. She won't find out," Gordy said. "She's on the phone with my dad, and she's pretty upset. I doubt she'll come out of her room until morning."

Bolter relaxed, his shoulders slumping once more, and he gave Gordy a sympathetic look. "Then I trust their journey went without a hitch?"

Gordy nodded. "Landed about three hours ago."

Tobias's farmhouse was no longer safe for any Stitser

unable to brew a potion, so right after breakfast that morning, Wanda Stitser, Gordy's mom and a celebrated Elixirist, fourth class, had Blotched her husband and the twins using a Tainted tube of toothpaste and then planted a jar of Haitian Konfizyon Cream in Mr. Stitser's suitcase. Then she had driven them to the airport, where the three confounded Stitsers boarded a plane believing they were going on an international vacation, when in reality, members of the Stained Squad had escorted Gordy's family to an undisclosed location where they would be kept safe for as long as needed.

Gordy had no idea when he would see his family again, but as long as his grandfather, Mezzarix Rook, was on the loose, it wouldn't be anytime soon.

Gordy's mom had been an emotional mess since the moment they had left. Blotching a family member was never easy and mostly frowned upon by the potion community, but by the tone of Mr. Stitser's voice on the phone earlier, it sounded as though he was in good spirits. Konfizyon Cream had a way of doing that.

"Have you finished it yet?" Gordy asked Bolter, glancing around.

Bolter had been at Tobias's for less than a week, but he'd already managed to transform the neatly kept garden shed into his personal workstation. Car parts were scattered everywhere. Several cardboard boxes floated lazily, like abandoned canoes, in an ankle-deep puddle of oil gathered in one corner of the room.

"I have!" Bolter exclaimed, clicking his heels together. "An hour ago. Though it was more difficult than I had originally anticipated." He directed Gordy to a table littered with a hundred automotive owners' manuals and a small Tupperware container.

Removing the lid from the container, Bolter withdrew a copper bracelet approximately two inches thick and wide enough to slip over Gordy's hand, fitting comfortably around his wrist. Four holes had been punched into the metal.

"Each of the notches is equipped with a launching mechanism," Bolter said, handing Gordy a magnifying glass.

Squinting, Gordy could see miniature cogs and springs inside the dime-sized holes, as well as a tiny hammer held in place by a lever.

"It's so small," Gordy said, marveling at the intricate contraption.

Bolter squealed. "I know! And it actually works!"

"Will it hold them in place?" Gordy glanced up from the magnifying glass.

"Let's find out," Bolter said. "I'm assuming you brought them."

Gordy opened his satchel and removed a jar of several colorful glass orbs, each one no bigger than a marble. Gordy handed a green one to Bolter, who carefully inserted it into one of the notches on the bracelet, locking the orb into place with a click.

"When pressed firmly, each notch acts as a trigger and releases the potion through a chamber at a rate of fifteen-hundred feet per second." Bolter slapped the table with one of his fingerless hands. "That's faster than a round fired from a .44 Magnum revolver!"

That *was* fast. "And the potion?" Gordy asked. "Where does it come out?"

"The liquid discharges from a pinprick hole along the edge," Bolter explained. "I've tested it multiple times with blueberry juice."

"Why blueberry juice?"

"Why not?" Bolter shrugged. "Anyhow, the trigger worked flawlessly. Though my aim is horrible. I made quite a mess, as you can see."

Gordy snickered, unsure of how he would be able to spot a specific mess in Bolter's disaster of a room.

Bolter pointed to a paper target pinned to an easel across the room. Splotches of blue syrup dripped from the wall behind the otherwise spotless target.

"I haven't figured out a way for the bracelet to automatically reload the trigger once a potion has been fired. That will be the next phase," Bolter said, gazing at the bracelet with pride. "For now, you'll have to bring the potions to me once you've emptied a full four rounds of ammo, and I'll manually reload them for you."

Gordy aimed the contraption on his wrist toward the target across the room and pressed his finger down on the orb fitted within the notch. There was a crinkling of broken glass, and a potion cylinder equal in diameter to pencil lead, fired from the opening. A splash of green struck the bull's-eye and instantly transformed into a web of writhing vines that wrapped around the target, snapping the wooden easel in two.

"How . . . how on earth?" Bolter stammered, his mouth dropping open. "That was a fully formed Vintreet Trap! As large as one from a regular-sized bottle."

Gordy laughed in surprise, holding up another color-ful orb containing bright-pink liquid. "I discovered how to distill potions into these containers. It takes longer than a normal batch and uses dehydrated ingredients and some fairly unique heating methods, but it yields the same re-sults."

Bolter screwed up his face incredulously. "Was there a manual on the process?"

"I don't think so, at least I didn't read any. It was the only way to make a potion that would work with the bracelet, so I started testing. And that's not real glass ei-ther." Gordy's voice grew excited. "It's candied sugar and emulsified corn syrup. I call it Ghost Glass. It doesn't in-terfere with the actual ingredients, and it breaks easily with a little pressure." He had already started transferring some of his potions into vials of Ghost Glass, figuring the odds were high that he'd find himself under attack by another army of Scourges at some point. Smaller containers meant he could carry quite the arsenal of weapons.

"So, is all that"—Gordy gestured to the grease and oil

stains dotting Bolter's face and clothes—"from working on the bracelet?"

Bolter flushed. "Of course not! I always have multiple irons in the fire. I'm nearly finished with another top-secret project. I hope I can complete it before I leave."

Gordy frowned. "You're still planning on going?"

Bolter nodded. "Early tomorrow morning. Before sunrise."

"Are you sure that's a good idea?"

Last week, Bolter had received a message from one of his associates in Michigan who needed help with a special assignment, which meant that it would definitely be centered around cars, trucks, or other automotive equipment.

"I do," Bolter said. "We all have to play our part, and while there will be plenty of Elixirists ready to charge into battle and face the danger head-on, I can help in other ways. Besides, I need my own workshop. This place is fine, I suppose, but I miss my things." He looked disdainfully around the messy room as if to imply he wasn't the one responsible for its current state of disarray. Rainwater trickled through the ceiling, dampening stacks of papers covered with Bolter's scribbled ingredient lists. "And I'm not on B.R.E.W.'s most-wanted list—not yet, at least—and I'd like to keep it that way."

Gordy suspected he was only telling part of the truth. Ever since Zelda Morphata had betrayed B.R.E.W. and joined forces with Mezzarix, Bolter had acted differently.

Her treachery had been a surprise, and the blow seemed to hit Bolter the hardest.

"You still haven't told my mom yet, have you?" Gordy asked.

Bolter gnawed on his lip. "No, but I intend to leave her a note."

Gordy scoffed. He couldn't wait to see his mom's reaction when she read that message.

"Don't worry about me." One of Bolter's eyebrows lifted. "I will be checking in with you as soon as I can. And I shall be leaving you a going-away gift."

"What is it?" Gordy asked cautiously. Many of Bolter's surprises were often worth avoiding.

"I can't tell you!" Bolter laughed. "That will spoil all the fun. Now, you'd better be off before someone notices you're gone."

On the eastern side of a mountain overlooking the grand expanse of a pale-blue ocean, Mezzarix Rook stood staring into the depths of an enormous hole. With craggy edges, crumbling rock footholds, and foul-smelling air rising from below, the hole looked far too treacherous for someone of Mezzarix's age and condition to be near. But he had no intention of climbing down.

He heard the distinct sound of metal hooks on stone growing louder as someone ascended. Soon, a white-haired head appeared, followed by the rest of an elderly man. All kinked elbows and knobby knees, the old creature wheezed and hacked before succeeding in hoisting his body from the depths.

"Here, Gabriel, let me help you." Mezzarix offered his hand. He nodded to Ravian McFarland, his companion, who for the greater part of the last hour, had been lying down with his legs draped over the ledge, whistling an annoying tune.

"He's back already?" Ravian inquired, frowning. His Irish brogue was thick with boredom. "That was at least a two-thousand-foot descent and then back up again. Should have taken him most of the afternoon."

"Stop questioning it and bring this poor soul something to drink." Mezzarix snapped his fingers, and Ravian produced a water bottle from a red cooler basking in the shade.

Plastic crinkled as Ravian opened the lid and passed the bottle to Gabriel. Sweat ran down Gabriel's face, drenching the collar of his tunic as he drank, slurping down the contents in one breath.

"How are you holding up?" Mezzarix asked, studying Gabriel with mild concern. He looked to be about eighty, but that was just a guess. In truth, Mezzarix had no idea how old the man was, or any of the Atramenti, for that matter. Age passed differently on the island, and Gabriel had been one of the first, or so Mezzarix had been led to believe.

Gabriel grimaced, pressing a hand to the small of his back, which popped in protest. "I am quite all right. Just exhausted, that is all," he replied in dulcet tones. "I am not as spry as I once was, but I am in excellent health, I believe."

"That was quite a climb." Mezzarix peered into the hole, knowing full well Gabriel's spine was crooked. The pain had to be immense, but he masked it expertly.

"It is nearly impossible to see down there, and the

keystones do not work as well in the depths of the moun-tain. I must feel around with my hands. And as I have said before, I have not made that climb in several years. But . . ." He withdrew a tiny vial of midnight-blue liquid from beneath his tunic. "I did manage to find a bit more." Lips quivering in a proud smile, he showed Mezzarix his prize.

Mezzarix snatched the bottle and held it up to exam-ine the inky syrup in the waning afternoon sunlight. The liquid, speckled with dirt and fine bits of rock, didn't look like much, but it was all that mattered at the moment.

"Is this it, then?" Mezzarix asked. "The last of it?"

"I am afraid so," Gabriel answered, his smile dissolv-ing. "It is not like a fountain you might see on the main-land. More like several springs buried beneath the rock. In some places, you have to dig deep and without tools—"

"This is fine." Mezzarix nodded. "Your people have brought me plenty."

"But will it be enough?" Ravian asked.

"Shall I go back?" Gabriel turned toward the crevice. "Perhaps I returned too hastily."

Mezzarix stroked the grizzled edge of his beard with his thumb and forefinger. How long could this old man possibly hold up? "That won't be necessary."

"Please, Master Rook, I have failed you." Gabriel stooped near the hole, searching for adequate footing, his sandals scrabbling on the loose rock.

"Stop," Mezzarix commanded, his voice a few notches above a whisper.

Dropping his hands to his sides, the old man obeyed the order at once.

"I am satisfied, and I want you to take the rest of the evening off." Mezzarix kept his focus on the vial, but his eyes flickered to Gabriel's hunched back, and he felt a twinge of regret.

It wasn't as though Blotching made Gabriel younger or stronger. The controlling effects of the potion could make a person do things that normally seemed physically impossible, as Gabriel and the other members of the Atramenti had proven, but in truth, everything they accomplished was within the natural capabilities of their bodies. The Blotching just removed their inhibitions and doubts. Still, if Gabriel kept at it too long, he would die. And though he was nothing more than a minion, like all the others on the island, Mezzarix wasn't ready to sacrifice his life just yet.

"You need to recover," Mezzarix said. "Get a hot meal and some sleep. I need you at full strength in the morning."

"Thank you, sir." Gabriel turned away from the hole to head back but lingered for a moment, eyeing the cooler of water.

Ravian narrowed his eyes as though considering withholding a bottle from Gabriel, but then he passed one over, and the old man bowed with appreciation. Unscrewing the lid with trembling hands, Gabriel didn't guzzle his drink as he had before but sipped it as he ambled down the path that led to the base of the mountain.

"Tell me again why you picked this island of all places to set up your base of operations," Ravian said, turning to Mezzarix. "We could've gone to the Motherland. My mother's island, rest her soul, would have been most ideal."

"We are hidden here, which gives us ample opportunity to set things in motion." This wasn't the first time Mezzarix had had to explain his plan to his companion. Since their arrival at the mystical island off the coast of Florida two weeks ago, every day had been riddled with Ravian's annoying remarks.

"Yes, but the Silt has run dry. What about all that talk from Ms. Bimini about filling our coffers with enough Silt to take over the world?" Ravian pawed at his eye, yawning. "What complete rubbish. We can't very well take on B.R.E.W. if they can see us coming from miles off the shore. And especially not now that the Vessel has confounded the great Mezzarix!"

A growl gathered in Mezzarix's throat, and his eyes flashed violently at Ravian. Oh, how he longed to shove him off the side of the mountain, but alas, he was one of the only skilled Scourges in Mezzarix's employ. Besides, the annoying Irishman was right. The Atramenti were faithful now that they had been thoroughly Blotched, but they were ancient and broken and limited in their capability to vanish on command.

Mezzarix had believed that once he seized control of the Vessel, he would have no problem in accomplishing his goal of destroying B.R.E.W. But some sort of fail-safe had been added to the roiling mixture inside the silver chalice, some powerful ingredient interwoven into the very fibers of the ancient potion, that prevented him from simply pouring out the Vessel's contents, setting it afire, and plunging the world into chaos.

Mezzarix could still use the Vessel in a number of ways, all of which would be devastating to the Community, but until he could remove that critical component from the mixture, his powers remained limited. He needed the Chamber members of the Board. More specifically, he needed to remove those members. And Silt had been his first plan to do that.

"Silt will not be required for every member of my army. A select few can do plenty of damage on the inside." Mezzarix always had a backup plan, and his next move would prove to be more chaotic than the first. He had already begun work on the second option, and it was taking all his energy to complete. He had spent many sleepless nights siphoning microscopic chemicals from the Vessel and compiling them in his cauldron. "Come along, Ravian. We have work to do."

ordy sat on a stool in Tobias's kitchen. It was not
quite seven o'clock in the morning, and the house
was completly silent. Just before dawn, his mom
and Aunt Priss had gone shopping for more ingredients.
They had been brewing tirelessly for most of the week and
had created enough Torpor Tonics, Vintreet Traps, and a
variety of other combative mixtures to start a full-scale war
on any of their enemies. Right now, that list of enemies
was exceptionally long. Tobias was walking the property,
mapping out more locations of his deadly plants, leaving
Gordy by himself to brew.

Rain pattered against the windows, with no end to the
storm in sight. The smooth surface of Gordy's silver cauldron gleamed as he heated the thick liquid to a boil with
his Bunsen burner. The five ingredients for his potion were
in a row on the counter: tow-truck axle grease, a Styrofoam
container of tapioca pudding, several caps of inga-berzina
mushrooms, a vial of coral-snake venom, and a bag of

oily marten fur. Gordy was concocting a Latvian Dunka Draught, one of his Aunt Priss's specialties, but without one key ingredient: sessile barnacles. Without them, the Dunka Draught was virtually impossible to brew, and yet Gordy had purposely left them out.

As the axle grease began to bubble sluggishly, Gordy licked a pewter spoon and dropped in a dollop of pudding. The creamy substance sizzled. Next, he tied several strands of the marten fur into knots before dipping them into the vial of venom and adding them to the mixture. Mashing the mushrooms into a pulp with his thumbs, he waited until the cauldron began to pulse rhythmically before tossing those in as well.

He was almost finished, but without the barnacles, a normal Elixirist could not turn the brown-colored concoction into an actual Dunka Draught. When it came time to add the three barnacle stems, Gordy allowed his eyes to roll to the back of his head and dipped his index finger into the scalding liquid.

The potion should have burned him, but Gordy felt no pain. After stirring the potion for almost an entire minute, he checked his creation. The once dark-brown color had become a vibrant lime green. The Bunsen burner flame whickered out with a soft pop, and Gordy placed four corked vials of perfectly brewed Dunka Draught on the kitchen counter.

This had been the third time in one week Gordy had brewed a potion using an incomplete inventory of ingredients. Each time, when the recipe required the missing element, Gordy had used his finger instead.

Something had changed inside of Gordy ever since he had brewed a potion in Sasha Brexil's basement without using a cauldron or heat source. Not wanting to scare his mom, Gordy had yet to ask her about what it might mean, but he had an inkling of what was happening.

⁓

A few hours later, Gordy still sat in the kitchen, but this time with Tobais next to him, a piercing ring trilling in his ears, and thick smoke in the air. Just moments earlier, the cauldron atop the stove had detonated, sending a mass of barely dissolved ingredients, including dead animal parts, showering down upon Gordy's and Tobias's heads. Crimson potion sloughed from the kitchen walls. They had both been wearing protective goggles and helmets but were completely drenched from head to toe in the foul-smelling goop.

"Told you these batches could be a tad testy!" Tobias shouted, hurriedly killing the heat on the stove and swatting at the smoke with an oven mitt.

Gordy gaped at the carnage. The better part of the kitchen's eastern wall as well as the windows facing the garden were thoroughly painted with a bloodred substance.

"A *tad* testy?" Gordy dug a pinky in his ear, trying to quell the ringing. Tobias's voice sounded as though he was underwater.

"Whatever you do, don't swallow any of it." After hurrying across the room to grab a bowl from the sink of dirty dishes, the redheaded man returned, hovering over Gordy. "Some of it is still salvageable, I think."

"What exactly was it supposed to do?" Gordy asked, not daring to move as Tobias scraped the potion from his goggles into the bowl.

Tobias's head bobbled. "Well, that there's a Sturmwolke Slosh. I mix it twice a month to keep the rain constant."

"And it *should* explode, right?"

"There's no other way to propel a Sturmwolke into the sky above my garden save for a right royal explosion, but usually I can set a timer and run away before she blows her top. I best go get a mop." Tobias scurried from the kitchen, grumbling under his breath.

Gordy's cell phone buzzed against his leg as a text arrived. It was from his best friend, Max Pinkerman.

To prevent anyone from discovering their whereabouts, Mrs. Stitser had warded Tobias's home to stop calls from coming into Gordy's phone. Everyone else's phone worked like normal, but not Gordy's. No calls. No social media. And almost no access to his old life. His mom did, however, allow for text messages to come through, but from only one outside source. It seemed fitting that Max had earned that right.

This Saturday, dude. No more putting it off. You've got four days to make it happen.

After wiping his face with a wet paper towel, Gordy typed a quick reply.

I can't this weekend.

Max had been trying to arrange a meeting between Gordy and Sasha, the daughter of B.R.E.W.'s former Chamber President, ever since the Stitsers had gone into hiding. It was the topic of every texting conversation.

After about a minute of waiting, another text appeared. This one was an audio message. Gordy pressed play, and Max's voice suddenly erupted from the phone.

"You're killing me! Do you know how many times Sasha asks me about you? A billion times. That's not an exaggeration. She's at my locker. She follows me in the hallways between classes. I have to eat my lunch in the bathroom just to avoid bumping into her in the cafeteria. Have you ever tried eating a ham sandwich while sitting on one of these toilets? I don't recommend it. She comes over to my house and throws rocks at my bedroom window. I'm serious, dude! She mopes around school all day like some sick, wounded animal. You have to meet with her. You have to. If you don't, I swear I will—" The message ended mid-rant.

Gordy snickered. It was good to hear Max's voice, even when he *was* shouting. In truth, he didn't feel too bad for his friend. Max could still go to school and have a normal life. Plus, it wasn't like this was all Gordy's fault. He honestly wanted to meet with Sasha, but he didn't dare ask his mom if she would let him head back into B.R.E.W.

territory to meet with the daughter of the woman who had made Gordy and his mom outlaws. Not a chance.

Gordy could almost sense Max's growing agitation at his silence, and he hurriedly typed a reply.

I promise I will get there soon. In the meantime, I've concocted some pretty amazing potions that you're going to want to try out. I'll bring them with me when I come. You're going to love them!

Max's response came almost immediately.

Consider me intrigued. Send me a pic!

Satisfied he had calmed down his friend, Gordy slid his phone back into his pocket. A picture wouldn't do it justice. Max would just have to wait.

"Something smells burned," Gordy's mom announced, entering through the front door and followed closely by Aunt Priss. Both women were toting paper sacks bulging with ingredients. "What were you brewing?" Her eyes narrowed in suspicion. It had been months since Wanda Stitser had been her cheerful and carefree self, and Gordy feared she might never act the same again.

"Uh . . . I was . . ." Gordy started, but Tobias cleared his throat.

"Since when do I have to explain my brewing techniques to you?" Tobias asked stiffly. "*My* kitchen. *My* equipment."

"Oh," Gordy's mom replied, her scowl softening. "I didn't mean anything by it, Tobias. It just smells . . . off, a little."

"Well, we all aren't as skilled as the great Wanda Stitser, are we?" Tobias said.

"What did you buy?" Gordy eagerly pulled open one of the bags and peered inside at a pair of hideous-looking dried fish wrapped in plastic. He removed a glass jar containing some shriveled fruit.

"Those are figs," Priss said.

"What's with the blue-and-white fuzz?" Gordy asked.

"They're moldy," Gordy's mom said. "And they smell awful. Don't open it, please. I'm going to have to shampoo the upholstery to get the scent out of the Subaru."

Priss innocently held up her hands. "Someone didn't secure the lids before she put them in the bag. I'm just thrilled we were able to find some. The clerk at the Mediterranean grocery store was certainly suspicious when I offered to buy them."

"Eunice?" Tobias asked. "She always gives me a look whenever I ask for rice weevils. She says they don't sell bugs! 'Well, I know you don't, Eunice! Just point me to where they burrow.'"

"Why did you buy moldy figs?" Gordy frowned at the jar, but then his eyes widened. "Oh!"

Priss's eyebrows crinkled as she grinned. "They need a few more days to fully turn, but you know what they're used for, right?"

"I do." Moldy figs were a key ingredient in brewing several complicated potions, including a Disfarcar Gel. "So, does that mean . . ."

"Saturday night," Gordy's mom said tersely. "We're meeting with Paulina in the Swigs."

Paulina was the leader of a group of Elixirists called the Stained Squad. She had been providing the Stitsers with information regarding several of the Banished Scourges who had personal vendettas against Wanda.

Trying his best to keep cool, though he could feel his pulse starting to quicken, Gordy carefully placed the jar of moldy figs on the kitchen counter. "Do I get to go with you?"

Gordy's mom continued sorting groceries, not making eye contact with him. He could see her nostrils flaring, which meant she was fighting back the urge to yell at someone. Gordy looked to Aunt Priss for an explanation, but she was too busy shaking her head at Wanda.

"Mom?" Gordy asked. "What's wrong?"

"Yes, you'll be coming with us," she said. "You can thank Bolter the next time you see him."

An hour before they had left that morning, Gordy's mom had discovered Bolter's note under her bedroom door. She hadn't exactly yelled at anyone after reading it, but her voice had definitely not been warm and welcoming. Gordy knew it hadn't been Bolter's intention to leave the Stitsers high and dry, but even Priss seemed annoyed by his departure. They hardly had anyone on their side as it was, and now they were down another man.

"Because of his decision to leave, we really don't have much of a choice. Don't pump your fist!" She glared at

Gordy, pursing her lips until they drained of color. "This isn't some field trip to the zoo. You're not going there to have fun."

"I know." Gordy hurriedly hid his hands behind his back. The fist pump had been a bit much, but he couldn't help himself. Finally, he would get a change of scenery and better yet, a trip to the Swigs!

"I don't think you do." His mom folded her arms. "These are dangerous people. They won't hesitate to capture you and . . . and harm you . . ."

Tobias groaned, slapping his forehead dramatically. "Oh, good grief!"

Priss covered her mouth, trying to conceal her grin, her shoulders starting to shake with laughter.

"What?" Gordy's mom whirled around, squaring off with Tobias. "I'm not joking. If you can't see the seriousness of what we're about to do, maybe you shouldn't come along with us."

"Fat chance getting into the Swigs without me, cupcake." Tobias stuck out his chin. "And we're not marching Gordy into the mouth of a volcano, for crying out loud. Nothing's going to happen to him, but we might need to sedate you before going down there."

"I'll be good," Gordy insisted. "I promise. I'll do whatever you say, and I'll stay out of trouble."

"You'll be fine," Priss said, winking at Gordy. "Your mother's just being protective, that's all."

A jarring crash suddenly echoed through the kitchen as

though an entire apothecary table had tipped over, sending its contents shattering. Gordy flinched in surprise as his mom spun around, glaring out the window.

"What was that?" she demanded, reaching for her satchel.

"That didn't come from outside." Tobias frowned, cocking his head and listening. "I think it came from . . ." He sputtered to a stop.

Gordy watched his mom's demeanor shift from annoyance to concern. Followed closely by Aunt Priss and Tobias, Gordy raced after his mom toward the stairs leading to the basement—to where Ms. Bimini and her son, Carlisle, had been held prisoner since the Stitsers first went into hiding.

Carlisle stood at the bottom of the stairs, bony hands dangling at his sides, staring up expressionless at Gordy and the others. With gray hair, weathered skin, and thin arms, Carlisle had always looked old, perhaps in his late sixties when Gordy first met him. Then, a few days ago, without warning, Carlisle's age began rapidly accelerating.

"What happened?" Gordy's mom demanded. "What was that crash?"

Carlisle's drooping eyes blinked slowly, and he cast a tired glance at the hospital bed in the corner behind him. An IV station and a ventilator were hooked up to a frail, gray woman lying under a mound of blankets. A plastic mask, foggy from her damp breathing, covered the woman's nose and mouth. Two trays and a few pans of food were scattered beneath Ms. Bimini's bed.

"If you didn't want meat loaf, you could've just

requested something else," Tobias said, descending the stairs and eyeing the mess on the floor.

"Are you all right?" Aunt Priss asked Carlisle. He didn't answer, but he never answered. Carlisle couldn't speak, though Gordy had never found out why. And though when they'd first captured Ms. Bimini and her son, they had been considered dangerous and a high flight risk, Gordy's mom had since removed the shackles latching them in the basement. Once their age began deteriorating, they were no longer a threat to anyone. Plus, it didn't feel humane keeping them chained to the floor.

Gordy's mom stood over Ms. Bimini, carefully cradling one feeble hand in hers. Deep-blue veins seemed to glow beneath the old woman's paper-thin skin, and her knobby knuckles jutted up at crooked angles.

"Tell us what to do for you," Mrs. Stitser said, her calm voice soothing as though addressing a small, injured child. "How can we help you? If you would just give us direc-tions . . ."

A harsh coughing fit overtook Ms. Bimini, and she im-mediately pulled down the mask from her mouth. Gordy's mom gently caressed her hand.

"Just draw us a map or something. Send us in the right direction. We could get to the island and bring back the Silt to stop this." She left out the part about hunting down her own father, Mezzarix, and putting a stop to his plans to overthrow B.R.E.W., but Gordy knew there was no need for her to say that.

The ancient woman's eyes opened, and her lips quivered in what might have been a smile. "No stopping this now," she wheezed. "It has been . . ." She broke into another fit of phlegmy coughing, burying her face into her blanket. "It has been happening for years and has finally caught up with me."

"We could still help Carlisle," Mrs. Stitser said, patting Ms. Bimini's hand. "Put a halt to his aging. Wouldn't you want that?"

Ms. Bimini's meager smile suddenly turned sour, and she glared fiercely at Carlisle. For a moment, Gordy thought she might spring from the bed and throttle her son.

"Don't fret over him. He'll hit his mark soon enough. I still have more than a hundred years before I finally catch up. Fortunately for me, I will be long gone before that happens." Ms. Bimini coughed again, eyes clamping shut in pain. This bout lasted for almost a minute before the old woman was able to catch her breath again.

Gordy looked at his mom, dread settling in his stomach. "What about Adilene? She drank Silt as well."

"So did we," Priss added, her brow furrowing.

The three of them had taken a few sips from a vial of Silt when they'd broken into Madame Brexil's home. Along with rendering them invisible, the Silt could possibly tamper with their age.

Adilene had swallowed the most—almost an entire vial—when Ms. Bimini, disguised as the young girl Cadence, had tricked her into doing so. What would happen to Gordy's best friend? No one was quite certain how that part of the Silt worked, whether it added years or removed them. One thing was for sure, though: a slew of horrible side effects took hold of the person once they stopped drinking the Silt, evidenced by Ms. Bimini's and Carlisle's current state.

Ms. Bimini's exact age was a mystery, but Aunt Priss suspected the woman might be at least a hundred and eighty years old. No one had ever lived that long—not naturally at least. The Silt Ms. Bimini had ingested over the years had made her age the most unnatural thing about her.

Tobias scratched the back of his head. "Oh, mercy, am I going to have to order more beds and meds for the lot of you? I didn't sign up to be a nurse!"

A puttering sound rose from Ms. Bimini's mouth. Gordy thought she was having another coughing fit, but then realized she was laughing.

"One sip? One vial?" Her thin shoulders trembled. "Foolish children, you know nothing. My blood is Silt. I am Atramenti. I've consumed thousands of sips. More than that—hundreds of thousands." She scowled at the ceiling, her upper lip curling into a snarl as she wriggled her hand free from Mrs. Stitser's grasp. "Drained the fountain, we did. We found another source, deep in the dark caves where no light reaches. But that pool ran dry as well. So much so that when the first of my people withered and crumpled to dust, the others believed it was fate—that, with the Silt dying, we were meant to die as well. And when I fought against them, fought for our very existence, they sent me away!" Her eyes glistened with tears.

Gordy had never heard her speak of what had happened on the island before or the reason why she had been banished from her people.

Ms. Bimini moaned, the whole bed rattling from her sobs.

"And you!" Ms. Bimini jolted up, finding enough strength to point an accusing finger at Carlisle. "You gave me to them!" Her once-whispering voice had turned deep and hideous. "You betrayed me!" Her energy spent, she collapsed back onto her pillow, chest rising and falling as though she had run a marathon.

Gordy felt his heart racing in his chest. What was going on? Carlisle hadn't moved, but he would no longer look at his mother. No one spoke, not even Tobias, who always had a way with words. He just stood by the door, eyebrows crinkling in confusion.

Ms. Bimini finally stopped crying and gazed up at Gordy, her expression softening. "Don't worry about Adilene," she said. "She didn't drink enough to experience all this. But she will see some subtle changes. As shall you all."

"Changes?" Gordy asked, worried. "Like what?"

Ms. Bimini chuckled. "One doesn't drink from the Elixir of Life and leave without wanting more. With power comes a price, and the payment is desire. And from what I know of your precious friend Adilene, she was already willing to pay the price. Oh, stop that!" Her voice rose with agitation as Gordy's mom prepped the next bag of fluids to connect to her IV. "That does nothing for me but make me disoriented." Her scowl returned, harsher than before.

"We have other medicines," Priss offered. "We can concoct potions to make you comfortable."

"I don't want your magic," Ms. Bimini said. "I never wanted it. I never should have involved myself with your kind. Go back to your pathetic attempts to save your world and leave us. I need what little time I have left in this life to curse my son." She closed her eyes, her jaw set in determination. "Alone."

L ater that evening, Gordy and his mom returned to
the basement carrying two trays of food for Ms.
Bimini and Carlisle's dinner. Carlisle sat in the chair,
hands folded in his lap, staring at the wall. Ms. Bimini's
bed had been stripped of its sheets and blankets, and the
medical equipment had been powered down and shoved
into one corner of the room. The ancient woman's faded
maroon pantsuit was splayed out on the bare mattress, but
the elderly woman was nowhere to be found.

"Your mother?" Gordy's mom waved her fingers in
front of Carlisle's vacant expression. "Where has she gone,
Carlisle?"

And why wasn't she wearing her clothes?

Carlisle lowered his eyes and studied his hands. They
were calloused and cracking at the knuckles. But they were
also arthritic. Gordy wondered if they caused him pain.

"She couldn't have just vanished," Mrs. Stitser said.

Then she glanced at Gordy, and they exchanged a know-ing look.

When Ms. Bimini had access to Silt, she frequently turned invisible whenever she fancied it. Maybe she had just been waiting for the right moment to try it again. And yet Gordy didn't believe that was what had happened. She had been too weak. He felt a chill in his shoulders, goose bumps prickling his skin as though he had seen a ghost. As an Elixirist, he knew there were weird things in the world, but of all the potions Gordy had mastered, he had never known of one that could make someone vanish for good.

"Is she gone?" Gordy asked Carlisle. "Really gone?"

Carlisle dragged his tongue across his lips, giving no indication he even understood the question. Gordy glanced at the mattress and the outfit Ms. Bimini had worn throughout her stay in Tobias's basement. He half expected he'd see gray dust buried under the maroon fabric if he examined it closely.

"Gordy, come with me for a moment." His mom pulled him back to the stairs by his sleeve, but they paused half-way up, the wooden boards straining beneath their weight. "We're going to let Carlisle go free," she said. "Saturday afternoon, before we travel into the Swigs, we're going to release him. It makes no sense to leave him here unat-tended. I doubt Bolter took that into consideration when he decided to abandon ship. In any case, Carlisle can't stay here."

"We're going to let him go?" Gordy asked a little louder than he intended.

She held her finger to her lips and fixed him with a stern glare. "We may be forced to relocate sooner rather than later, and there's no need to keep him prisoner anymore," she said. "He's not a threat."

Gordy shook his head. "That's not what I meant. Carlisle's old. Way old. And if . . ." He swallowed, his mouth dry. "If she's really gone, what's he going to do?"

He felt a little weird worrying about an eighty-plus-year-old man now that his one-hundred-and-fifty-plus-year-old mother had . . . well, disappeared, but Carlisle's situation felt different. He needed assistance and someone to watch over him, especially if he was still aging rapidly. What would happen to Carlisle if he woke up one morning unexpectedly ten years older and unable to walk?

"If we're on the move, we can't worry about transporting a prisoner." His mom looked away guiltily for a moment. "I don't want you blaming yourself for any of this."

"But it's not right, Mom." Carlisle may have once been an enemy, but all that changed the moment he aged twenty years in a couple of days. And since his capture, Carlisle had been nothing but cooperative.

"What's right is making sure he's as safe as we can make him. We'll see that he has plenty of supplies, anything he needs. But, Gordy, we're headed into a potion war with a dangerous enemy. These other inconveniences we've had this past year—"

"Inconveniences?" Did she really consider Esmeralda Faustus and Ms. Bimini nothing more than inconveniences?

"Listen!" She squeezed Gordy's arm while raising a warning finger. "Mezzarix has control of the Vessel. You have no idea what he's capable of. Nothing can get in the way of us stopping him." She closed her eyes and exhaled before rubbing Gordy's arm affectionately. "If Carlisle remains with us, we'll be dragging him into the cross fire. Do you understand?"

Gordy thought for a moment, struggling against the idea, but then finally nodded. When the potions started flying, the real nasty ones Mezzarix was skilled at concocting, Carlisle would be in danger—they all would.

Gordy ducked down a little to glance back into the room. Carlisle still sat in his chair, hands still folded in his lap, gazing at the floor, eyes unfocused. He wasn't listening. He might not have even cared.

Poor guy. Where would he go? Gordy wondered. In any case, he had a few more nights to sleep in Tobias's musty basement. By Saturday afternoon, Carlisle would be gone.

CHAPTER

6

Mezzarix and Ravian strolled beneath a cedarwood trellis where baskets of flowers hung from hooks. The warm evening breeze carried with it the smell of brine and perfume. Overripe papayas, like enormous colorful beehives, drooped from tree branches, mere days from splatting along the cobblestone walkway.

The Atramenti called this place the Palace of Puerulus, and it sat on the southern shore of the island. There were several fresh pools of dark-green water beneath the canopy of palm trees where flocks of a wide variety of birds gathered, many of which paused in their bathing and preening to watch as the two Scourges passed by. The whole island was a paradise, a haven from the outside world, dripping with beauty and serenity.

And Mezzarix had no need for it.

After plucking a papaya from a nearby tree, Ravian pressed his thumbs into the flesh, splitting the fruit into two glistening chunks. He took a bite, and the orange juice dripped down his chin and onto his collar.

"You know? It sort of tastes like soap," Ravian said, his mouth full. "But like fruity soap. You've eaten fruity soap before, haven't you? My mother used to flog me with a switch whenever she caught me eating soap. Said it would make me go mad if I ate enough of it." He wiped his mouth with his sleeve. "Little did she know I ate grundles of the stuff. It reminded me of cheese just about to turn. The best kind, really. And look how I turned out."

"You are mad," Mezzarix muttered.

Ravian knitted his eyebrows. "Mad or brilliant. There really isn't much difference if you ask the right people."

They entered through the palace gates and climbed a flight of steps to a great hall where several long tables and ornate wooden chairs sat empty. At the far end of the room stood six marble thrones encircling a dais where a single bowl of white opal rested at the center. The bowl was empty except for a sticky residue of the Silt that had once filled it.

A miniature woman with green hair and white eyelashes lounged in the throne second from the left, her painted toes wiggling in the air as she stared at the ceiling.

"Zelda," Mezzarix said, stopping next to the dais. "How are things coming with our project?"

"Finished," the woman replied in more of a squeak than an actual voice. She swung her legs off the armrest and sat up. "Your recipe was easy to follow, and the Vessel is the perfect mixing bowl. There are so many amazing potions we could make with it." Her eyes drifted wistfully out of focus for a moment before returning to the present. "Anyway, they're ready to be sent. All they need is for him"—she pointed at Ravian—"to do the honors." Then she knelt on the floor, dragging a heavy leather bag three times the size of a standard satchel from underneath the throne. "They're all in here. Every one of them carved and ready."

Mezzarix smiled. "You've done well." He turned to Ravian. "And you're sure these animals will know where to go?"

Ravian shrugged, weeding a sliver of papaya out of his teeth with his fingernail. "They've always done as they've been commanded. Of course, I will have to manipulate their minds a bit, but that shouldn't be a problem. Not with the Vessel. What sort of creatures should I beckon?"

Mezzarix frowned. "I wasn't aware you McFarlands could control anything other than birds."

"Well, there are large birds, like storks and cranes and ostriches. There are wee tiny birds, like sparrows and finches. I need to know what you require and where they're going because climate could affect their flight patterns, and if they have weak constitutions, then—"

"I get the idea." Mezzarix cut him off, rubbing his forehead in annoyance. He nodded at Zelda. "How big will be necessary?"

Zelda curled her lip and then held her hands about two

feet apart. "And they'll need to be able to carry at least a half a pound of weight."

Ravian wiggled his fingers. "I think I know a few love-lies for the job. I'll get started now." The Irishman took the satchel from Zelda and hobbled away, heading for the water.

"I also have this one ready to go." Zelda held up an object wrapped in cloth. Wooden ends poked out from beneath the fabric. "Should I have him send this off by bird as well?"

Mezzarix took the object from her, cradling it gently, gazing upon it affectionately. "I will send it by other means. This one deserves a proper delivery. I don't want it simply dropped at the doorstep."

Zelda giggled, a shrill, bothersome sort of noise, and Mezzarix closed his eyes, wincing at the sound of it. "And you don't plan to send it directly to him? We know where he's hiding."

Mezzarix shook his head. "Wanda would never allow him to touch it. I shall send this via an alternate route." Sauntering over next to her, Mezzarix eased into one of the thrones. "Are you bored, Zelda?"

"Bored?" she replied.

"Someone like you, who has always been on the ground causing the explosions, must consider your time away from the action a bit of a bother."

"I don't mind, really," Zelda said.

"Come now," Mezzarix tutted. "I know where your

heart lies. And it's not on this island. Ravian is a coward who works best in the shadows—scheming and playing his role from afar. You, on the other hand, need to stretch your wings, much like his birds."

Zelda forced a smile, but her eyes narrowed. "What is it you want me to do?"

Mezzarix reached beneath his cloak and produced a wooden box containing several glass vials of Silt. There were twelve in all, each containing every ounce of the precious liquid the Atramenti had been able to siphon from the underground fountain.

"This is all we have," Mezzarix said. "But it should be enough for you and a few of your choosing to sneak back into the city without B.R.E.W. becoming aware of your presence."

Zelda scowled. "Go back? Why would I do that? Once all the Scourges are unleashed, it will be pure insanity."

"And that's why I need someone on the ground when they start arriving. You know how they can be after having been cooped up for so many years. You will be my eyes and ears on the battlefield. The one who will spring the trap."

She cocked an eyebrow. "You want me to lead the search?"

Mezzarix pulled another bottle from beneath his cloak. The potion resembled swamp water, only thicker in consistency and with a smattering of tiny, shimmering crystals floating in the mixture. Mezzarix rotated the bottle in his fingers before handing it over to Zelda. "This is also for you."

Zelda's eyes brightened as she inspected the bottle. "What is it?"

"This has consumed all my energy and thoughts. In my studies of the Vessel, when I realized the limitations facing us in truly unleashing my ultimate plan, I discovered I had the ability to create something on a much smaller scale." Mezzarix nodded at the potion. "With this concoction, many of B.R.E.W.'s advancements will revert to their original condition."

Zelda studied the potion closely, one eye peeking above the bottle. "Are you telling me this will turn the power off?"

Mezzarix grinned. "To all technology. All scientific marvels will be placed on hold—within a confined area, of course."

"How confined?" Zelda asked.

Mezzarix hummed for a moment, pondering her question. "Oh, eight to ten miles, I suppose. And there are other properties to the potion as well. Ones that will make things easier for us in the long run, including allowing our forces to carry out their assignment in relative peace and quiet.

"But I need someone to ensure this potion lasts as long as it can, and that is why I'm sending you. Someone with my shared interests. The potion will trigger the technology outage, which will be the signal for the Scourges to begin. And you shall lead them. I would go myself, but I must stay here to prepare for the next phase. This won't be a simple assignment, but I trust you'll know how to handle it."

"What about the boy?" Zelda asked, her glance flicking to the object in Mezzarix's hands.

"What about him?"

"Once we begin, the city will be overturned. I cannot be held responsible for every Scourge attack," she said. "There will be casualties."

"Which is to be expected," Mezzarix agreed.

"And what happens if the members of your family are caught in the cross fire?"

Mezzarix stroked his chin. "Should it come to that, I shall understand. You have my permission to take any means necessary to ensure the job is done. But I have no concerns about the boy's welfare. I feel confident in his abilities to endure."

"What makes you so sure he'll go unharmed?"

"Because deep beneath his exterior, Gordy Stitser is a Rook." Mezzarix smiled, carefully wrapping the wooden object within the cloth again. "And Rooks have always found a way to survive."

A black-browed female mallemuck unleashed a cackle as she dipped through a patch of cloud hovering above Águila Islet, an island five hundred miles north of Antarctica. The bird landed clumsily upon the only spot of earth not blanketed by snow and promptly spouted water from her beak. Hobbling back and forth, the mallemuck flapped her wings anxiously, and though capable, the bird did not immediately take flight.

"What's that you brought me?" a raspy voice sounded from close by.

The mallemuck leaped backward, screeching in fright, beady eyes concentrating on the figure emerging from behind a boulder.

"Easy, love." The man wore tanned animal skins, and his salt-crusted hair hung about his gaunt face in ratted clumps. The patch over his right eye bulged to a point beneath his brow, while his left eye barely peeked out from a sunburned lid. A slew of freshly scabbed wounds pocked his bare feet.

The bird launched upward, beating her wings against the wind before settling once more upon the ground.

"Steady now." The man extended a hand toward the frightened creature. "You can't have flown all this way to just tuck off without no more than a squawk."

He sprung upon the mallemuck, pinning her to the ground with his powerful hands. As she struggled against him, the man's deft fingers slipped beneath her left wing, unlatching a wooden tube.

"Thought you were acting odd." He pried a tiny lid from one end of the tube, and the mallemuck jabbed her beak into the man's thumb. The man paid no attention despite the thin stream of blood seeping from the wound.

The bird wriggled free of his grasp but still refused to fly away.

Eyeballing the creature curiously, the man unrolled the unexpectedly long message.

Steffan Musk,

Based upon your good behavior, the terms of your Banishment will be lifted temporarily for one week of freedom. Compliments of B.R.E.W.'s newest Chamber President.

Steffan scowled, his single eye narrowing to a slit.

"Week of freedom?" he asked gruffly. Seeing how his Banishment had been a life sentence, that made little sense.

And what good behavior had he done to garner such leniency?

> *Consider this an opportunity to travel to balmier climates or make a quick pit stop to nearby civilization to gather much-needed supplies. Surely someone of your expertise could benefit from a cauldron and an inventory of fresh ingredients.*
>
> *However, should you feel the itching for immediate work, I am in need of some hired help. Perhaps you and I might collaborate once more for old time's sake. I, in turn, shall reward you by ending your Banishment for good.*

This message couldn't be real. Flipping over the parchment, he read the scrawling signature written in purple ink at the end of the letter.

"Mezzarix Rook," Steffan muttered. "What are you playing at, you sly fox?"

Mezzarix had always been ambitious, with lofty aspirations of seizing power over the potion-making community, but the old fool had been banished a year before Steffan had. And now he had somehow escaped and become the Chamber President of B.R.E.W.?

"You expect me to believe this?" Steffan asked the bird, crinkling the paper in his fingers.

The mallemuck responded with a piercing cry.

Flipping the message over once more, he continued reading.

I expect you'll find it difficult to believe me at first. For that reason, I'm giving you twenty-four hours to ponder the terms of our agreement. After that, you'll feel the binding cords of your Banishment unravel. Then you shall have one week to spend as you wish—either lazily relaxing on holiday or venturing north to join me.

You and I shared a vision once. A vision of chaos. The world we live in has been hampered for far too long by those who have never known of our greatness. I stand at the precipice, on the verge of realizing my Manifesto, and I have chosen you to be there with me. I hope you will accept my offer.

To help with your decision, I've also sent you a gift. Just say the magic word: Upsy-daisy.

Steffan scowled as he scanned the ground in search of Mezzarix's present. There didn't appear to be anything else strapped to the bird.

"Upsy-daisy?" he mumbled.

The mallemuck immediately began to gag as if it had swallowed an enormous acorn. Baffled, Steffan watched as the bird writhed and wriggled. Something dislodged from its throat, and it spat out a slender piece of wood from its beak.

"What the devil?" Steffan recoiled in disgust.

The mallemuck shook its head, dazed.

Steffan snatched up the bird and crammed it into the pouch attached at his waist. The mallemuck squawked in protest, but Steffan ignored its cries. He knelt down to examine the object.

"Is this what I think it is?" It certainly looked as though it possessed the necessary chemically enhanced runes carved into the wood. But how on earth had Mezzarix come into possession of such a thing? They were only used by the upper echelon of B.R.E.W. Maybe he really was the new Chamber President. The thought was enough to make Steffan's head explode.

Be careful how you wield it, as its effects are irreversible. And while I'm sure you have a long list of enemies, I'm giving this gift to you with the hope you will use it on targets we both can agree upon.

It had been several years since Steffan had thought of confronting his enemies. Lifetime Banishments had a way of dulling the senses, but now he felt a sudden burning hatred ignite within his heart. This was his chance for freedom and revenge. Clasping the weapon in his hand, he could feel the dangerous power coursing through the wood.

Lip curling into a snarl, Steffan turned to head toward his shelter. Though his supply was limited, there were a few vials and ingredients he needed to gather before he embarked on his journey.

He felt the soft fluttering of the mallemuck's wings from inside his pouch, and his stomach gurgled, reminding him of his hunger. Then he realized there was still one final paragraph remaining of Mezzarix's message.

> *I do hope you have held off butchering the poor bird that delivered this gift to you. She has been charged with gathering a few more necessities for you in the days to come—potions and ingredients that will help speed you on your journey. Be gentle with her as she will do this task willingly. And she will be your guide to your destination, so take care of her. It is a big ocean, my friend. I would hate for you to lose your way.*

Steffan groaned in annoyance. Most birds he encountered on his island had too sharp of instincts to be caught without a fight. This one had been practically hand-delivered to his doorstep.

Now what was he supposed to eat?

I need some of your blood."

Adilene Rivera heard the voice behind her and knew who it belonged to, but that didn't make what was said any less creepy.

"You . . . you need my what?" Adilene closed her locker and spun around.

Sasha Brexil showcased a confident smile, her teeth practically sparkling. "I said I need some of your blood." Her tone sounded casual, but she did lower her voice, as several other students moved down the hall toward their first-period classes.

Adilene immediately noted that Sasha was wearing a dress, makeup, and bright golden earrings. She had worn those sorts of things at the beginning of the school year, but all that had changed the moment her mom had been ExSponged by Mezzarix. Gone was the sassy, perfectly manicured Sasha. In her place was a broken girl with a nasty temper and a short fuse who wore sweats to school and sunglasses to hide her wet eyes from everyone else.

But today the old Sasha was back.

"I figured it out." Sasha leaned in close to Adilene.

Adilene could smell spearmint gum on Sasha's breath as she smacked her lips, chomping noisily. She pressed her back against the lockers, feeling the combination lock digging into her shoulder.

"The tracking potion," Sasha said before Adilene could ask. "Well, not *the* tracking potion. That one's worthless. I don't know how my mom managed to destroy the most important steps of the recipe, but I'm getting nowhere with it. But I found a new one. It should work if I have the right ingredients."

Over the past couple of weeks, Sasha had been obsessed with finding a way to pinpoint where Mezzarix had taken the Vessel. Her mom had had a recipe, but most of the instructions had somehow been lost. And since she no longer had any potion-making ability, or even any memory of how to brew, Mrs. Brexil's incomplete tracking potion was impossible to recreate.

Adilene knew Sasha was waiting for Gordy to come back to town, because she believed he had the ability to fill in the missing pieces, but the girl was too impatient and determined to figure the potion out herself. With her mom's ExSpongement, the Brexils had lost their prestigious position within the potion-making community, and Sasha had lost most of her edge.

"Okay . . ." Adilene cast a wary glance around the hallway. "But what does that have to do with me?"

"You drank a whole vial of Silt. This new tracking potion works like a magnet. It can take a sample of any substance and lead you to where more can be found. And since we're certain Silt doesn't exist anywhere else in the world . . ." She clicked her tongue and beamed with enthusiasm. "There you go. Problem solved."

"Where did you find this recipe again?"

"Online," Sasha answered.

"You can find them online?" Adilene asked, suddenly interested. She had never thought to turn to the internet for potion recipes. "I mean, you know, ones that actually work?"

"Um, yeah. If you know where to look. This potion is not exactly legal with B.R.E.W, but like I care anymore." Sasha glanced down at her fingernails. They had also been painted recently. Discovering this lead had clearly breathed new life back into her.

"Sounds tricky. What do you need to make it?" An illegal potion probably required illegal ingredients. Sasha may have been harboring ill feelings toward B.R.E.W. because of what happened to her mother, but Adilene doubted she suddenly had access to those types of substances.

Sasha smirked. "You're not seriously questioning my ability, are you? I'm almost an Elixirist—something you'll never be—and I have practically everything I need. I'm just missing one key ingredient." She raised her eyebrows at Adilene, her glare vanishing in an instant and replaced by one of faux innocence. "Dearest Adilene, won't you help me? You're the only one who has swallowed Silt."

"Gordy drank some," Adilene reasoned. "And his mom and—"

Sasha held up her hand impatiently. "I meant the only one . . . here." She jabbed a finger at the floor. "If Gordy really wanted to help, he would've come back, and I wouldn't be forced to take these measures. So, I'm sorry, but I'm going to need your blood."

"Whoa!" Max suddenly rounded the corner from a side hallway and strolled up to the two girls. "Did you just ask her for her blood?"

"Shut up, Maxwell!" Adilene hissed as a few other students turned their heads toward them. Gordy would have thrown a fit at how blatantly indiscreet the three of them were being. They were breaking the first rule of an Elixirist: never draw unnecessary attention to the potion community. Adilene had the rules memorized.

Max laughed maniacally, then deepened his voice. "And so it begins! Sasha's final transformation into a vampire! I knew we were close." He pressed his hands together as if praying and closed his eyes. "I could sense it among the stars."

Sasha glowered at him, but she didn't seem to care that several of her classmates could hear the conversation. "You are a moron," she said.

"A moron?" Max looked appalled. "Yeah, well you . . . are a *pupitre*."

Sasha opened her mouth but then screwed up her face in confusion, glancing at Adilene for an explanation.

Adilene rolled her eyes. "You don't know what you're saying, Max."

Max grinned with pride. "I know exactly what I'm saying."

"You just called her a desk."

"Exactly." He leaned into the lockers, the clink of glass bottles suddenly loud in the hallway.

Adilene noticed that Max's backpack seemed more jam-packed than usual. "What did you bring with you?" she demanded, her eyes narrowing.

Max's eyes shifted between the two girls, and he turned away, but Adilene grabbed his backpack by the straps and removed it from his shoulders.

"Hey!" he shouted, but she had already unzipped one of the pockets, revealing at least half a dozen corked vials of various substances tucked inside.

"What do you think you're doing with these?" Adilene asked.

"I made them," he said. He lunged for the pack, but she pulled it away from his grasp.

"You made them?" Sasha snatched one of the bottles and removed the cork stopper, sniffing the opening. Gagging, she immediately held it out in disgust. "I'm pretty sure this is essence of choresine."

"Yeah, I know. I made it," Max said. "Corta . . . uh . . . cortisone."

Sasha rolled her eyes and recorked the bottle. "Not cortisone—*choresine*. And it's not a potion, dummy. It's a highly toxic poison found in a beetle from New Guinea."

"Really?" Max gaped eagerly at the vial. "How toxic? Are we talking, like, melt-off-your-skin toxic?"

"Where did you get these?" Adilene eyed the other bottles in the pocket. Some were fizzing and bubbling, while others were letting off steam beneath their lids and rattling their corks. None of the potions were labeled. They could have been anything, and Max wouldn't have had a clue of their contents.

Max puffed out his cheeks, obviously preparing some sort of lie, when Sasha grabbed his arm with her fingers and started pinching.

"All right, all right!" he shouted in pain, shaking his arm free from her grasp. "I got them from Gordy's, okay?"

"From Gordy's?" Adilene looked appalled. "What were you doing there?"

"What?" Max rubbed his arm, glaring at Sasha. "I know the garage code. I went there hoping to . . ." He trailed off.

"Hoping to what?" Sasha held out her fingers, threatening to pinch again.

"Hoping to find my rock," Max finally answered.

Adilene frowned. "Your rock?" Then she nodded, understanding. "You mean Cadence's rock. Max, Mezzarix took it with him. It's gone."

"Yeah, I know, but I was in the area, and I forgot, okay? And then I was hungry and I started thinking about all the snacks the Stitsers always have in their pantry, so I went inside anyway. It's not like they're coming back anytime soon."

"Do you realize you could've been caught by B.R.E.W. and questioned about Gordy?" Adilene said.

Max rolled his eyes. "No one was there. The house was empty, and besides, it was the middle of the afternoon. Who breaks into someone's house in the middle of the afternoon?"

"You do," Sasha answered, folding her arms.

Max chuckled. "In and out, two minutes flat. Like a ninja! And the lab had already been ransacked, but I know where Gordy keeps the good stuff—in his closet. I just wanted to make sure we were armed if something bad were to happen."

A warning bell rang, and Adilene's eyes shot up to the hallway clock on the wall. "I've got to go. I can't be tardy."

Max reluctantly surrendered his stolen potions to Sasha, who wouldn't let him sneak by. He muttered something in Spanish under his breath, though Adilene wasn't sure it was an actual word. Max was horrible at Spanish. He shouldered his way past them and disappeared back around the corner. Adilene turned to leave as well, but Sasha stepped in front, blocking her path.

"Not so fast, friend," she said. "We *are* friends now, aren't we?"

"I guess." More like mutual acquaintances. Most of their interactions ended with Sasha insulting Adilene in some way.

"Friends help each other, so you have to help me."

"And give you my blood? Right here?"

"No, of course not," Sasha answered. "We'll meet somewhere tomorrow night. That way no one will find out. You can even set the rendezvous point if that makes you feel better."

"It doesn't," Adilene said. "I don't think I can do this." How would Sasha even extract her blood? With a needle? It sounded sketchy.

"It's not going to hurt, and yes, you can do this. Because you wouldn't be just helping me. You'd be doing it to stop Mezzarix, and that helps Gordy too." Sasha pouted, her lips puckering into a hopeful expression. "Poor Gordy. Whatever will he do without his brave Adilene?"

"You're doing a horrible job of convincing me." Adilene started to push past her.

"All right, fine. Don't do it for honor. Do it for money. I can pay you."

Adilene scoffed. "I don't want your money."

"How about I do your homework for a month? No—for the rest of the year. I get straight As, and you know my father's the big cheese around here."

Sasha's dad wasn't an Elixirist, but he was the principal at Kipland Middle School. At least he was for now. Adilene had heard rumors spreading through the school that Mr. Brexil's time at Kipland may be running out.

"I don't need you to do my homework either." Adilene didn't mind doing homework. It was the only thing she could do now that Gordy and all access to his lab were gone.

Sasha had a point, though. Locating the Vessel meant they would be able to find Mezzarix and stop whatever horrible things he was planning. And there was one other thing. Adilene thought of at least one favor she could ask of Sasha that would maybe make it worth it.

Closing her eyes, she sighed. "Okay. I'll do it."

Sasha grinned. "I knew you would."

"I'll text you later with the address of where we'll meet," Adilene said. "And I have a request in exchange for my, you know . . . my blood." It felt weird saying it.

"Name it," Sasha said. "I'm good for it."

Adilene hugged her backpack and nodded. "I'll text that to you later as well."

Gordy had taken potions that had transformed his body before. He'd once taken on the appearance of a hideous beast, large and blubbery, trailing slime. The effects of that potion hadn't lasted long, but he could still remember how it felt being heavier and discombobulated. Gordy had recently turned invisible as well, after ingesting less than an ounce of Adilene's Silt. But aside from translucent skin, that potion had left Gordy in pretty much the same condition.

Tonight, however, was the first time Gordy had ever transformed into someone else. An actual someone, as though he had suddenly become some kind of body snatcher. Gordy now had dark-brown skin with coarse hair carpeting his forearms. Muscular forearms. He had never really had muscles before. He wasn't a weakling, but he was only thirteen years old.

He wore baggy cargo pants, a camouflage jacket, and combat boots. Clearing his throat, Gordy's voice came out deep and raspy. He wished he had his phone so he could snap a picture and send it to Max. But Gordy's mom had refused to let him take any of his personal belongings, other than his potion satchel, with him.

"Knock it off!" Mrs. Stitser stood a few paces away, gazing off into the foggy darkness and leaning on the brick wall between a vacated building and a row of dying bushes. Like Gordy, his mom looked nothing like herself. She was still female in appearance but considerably wider and more compact, with a hawkish nose that looked sharp enough to puncture a tin can and cropped, raven-black hair. Clenching her hands, she shot a beady-eyed glare at Gordy. "Eyes up, and no goofing around, Scheel."

Scheel. That was Gordy's code name for this mission. It had belonged to one of Aunt Priss's former acquaintances, someone she had done business with in the Swigs, and someone who was abroad in the Middle East at the moment. Until they were back at Tobias's farmhouse, Gordy was to be addressed as Scheel while his mom was to be called Akerberg. The real Akerberg had been ExSponged by Madame Brexil three months ago and exiled to an island off the coast of Cape Horn, South Africa, so there was no chance she'd suddenly pop up in the parking lot that night.

"Got it," Gordy muttered, his voice sounding like a belching toad. He almost snorted with laughter again but managed to gain control before seriously upsetting his mom. She held the vial of Torpor Tonic so tightly in her hands Gordy feared she might shatter the glass and knock herself unconscious. Though maybe then his mom might actually settle down.

Earlier that afternoon, they had told Carlisle he was no longer a prisoner at Tobias's home, and he was asked to leave. For the first time since his capture, Carlisle had shown a hint of emotion, even more so than when Ms. Bimini had blamed him for everything that had gone wrong in her life. When he learned he was free to go, Carlisle had appeared confused, but not in his normal space-cadet way. It seemed almost as though he had no desire to leave, that he actually enjoyed staying cooped up in Tobias's basement.

But Carlisle didn't argue. He accepted a small suit-case filled with food, water, and various camping supplies. Then he left, lumbering out the door toward the path that would lead him to the road. Gordy's mom had looked sick, and Gordy feared they had made a terrible mistake.

Tobias had watched Carlisle through his binoculars to make sure he didn't wander off the path and into the dangerous territory surrounding the property. Accidentally triggering a Boomclobber was the last thing the old man needed.

Shortly after Carlisle's departure, the four of them squeezed into Tobias's pickup truck and headed out for the Swigs.

Gordy's mom straightened, brittle branches scraping at

her jeans as she retreated a step from the edge. "Here they come."

The sound of hurrying footsteps and Tobias's heavy breathing filled the air as he and Aunt Priss rounded the corner, then squeezed into the narrow hiding space.

Gordy eagerly scrambled to his feet, and Priss held out a hand to calm him, offering him a faint smile. She looked the same as always, long auburn hair, steely-eyed, and determined.

Tobias wasn't wearing a disguise either. He and Priss were regulars in the Swigs, not like the Stitsers, who were fugitives from B.R.E.W.

Tobias spent most nights in the Swigs, where he peddled minor weather potions. It was the type of business that could get him in trouble with B.R.E.W., but the penalty would be a fine and having his supply confiscated. Selling high-intensity weather potions like the Sturmwolke Slosh would land him in a bit more trouble should he ever get caught.

"Entry location hasn't changed," Tobias said. "We should all be clear."

"Who all is there?" Gordy's mom asked, returning the vial of Torpor Tonic to her satchel and tightening the strap over her shoulder.

Tobias shrugged. "It'll be a full house, that's for certain. Gibbous moons always bring out the lot of them. A prime time for bartering and brouhaha."

Gordy's mom gnawed on her lower lip with noticeably

jagged teeth. Akerberg needed serious dental work. "But who exactly? Will we run into trouble?"

Tobias grunted. "I have no way of knowing for sure. It's not like your sister and I took a leisurely stroll to hand out questionnaires. We didn't make it past the bouncer, you know."

"Keep your voice down," Aunt Priss said. "It's all right, Wanda. It doesn't matter who we see down there because no one's going to know who you really are. Your disguises are spot-on, thanks to Gordy."

Gordy felt his cheeks flushing. Earlier that evening, he had brewed a flawless batch of Disfarcar Gel in the lab. Even his mom had been impressed with the perfect vial of broccoli-colored liquid, and nothing seemed to impress her lately.

Mrs. Stitser squared her jaw and nodded at Tobias. "You're right. I apologize for snapping at you."

"Apology accepted," Tobias replied with a smile.

A rust-covered school bus idled next to the only lamp-post in the otherwise empty parking lot. The rotting asphalt had cracked in multiple spots where tree roots had broken the surface and sprouted free. No movement. No voices. Not a soul in the area.

Tobias led the group toward the bus, the crunch of gravel underfoot.

Gordy squinted at the windows, but some sort of

reflective material covered the glass, blocking his view inside.

"That's the Swigs?" Gordy whispered. It wasn't even a full-sized school bus and couldn't have had more than a couple dozen seats.

"Shush." Tobias held a finger to his lips. "The fella guarding the entryway is not exactly the friendly sort, and he knows everyone who does business in the Swigs. He wears special glasses that can identify any B.R.E.W. official who might try to sneak in. Don't worry"—Tobias shot out a hand to calm Gordy's mom—"it doesn't see through disguises. It only detects whether or not someone is Bloodlinked to the Vessel, which you no longer are." He raised his eyebrows, and Gordy caught a hint of satisfaction in Tobias's smile. The Irishman loved that Wanda had gotten herself fired and said so whenever he had the chance. "It's best that I be the only one negotiating our way in tonight. Are we clear?"

The door to the bus folded open before Tobias could knock, and a man stepped down, blocking the entry with his tall, lanky frame. He had dark brown skin, thinning hair, and he wore a hoody, his hands slipped into the side pockets. He had on a pair of basketball shorts that ended at least a foot above his bony kneecaps. Despite the darkness of the parking lot, he also wore sunglasses, the lenses glinting with an unnatural sparkle.

"McFarland," the man spoke, his voice hoarse.

"Spider," Tobias replied, nodding in acknowledgment.

Gordy caught himself staring at the man with mounting interest. Was that his nickname? And if so, what had earned Spider his strange moniker? Did he like spiders?

"And you brought friends, I see." Spider frowned. "And your business is . . . ?"

"None of yours," Tobias answered. "Now, shove off and let me through. I'm in a hurry."

Gordy waited for Spider to retaliate, but the lanky man merely grunted and stepped to one side of the door, allowing Tobias access.

"No rain this time," Spider murmured as Tobias shuffled up the stairs. "Or hailstones. Or whirly-whirls, or whatever it is you do. Keep it corked."

"I'll try my hardest," Tobias answered before vanishing into the bus.

Spider bowed his head slightly at Priss but issued no warnings to her as she walked in next. Gordy's aunt hardly gave Spider a glance. Gordy wasn't sure if it was because they had a mutual understanding or if what Tobias had told him about Priss's reputation in the Swigs was accurate. Few people dared cross Priscilla Rook. His aunt was always such a pleasant person it was hard for Gordy to believe it. Of course, he had never seen Priss unleashed in her actual element.

"Thought you were dead," Spider said to Gordy's mom disguised as Akerberg.

She hesitated before replying, "Might as well be."

That seemed to satisfy Spider, and he let her pass with-out any further discussion.

Then he shot out a hand, his long arm blocking the opening, as Gordy tried to sneak by. "Where do you think you're going?"

"Uh . . . the Swigs?" Gordy said, hopeful. He had deepened his voice on purpose, which made him sound ri-diculous, since Scheel's actual voice already bellowed with-out any effort.

"Oh, you think so?" Spider asked.

"What seems to be the problem?" Gordy's mom asked from behind the man, her hand slipping into her satchel.

"This problem doesn't concern you, Akerberg," Spider said. "This is between me and him." He jabbed a sharp fingernail into Gordy's shoulder.

Gordy felt his stomach tangling up in knots. Had his Disfarcar Gel already worn off? Had Spider seen through his disguise with those magic glasses? By the looks of things, Gordy wasn't going to catch even a glimpse of the inside of the bus, let alone the Swigs.

"My Nipsy still walks around on her back legs every-where she goes." Spider's narrow jaw shifted from side to side. "How long is she going to do that?"

Confused, Gordy's eyes shot up again behind Spider, but this time he found Tobias standing in place of his mom at the top of the stairs, silently mouthing a word over and over. It looked like he was saying . . .

Spider dug his fingernail into Gordy's shoulder.

"Cat?" Gordy blurted out, and Tobias nodded rapidly. "Ah, you're talking about your cat, aren't you?" Gordy floundered, fixing his nervous gaze upon Spider.

"Yeah. My Nipsy. She looks like a fur-covered imp. Even sits on the couch and crosses her legs, one over the other, just like a person." Spider jabbed at Gordy's shoulder with each word. "I don't like it." He shoved his hand back into the pocket of his hoodie. "I don't think she was supposed to do that, was she? And definitely not for this long."

Gordy puffed out his cheeks, trying to recall a potion that could do that. Why would Spider ever need his cat to walk around on its hind legs at all?

"Well?" Spider demanded. "When does it end?"

"Uh . . . how many spoonfuls did you give her?" Gordy had no idea if the potion was even administered by spoonful. He just had to guess.

"All of them," Spider answered flatly. "The whole stinking vial."

"Oh!" Gordy looked at Tobias, who was twirling his hand, implying Gordy should wrap things up. "Then she should be fine in no time."

Spider harrumphed, then leaned close, lowering his voice. "I'm going to come looking for you when I'm off duty," he said. "And you best have an antidote for me when I do."

The inside of the bus was empty save for one folding chair next to a small cooler packed with ice and a paper sack, which Gordy assumed held Spider's dinner. Directly in front of the chair was a square hole in the ground, a ghostly pink hue lighting up the opening.

Gordy hesitated, staring down into the space that seemed to go on forever below the bus. Gordy's mom was about halfway down when she glanced over her shoulder and urged Gordy to follow.

The pink lights came from bottles of glowing potion resting upon hollowed-out recesses every ten or so steps down the corridor. Gordy flicked one of the bottles as he passed by, and the pink liquid sloshed against the glass. He had made Luminescent Lamps before in his mother's lab, but they could barely light up a darkened closet for a few minutes. These filled the stairwell with ample light and showed no indication of weakening anytime soon.

After what had to be close to two hundred steps, the stairwell ended at a closed door. Gordy looked back up the stairs and could see the outline of Spider standing at the top. From that distance, Spider actually looked like a spider, one who happened to be missing most of its legs.

"Stay to the right of the road," Tobias whispered. "Don't talk to anyone if you can help it. Your disguises should keep you out of trouble as long as you don't stir any up yourself." He glanced at Wanda and chuckled. "I half expected Spider's glasses to trigger an alarm, but now I'm convinced you truly have been banned from B.R.E.W."

"I'm glad you find that amusing," Gordy's mom said, glaring at Tobias.

"Just ironic, I suppose. Now, act like you belong. Avoid

questions and don't stare too long at the locals and you should be fine. There's a cookery just off the main strip that has good food, and the customers generally keep to themselves. I know the owner. We go way back." Tobias grabbed the doorknob and gave it a slight twist. "That's where I'll take Scheel, and you can join us after your meeting."

"We're not going with them?" Gordy asked, feeling dejected. He'd wanted to meet Paulina Hasselbeck and her secretive Stained Squad.

Gordy's mom looked like she was struggling with the decision, her face contorted in frustration. "As much as I hate leaving you alone in the Swigs, this is a private meeting with Paulina. Priss and I are the only ones with invitations."

"He won't be alone, lass. I'll keep a good eye on him," Tobias said. "Your meeting place with Paulina should be about a mile in."

"A mile in?" Gordy asked, baffled. How was that possible?

Tobias's eyes sparkled as he swung the door open. "Welcome to the Swigs."

10

Before he had a chance to see anything, the fumes of the Swigs struck Gordy squarely in the jaw. A fragrant whirlwind seemed to blow through the opening, bombarding his senses all at once. Gordy's Deciphering skill kicked into overdrive as he caught the pungent scent of spilanthes and putrescine. The tang of wilting lotus flowers and bombardier beetle husks melded together with boxwood bark and what had to be peafowl feathers. It was as if someone had tipped over the world's largest spice rack and swept everything together in a massive pile on the kitchen floor.

Gordy immediately clamped a hand over his nose and mouth, trying to block the wave. He noticed his mother doing likewise, but Priss and Tobias seemed to be unaffected by the swarm of smells. Then Gordy caught sight of several dozen Elixirists beyond the door, crowded in a bustling group, and he forgot about the smells.

"No way!" he exclaimed. "Who are all these people?"

Most of them looked normal, wearing business suits, but mingled among them were more than a few oddballs. A woman—at least Gordy thought she was a woman—wore a hat made of some kind of beaded curtain that covered her body completely. The colorful beads swished back and forth, making the woman look like an undulating caterpillar standing on one end and weaving her way through the middle of the crowd.

Tobias squeezed Gordy's shoulder and whispered in his ear. "Careful now, Scheel. People might start to question your frequency here if you ask such things."

Gordy gritted his teeth and nodded. He had to somehow keep his cool, which was turning out to be harder than expected. The Swigs were basically a long tunnel with a high ceiling. There were pathways splintering away from the main strip and additional closed doors, some of which were guarded by unfriendly looking Elixirists.

The crowds of people made it feel more like the entryway into an amusement park. More glowing pink potions lit up the tunnel from the tops of poles, but other lights poured out from beneath the awnings of shops, which were separated by nothing more than a piece of sheet metal. Animal carcasses dangled from hooks in the entryway of one shop while dried herbs hung from another. Gordy recognized several of the herbs immediately and grinned with eagerness. Most of what he saw couldn't be found anywhere in the country, and here they all were, within arm's reach.

"Are those Gloriosa petals?" Gordy kept his voice low as he pressed close to Priss. Unlike Tobias and Wanda, Priss seemed to revel in Gordy's excitement.

"That's the only shop in more than two thousand miles where you can buy them," Priss replied. "And they have Kadupul seeds as well."

Gordy trembled with excitement. "Shut up! For real?"

"Highly illegal, though," she said, nodding. "Should you be caught with even a couple ounces of those seeds in your satchel, you'll land yourself with a six-month-long Sequester Strap from B.R.E.W."

"How much are they?" he asked. His mom shot him a deadly look, and Gordy cringed apologetically. "I'm not going to buy any. I'm just curious."

"Your curiosity can be dangerous here," his mom said and then glared sharply at Priss. "Stay on task, please. This is not a grocery store."

Priss snickered. "At ease, Akerberg. Kadupul seeds are two hundred dollars each, and you need at least eight to concoct an effective Terramoto Tonic. So unless you've significantly upped this boy's allowance, I wouldn't worry too much about it."

"Sixteen-hundred dollars!" Gordy's mouth dropped open. Who had that kind of money to blow on seeds? Still, he had been dying to brew a Terramoto Tonic since he first read about the rare and dangerous earth-shifting potion more than a year ago.

Gordy's mom pushed through the throngs of people,

fixing almost everyone with the deadliest stare Gordy had ever seen. Even without the appearance of Akerberg, she would have looked ruthless.

"Probably not the best time to go shopping." Tobias slapped a hand on Gordy's shoulders. "Your mother has spent the greater portion of her life as B.R.E.W.'s Lead Investigator, trying to find her way into the Swigs. What she wouldn't give to take down most of these establishments."

"But they're just selling ingredients. Is it really that big of a deal?" Why wouldn't his mom be happy for the chance to purchase these items? It seemed that the Swigs acted more as a shopping mall for Elixirists. What could be the harm in that?

"You wouldn't think so," Priss said. "But the Swigs have always stood in opposition of what she has been taught at B.R.E.W."

Once away from the exit and farther down the road, the initial wave of overlapping smells transformed into something more appetizing. Aside from potion booths and shops, vendors peddled food items. Several large Polynesian men turned an entire skewered pig on a spit. But instead of a fire or coals, a luminous substance coating the animal's flesh glowed rosy in color as the spit rotated.

"They're using modified ogon oil," Tobias muttered. "Cooks in half the time but leaves an aftertaste of musk-deer tongue. I'd rather wait for a proper roasting myself."

One of the Polynesian men wearing a grease-stained

apron, his hair pulled back in a bun, sifted a large salt-shaker over a steaming wok of what looked like roasted nuts. A butane torch blazed beneath the bottom of the wok, and the nuts started popping and cracking open, their insides sizzling against the hot, oiled metal.

"Garlic-buttered phasmid eggs," Priss said, noticing Gordy's interest. "They've purposely made them bigger, otherwise you wouldn't have much of a bite."

Upon hearing Priss, the man glanced up from his wok and motioned them over. He pointed to a tray of white paper sacks, each one filled to the brim with the glistening, blackened nuts.

The oil and garlic smelled wonderful; Gordy's stomach gurgled.

"Six dollars and seventy-five cents," he said. "Or two bags for ten."

Priss waved him off politely just as the vendor starting lowering his prices. "Trust me," Priss said to Gordy as they walked past. "Those aren't something you'd want for a snack."

"What are phasmid eggs anyway?" Gordy had never heard of them.

"You ever seen a giant walking stick before?" Tobias asked. "You know—the ones in Asia?" He held his hands a foot apart to show the size and grinned. "Some are as big as your arm."

Gordy shuttered, the gurgling in his stomach ceasing almost at once. "Please tell me you're kidding."

Tobias licked his lips and rubbed his belly. "They have the same effect as a five-hour energy drink."

"Joslat Juice here!" A woman who could have been Gordy's Grandma Stitser's twin had her hair been slightly grayer sat on a stool next to the phasmid egg vendor. A tray containing vials of opalescent liquid rested in front of her. "There's a strong brute for you." She nodded at Gordy. "But all those muscles can't stop what's coming. Better to know than to not."

Muscles? Strong brute? Gordy wasn't sure what she was talking about, but then he remembered how he looked in his Scheel disguise and it all made sense.

"You have enough money," the woman said, eyes twinkling. "I can sense it. And if you feel you're a bit shy on coins, I'm sure you'll know how to get some."

"Not interested," Gordy answered, though he felt drawn to the strange vials. Joslat Juice? Had he read about that in one of his mom's manuals? If so, he couldn't remember.

The woman's eyes twinkled with delight as Gordy stepped toward her stool. "Want to see your future in a dream? Sip this on an empty stomach at midnight and your vision is guaranteed to come true!"

No way! Gordy thought. Less than twenty yards into the Swigs and Gordy had already discovered something his mom had never told him about.

"I told you this place is dangerous." Gordy's mom glared at the woman, who met her gaze with a puzzled expression. "We're not interested in purchasing your wares."

"Strange talk," the woman said, eyes narrowing in suspicion. "Do I know you? Done business in the past?"

"That's bogus, you know." Gordy's mom jabbed her index finger at the vials. "There are no such things as prophetic potions. That myth was debunked years ago. You should be locked up for even trying to sell them."

The woman shrugged. "Locked up? As in taken before a B.R.E.W. tribunal and Banished, maybe?" She cracked a smile, and Gordy could see through the gap in her front teeth to her tongue. "That's no way to talk to an honest peddler." She held up a finger, a thought striking her. "I do know you," she said, and waggled the finger at Gordy's mom. "But not this you."

"You're not making any sense," Gordy's mom replied. "You've probably ingested too much of your own product."

"Come on, guys. Let's make way for paying customers." Tobias nudged Wanda with his elbow, the tension rising. Gordy was eager to get away from the argument as well and felt relieved when Tobias finally succeeded in pulling his mom a few steps away. "How quickly you forget who you are, *Akerberg*." He squeezed her arm. "You can't talk to people like that here."

"I don't know how many Scourges I put away who believed they were destined for greatness because of some ridiculous Joslat Juice prophecy." Wanda shook her head in frustration. "This is a horrible place. Don't you see how it can alter reality? Some poor, down-on-his-luck Elixirist drinks a Tainted potion and goes on a rampage. B.R.E.W. has laws specifically to protect us from this nonsense."

"Oh, Wanda," Priss scoffed. "That woman's selling a dream potion. That's all. And you're turning her into some criminal mastermind."

"I see straight through that façade, dear," the older lady called out from behind them. "You and the man!" Her loud voice cut through the commotion of chattering vendors and made Gordy's skin crawl. She was still holding up her finger, shaking it as though she had realized the truth. "Fairly decent disguises, I must say. Someone is gifted at brewing Disfarcar Gels, but it makes me wonder." She tapped her finger to her pursed lips. "Why would someone need to hide their identity in this place?"

Tobais turned around and took the few steps back to her table. "Settle down, now. No one's disguising themselves." He passed her several crinkled bills and selected a vial from her tray. "You swear by this mixture?"

Eventually she broke eye contact with Gordy, then turned and tendered Tobias's transaction. Both she and Tobias spoke in hushed voices, and after some coaxing, the woman smiled and thanked him for his purchase.

"Just ignore her," Priss said to Gordy under her breath. "Everything's fine."

"Are you sure?" Gordy asked, feeling a nervous jolt in his stomach. Had the woman really seen through their disguises, or was she just babbling nonsense?

"Nothing to worry about." Tobias ambled up with a new potion in tow. "Folks here will say anything for a sale. But just to be safe, you should probably get off the main road. Let the mood soften a bit." He slipped the bottle into his satchel and clapped his hands. "Okay, this is where we go our separate ways. Come along, friend." He nodded at Gordy. "We have business elsewhere, and bowls of creamed ham to consume."

"Yuck," Gordy muttered.

"Don't knock it until you try it." Tobias pointed to a spot less than thirty yards away where an enormous multi-colored pig had been painted on a sign above an entryway. "See you two in an hour."

Gordy thought about hugging his mom but then changed his mind. They were already treading lightly. What would people think if Scheel suddenly embraced Akerberg out in the open? Tobias would have to buy the rest of that woman's fortune-telling potions just to shut her up. Instead, Gordy extended a hand to his mom, and she squeezed it warmly, her calloused hands scratching his palms.

"Stay out of trouble," she whispered. "But if trouble finds you . . ." She looked pointedly at Tobias. "You leave right away. Don't wait for us."

"Got it." Gordy let go, and Tobias nudged him into the flow of traffic. Before he had time to consider changing his mind about separating, his mom and Aunt Priss were gone.

11

It had been at least two years since Adilene had sat on the swings in the park at the end of her neighborhood. Life was busy for an eighth-grader, and even busier for one who was best friends with Gordy Stitser.

Her swing creaked as she dangled, the vinyl seat digging into her hips. The smell of rusted chains mixed with the crisp scent of pine needles brought on a hint of nostalgia. She used to love to ride her bike to the park after school and read a book while she occupied a swing. Tonight was the first time she had ever come to the park so late, and though she didn't have an actual paperback book, she *was* trying to read something but struggling mightily.

"Come on," Adilene muttered, squinting in the dark.

The words on her phone jumbled together, her eyesight blurring, as she held the screen up close and blinked. Why was she having such a hard time reading it? Adilene's head ached, and she gnawed her lip in frustration. She had increased the size of the text on her e-reader app by fifty percent, and it still looked like someone had smudged grease all over her screen.

Adilene wiped the glass with her sleeve and flipped through another couple of pages, which took way longer than it should have. She closed the app and lowered her phone into her lap.

A snapping twig announced a visitor, and Adilene shot an anxious glance over her shoulder as Sasha emerged from the wooded area behind the park, wearing a long-sleeve T-shirt and blue jeans. She carried a flashlight, narrow beam homed in on Adilene, and a leather satchel draped over one shoulder, which swished back and forth as she strolled up to the swing set.

Adilene stood, folding her arms tightly across her chest. "Were you followed?"

"Oh, yes, they're right behind me," Sasha Brexil replied sarcastically. "I wasn't followed, and even if I was, I know how to lose a tail."

"That's good," Adilene said. "I wasn't followed either. I don't think."

Sasha snickered. "Yeah, no big shocker there."

"Why do you say that?" The park may have been less than a quarter of a mile away from Adilene's house, but that seemed an adequate amount of time to be followed. "There could be B.R.E.W. investigators anywhere."

"I hate to break it to you, but you're not important enough to B.R.E.W. to warrant following. They have no reason to tap your phone lines or to ransack your room. It's not like you're Gordy's girlfriend. Or are you?" Sasha asked.

"I'm Gordy's *best* friend," Adilene fired back.

"That may be true, but they don't see it that way. Now, Max, on the other hand, might want to stop drawing so much attention to himself." Sasha gestured to Adilene's phone. "What were you reading just now? Was that a message from Gordy?"

"No, it was just a book. Only Max can receive texts from him, remember?"

Sasha huffed, turning up her nose. "Some best friend you are."

Adilene shifted her weight to her other leg and pursed her lips. Trying to be cordial to Sasha was requiring all her energy. She'd agreed to come here to help Sasha, so why was she always being so difficult?

"Do your parents know you've snuck out?" Sasha's eyes darted over to the road as a car drove past the park. The vehicle's headlights illuminated Sasha's face, and her golden earrings sparkled.

"My dad's asleep on the couch in front of the television, and my mom is at her book group," Adilene said. "She'll be there for a while."

"And when your dad wakes up and goes to check on you in your room . . ."

"He won't," Adilene answered. Why did it matter? It's not like Sasha had to worry about the Riveras being angry with her. "What about your parents?"

"I gave my mom one of my special sleeping potions an hour ago, and she downed the whole thing. My recipe is way better than the ones they teach you during training." She glanced arrogantly at her fingernails as if to showcase the hands that had expertly brewed her potion, but Adilene could tell it was just an act. Sasha had talked a mean game from the moment Adilene had met her, and a few weeks ago she may have meant every word of it, but not anymore. Now, every harsh thing she spat out was another block trying to hide her sadness.

"My father's still at the school," Sasha continued. "He had a meeting with the superintendent earlier this afternoon that lasted like four hours. He just texted me to say he won't be home until after midnight."

"On a Saturday?" Adilene asked. "What was the meeting about?"

Sasha glared at her. "That's none of your business."

Adilene held up her hands apologetically. "You don't really think he's getting fired, do you?"

"Who did you hear that from?" Sasha demanded in a clipped tone.

"Uh . . . no one!" Adilene retreated a step, nearly tripping over the swing behind her. "I mean, it was some kids in the cafeteria. I overheard them, but they were just talking."

"Well, I'm sorry to disappoint you, but he's not getting fired."

"That doesn't disappoint me. I like your dad." That

wasn't a lie. Mr. Brexil was friendly and almost always re-membered Adilene's name when she saw him in the halls.

"Yeah, whatever." Sasha shrugged. "Anyway, he told me in his text that everything was fine. The superintendent was just going over some policy changes for the schools. That's all."

Adilene nodded and looked away from Sasha's glaring eyes. "That's great. I'm glad."

"But if he does get fired or we're forced to move away, you'll know why, right?"

"Because of B.R.E.W.?"

"That's right. Because B.R.E.W. wants the Brexils to disappear. They want to wash their hands of our family. And if you don't think they have ways to make that fat superintendent fire my dad, then you obviously have a lot to learn about B.R.E.W."

Adilene swallowed. Even if Sasha was hiding her sad-ness behind a mask of arrogance and anger, she still wasn't someone Adilene wanted as an enemy.

Another car drove by, slower than the first, and Adilene ducked her head so that her ears crept between her shoulders. Was it a police car patrolling the neighborhood? Adilene braced herself to hear a sudden siren and see flash-ing lights, but the car drove on, leaving the two of them in darkness.

Sasha waited until the car was gone, then said, "I need to get back in case my dad decides to come home early, so let's hurry this up."

"Oh yeah," Adilene replied, but there was no enthusiasm in her voice. She had been hoping Sasha would change her mind. "How do we do this?"

"I brought a lancet with me," Sasha answered.

"A what?"

Sasha showed Adilene something that looked like a syringe, only one with a thicker tube. It was what Adilene had feared—a sharp object. Sasha intended to cut Adilene.

"Hold out your finger," Sasha said.

Adilene frowned. "Will it hurt?"

Sasha looked down at the lancet and shrugged. "Probably. Like a beesting. If you hold perfectly still, it will hurt less."

Adilene didn't like the idea of having her finger pricked. Was that device even sanitary? But she knew there was no way around it. Surrendering, she braced herself as Sasha wiped her fingertip with something wet that smelled strongly of rubbing alcohol. Adilene refused to look as Sasha touched the rubber end to her skin and firmly pressed down.

"Ouch!" Adilene winced, but though it did sting, it wasn't as bad as she'd feared. Sasha even dabbed her finger with a cotton ball and placed a bandage over the wound.

"Are you crying?" Sasha mocked.

"No," Adilene snapped. "My eyes are just watering a little bit."

Sasha checked the contents of the tube with her flashlight. Adilene could see the red glowing in the light. "This should be enough," she said. "But if I need more . . ."

"Forget it," Adilene said. "You've poked me one time too many."

Carefully returning the lancet to her satchel, Sasha started to zip up the pocket.

"Aren't you forgetting something?" Adilene asked. "We're trading, right?"

"You weren't serious, were you?" Sasha scrunched her nose. "Haven't you been humiliated enough?"

"That was the deal." Adilene moved forward a step and held out her hand—the other one, without the wounded finger. "You said you would do whatever I wanted, and I kept my end of the bargain."

Exhaling obnoxiously, Sasha opened another pocket in her satchel and pulled out a grocery bag, a vial of dark liquid, and a folded piece of paper.

Adilene moved closer and used the flashlight app on her phone to see better.

"This is the recipe for a basic Moholi Mixture." Sasha passed the folded paper to Adilene. "I make it all the time. It's one of the easiest potions to master. First-year Drams learn this on day one." She emphasized her words as if trying to insult Adilene. Adilene ignored her. "Five ingredients. Seven simple steps. No special cauldron necessary. You can brew it in any metal pot, and it doesn't require much heat."

Adilene opened the paper, narrowing her eyes to try to read the recipe, but it was too dark and the words blurred together. Maybe she needed to get her vision checked.

"What does it do?" Adilene asked.

"Melts metal," Sasha said. "Turns it into vapor."

"Really?" Adilene caught herself from laughing. That sounded amazing. "Is it safe?"

"Totally safe. You could drink this whole vial and be fine," Sasha said and then gave an annoyed sigh. "You're probably naïve enough to do that, so don't drink it. But yeah, it's safe. It will only melt metal, nothing else, and just equal to the amount you pour out. A vial this size"—she held up the small bottle of potion—"could dissolve maybe a toaster or the handlebars of your bicycle. But it works instantly. If you accidentally spill it on the hood of your dad's car, don't come running to me, begging for a way to plug up the hole."

"Wow." Adilene eyed the vial of Moholi Mixture and smiled. What if she could somehow make something like that herself? The thought gave her goose bumps.

"Here are the ingredients." Sasha plopped the grocery bag of supplies into Adilene's arms. Next, she handed Adilene the vial of liquid. "I'm giving you the actual potion so you can see what it is supposed to look like when yours doesn't work." She grinned obnoxiously, and Adilene had to bite her tongue to keep from being baited into an argument.

"Thank you," Adilene said.

Sasha shrugged. "Don't thank me. You're going to fail—and most likely in a miserable way. I know you think I'm saying that to hurt your feelings, that I'm some horrible monster who wants nothing more than to rub your face in the fact that Gordy and I can do things that you can only dream about, but I'm not. I'm trying to help you. You're not a Dram, Adilene. You won't become one. And the longer it takes for you to accept that fact, the more painful it will be for you in the end."

Adilene hugged the bag in her arms. A stalk of some sort of vegetable—like celery but oddly fluorescent—poked out from the opening. She knew Sasha was right. Nothing had changed. She had failed at every attempt to brew an actual potion on her own. Sure, she had experienced some success while Gordy had been with her, but that didn't count. He had only been using Adilene as an instrument, projecting his ability through her.

"Well, just so you know, I appreciate you giving me the recipe and the ingredients." Adilene fought back tears. "I have to keep trying."

Sasha tilted her head. "I don't take any joy in proving you wrong. I hope you know that."

"I know." But she sensed obvious joy pouring out of Sasha whenever she put Adilene in her place.

Adilene dropped the recipe and the potion vial into the bag of ingredients and then tucked everything neatly into her backpack next to her notebook—the one containing her own notes of recipes and ingredients she had jotted down while brewing with Gordy. She turned to say good-bye, but Sasha was already halfway across the park, ducking beneath the branches of the wooded area behind it. She didn't even acknowledge Adilene as she left.

12

Tobias's preferred cookery was a hole-in-the-wall dive with three battered tables and a few splintery chairs scattered about the meager establishment. A single ceiling fan wobbled precariously overhead with cobwebs clinging from the blades, whirling in a circle like carousel swings at an amusement park. There was a bar with glass mugs on the countertop, a couple of jars of murky liquid crammed on the shelves behind them, and a window opening into a back kitchen area where a cloud of steam hindered almost all visibility. Gordy couldn't see any employees behind the bar or in the kitchen. And as far as other customers were concerned, there was just one, and he was snoring loudly upon a table by the far wall.

Gordy had been to lots of restaurants with his family over the years, but this one was by far in the worst condition. His combat boots felt extra heavy as he attempted to walk into the room, his heels sticking to the floor.

"Ah, can you smell it?" Tobias asked, grinning blissfully

and plopping into one of the chairs at the center table. The rotted wood nearly collapsed beneath his weight. "Creamed ham is a delicacy."

Gordy cautiously took the seat next to him. Considering the state of the restaurant, the garlic phasmid eggs out on the street were starting to look far more appetizing than whatever entrée he might find here.

Something whistled from the kitchen, a sort of tinny, metallic shriek, like that of a raging teakettle, and the snoring customer shot up from his table. Gordy jumped as the man's chair clattered to the floor and several insects scurried for cover.

"Fine, fine. Don't trouble yourself one bit," the man grumbled, yawning. An unhealthy number of joints in his back crackled as he stretched and shoved one loose end of his shirt beneath his belt. He appeared to be of Asian descent, with dark skin and long, unkempt hair as black as coal that fell about his shoulders in knots.

The man stumbled out of the eating area, nearly tripping over the leg of Gordy's chair as he brushed past. Muttering incoherently and possibly in a foreign language, he meandered groggily toward the bar, and then, to Gordy's surprise, nimbly leaped over the countertop before vanishing into the gathering steam. What followed next was a cacophony of glaring shouts of anguish, a few more unrecognizable words that Gordy assumed were unpleasantries, and the sound of clanging metal. The whistling teakettle ceased abruptly, and the cloud pouring from the kitchen cast the restaurant in a much deeper haze.

"That guy works here?" Gordy pointed to the kitchen.

Tobias nodded. "That's Yosuke. Listen—he's not to be trifled with. He's irritable, insulting, and prone to violence."

"What do you mean—prone to violence?" Gordy looked nervously toward the kitchen.

Tobias leaned closer. "How are you at defending yourself from say . . . a knife attack?"

"What?" Gordy croaked. Knife attack? Who would be wielding a knife?

Tobias held up a hand, trying to keep him calm. "Keep your voice down. Don't make a scene. Nothing will happen—probably. Just be on guard. Yosuke and Scheel never got along well. Their last exchange ended in fisticuffs."

Gordy stiffened and started to climb out of his seat. "Then we should leave." There were plenty of other places to grab a bite to eat while they waited for his mom's meeting to end.

"Too late." Tobias clicked his tongue and gestured hastily at Gordy's chair. "We're paying customers now. If you try to leave, it won't bode well for either of us."

"Um, I don't think I'm that hungry . . ." Gordy started to say but was cut short as something heavy thudded upon the table.

Yosuke loomed above him, glaring down in disgust. Somehow the man had vaulted back over the bar and covered the distance from the kitchen while balancing three wooden bowls of soup in the crooks of his elbows without making a sound. Gordy could see the pencil-thin wisp of a mustache twitching beneath the man's pudgy nose. He looked much older than Gordy expected. The corners of his eyes bore deep creases, and a webwork of wrinkles was etched into his skin, along with an ancient-looking scar that traveled down the length of his face. The old wound looked to have been crudely stitched back together at one time, and from a distance it made him appear even more menacing.

With a raspy exhale, Yosuke tossed two bowls on the table, one in Tobias's direction and one in front of Gordy. The bowl wobbled, its contents sloshing sickeningly. Yosuke dragged over a chair and sat down to join them. No words were spoken as he divvied out spoons, and then he grunted, which apparently was code to start eating.

Tobias immediately began scarfing down his soup, hardly pausing to breathe.

Gordy stared down at his bowl. He was definitely hungry. His nervousness about his trip to the Swigs had prevented him from eating all day, but consuming anything creamed from that kitchen would most certainly land Gordy in the emergency room. Coming to this restaurant had been the worst idea ever.

"Very rude to turn away an offered meal," Yosuke said, slurping a spoonful. Gordy couldn't place his accent, but he didn't think it was Chinese. "Where I come from, that could be taken as an offense."

Gordy's stomach folded upon itself as he eyed the pink glop. What if he threw up? Wouldn't that be worse than not eating? Hand trembling, he raised his spoon and slid the warm mush into his mouth.

It took most of his strength to not gag, but then Gordy realized the soup didn't taste all that bad. It was like a ham sandwich, only blended up with chunks of . . . What was that? Corn? Gordy hoped it was corn.

"What's wrong?" Yosuke asked, eyes narrowing. "You don't like it?"

Gordy swallowed. "No, no, it's awes—" He coughed into his hand, creamed ham rising back up his throat. "So awesome. It's my favorite!"

Yosuke produced a hissing sound in his throat and slammed his spoon down next to his bowl. "Just like the last time when you insulted my family!" Chair legs screeched against the floor as he shoved away from the table. He slipped his hand beneath his shirt, snagging hold of something out of view. Was he carrying a knife tucked into his waistband? "Then you have the nerve to come here and sit in my restaurant?"

"Look, sir, I honestly—" Gordy shot a panicked glance in Tobias's direction, searching for help, but Tobias was devouring his own meal and not paying attention.

"I always repay my debts, Mr. Stitser. Always." Yosuke whipped out his hand, and Gordy gasped.

There wasn't time to be picky. Any potion would delay the attack, but as Gordy's fingers fumbled with the zipper, his satchel fell from his lap.

A warm substance splattered against his cheeks. He shrieked, shielding his eyes. Yosuke had struck him with some kind of potion. Something that felt oddly like . . . water.

Gordy opened his eyes and saw that Yosuke was not holding a knife but instead a green, plastic water gun. The man was grinning.

"I should take a picture!" Tobias smacked the table, laughing. "There's no way to recreate your expression right now."

"What's going on?" Gordy stared at Yosuke. "Wait—you called me Mr. Stitser. Not Scheel."

"I did," Yosuke admitted thoughtfully.

"You can see through my disguise?" First that strange lady and now this guy. If everyone in the Swigs could tell his identity, maybe Gordy's Disfarcar Gel brewing skills were less effective than he thought.

Yosuke paused before shrugging. "What disguise?"

"My . . ." Gordy looked down, and to his shock, he no longer resembled the burly Scheel. Gone were the stiff black hair covering his arms and the rippling, corded muscles. Gordy cleared his throat and realized his voice had changed as well. He shot a look in Tobias's direction, but the man didn't seem worried.

"That Disfarcar Gel was worthless!" Gordy shouted.

"I'm sure it was a perfectly brewed dose," Yosuke said. "But I may have slipped a little glowworm oil into your soup."

Glowworm oil was odorless, tasteless, and instantly removed any potion-induced disguises.

"I hope you don't mind, but you have no idea how difficult it is for me to have a heart-to-heart conversation when you look like Scheel." Yosuke snorted, and Tobias erupted in laughter once more.

"It's not funny," Gordy said, but the two men were beside themselves with glee, which made it difficult to keep from smiling. Gordy thought he had been one second away from being stabbed by a lunatic. Puffing out his cheeks, exasperated, Gordy glared at Tobias. "Did you bring me here just to play a prank?"

"Of course not. Creamed ham is my all-time favorite dish, and I wanted to introduce you to my good friend, Yosuke." Tobias gestured grandly to the man next to him. "The founder of the Swigs."

Dipping his head in a humble bow, Yosuke pressed a hand against his chest. "In truth, I'm more like the custodian of the Swigs," he said. "I keep the silver shining and sweep up the messes when required. Oh, and my apologies for our playful introduction. I am truly honored to meet the fabled son of Wanda Stitser. I've known about you for a long, long time."

"If you're really the founder of the Swigs, why don't you have a better place?" Gordy felt embarrassed about asking, but he wasn't sure he believed the man. This place had bugs and rats and who knew what else burrowing in the kitchen.

Yosuke raised an eyebrow. "Ah, judging a book by its cover? This is my home. My sanctuary. I have had many wonderful memories here. Far too many to count. Why would I give this up just so I can have cleaner floors and a kitchen that doesn't breed mildew and mold?"

"Are you the one who changes the entrance to the Swigs?" Gordy asked.

Yosuke nodded. "There are miles and miles of underground passageways. Most are no longer in use, but I'm afraid we've become the world's largest and peskiest termites."

"Yosuke's also the one who grants permission to new vendors," Tobias added. "He revokes rights to all who break our rules. There's not a transaction that transpires down here that he doesn't know about."

Gordy gnawed the inside of his cheek. "Then you know about my mom's visit."

"I do," Yosuke answered.

"And you're not stopping it?"

"Why would I? Your mother's intentions are wholesome. She's a good person." Yosuke cleared his throat. "Besides, I am one of the Stained Squad's benefactors. I have fully funded many of their missions, and before that"—his eyes twinkled—"I was a senior member of the Chamber of Directors."

Gordy started in surprise. "B.R.E.W.'s Chamber?"

"Is there another?" Tobias asked through a mouthful of soup.

"When did you work for them?" A senior member of the Chamber was one of the highest-ranking officials for B.R.E.W., second only to the Chamber President, a title which, until recently, had been held by Talia Brexil.

Yosuke closed his eyes as if caught up in a nostalgic

memory. "Many years ago. I worked my way up from the bottom and served for more than a decade in the Chamber."

"But then you did something bad at B.R.E.W., and my mom uncovered it, and she had you kicked out, right?" That seemed to be a constant theme in the Swigs. Elixirists who had once been employed by B.R.E.W. who now had personal vendettas against Gordy's mom.

"Not exactly," Yosuke said. "One of my last official acts as a member of the Chamber was to pardon Wanda and Priscilla for their crimes against the Community." He focused on Gordy. "I'm sure you've heard of what became of your grandfather, Mezzarix Rook."

"Yes," Gordy answered, feeling his cheeks surging with heat. "My mom Banished him to Greenland." But he had never heard that his mom had needed to be pardoned by B.R.E.W. Pardoned for what?

"Only at the end of his reign." A wry grin tugged at the corners of Yosuke's lips. "Before that, Wanda was his follower, and one who succeeded in doing damage to our Community. There are Scourges, and then there are Rooks. Volumes have been written about that family—your family." He pointed a long finger at Gordy.

"Are you saying my mom was a criminal?" Aunt Priss frequently had trouble with B.R.E.W., but not his mother.

"Not a criminal. Just misguided. We took into consideration the impact her father made on her decisions. Mezzarix was gifted at brainwashing," Yosuke reasoned. "If he could convince so many to adopt his ways, what chance did his own daughters have in refusing his wishes?"

Unable to hold back his anger any longer, Gordy leaped up from his seat, jarring his bowl of soup. "My mom was Lead Investigator!"

Tobias scowled at Gordy, but if Yosuke was outraged by the eruption, he masked it well.

"And she was good at it too," Yosuke said calmly. "She knew what to expect from the Scourge attacks and where to find their hiding places. She knew how to think like one. Easy to do since she was almost one herself."

"This is another one of your pranks, isn't it?" Gordy whirled on Tobias. B.R.E.W. meant the world to his mom. She stood for justice and fought against evil. She was his hero, and he wasn't about to let this stranger drag her reputation through the mud. "My mom is one of the good guys!"

"She is now!" Yosuke finally raised his voice. "But we all have a past, don't we? Some are more complicated than others. In the end, when it truly mattered, Wanda made the right decision. Both she and Priscilla did. They put a stop to Mezzarix's Manifesto and sought for mercy from the Chamber."

"The what?" Gordy asked. There was so much running through his mind he didn't know what to think anymore.

"Of course, you wouldn't have heard of it before. The Manifesto went away with your grandfather's Banishment. Mezzarix believed that in order to truly create greatness among the potion masters, there first had to be an elimination of prisons, governments, and secrets." Yosuke's eyes narrowed. "B.R.E.W. would be the first to crumble, and then everyone in the world would learn of our existence. There would be no need for rehabilitation or judgment from society anymore. Good intentions or ill, it made no difference to him. At that time, no one could match Mezzarix's power and ability. Certainly not myself or anyone else at B.R.E.W." Yosuke shook his head. "He would often say 'Take whatever you can,' because he knew he would be the ultimate taker. Allow the wicked to stake their claim on whatever they desired, and the cream would rise to the top. Your mother was once a firm supporter of that mentality."

Why had his mom kept her past a secret from him? She had allowed Gordy to believe Mezzarix had been a farmer and had died in an accident before he was born. Gordy had only thought she had lied because she was embarrassed about her grandfather's history. Had she been trying to keep the truth about *her* history from him as well?

Easing back into his chair, Gordy looked at Tobias. "You knew about this?"

Tobias dabbed at his mouth with the back of his sleeve. "I knew of the Rook family from when I was employed by B.R.E.W., but I didn't know the extent of your mother's mischief until much later. By then, Wanda had already betrayed me, given me the boot, and sent me scrabbling for scraps in the Swigs." He glanced at Yosuke, his lips forming a taut line. "It wasn't until I became associated with Yosuke a couple of years ago that I learned the rest of her tale."

"And you just forgave her for everything she did?" Gordy was still unconvinced. "Just like that?"

Yosuke nodded. "We became close friends. I was her trainer. She was talented already, but I helped guide her brewing in the right direction. Teaching her was my request—my final request." He patted his chest as though relishing his finest moment, then his countenance changed from pride to disappointment. "I don't expect you'll understand, but I believed someone with her sense of purpose would be just what B.R.E.W. needed. I saw her potential. Saw what she could offer. Then, shortly after Wanda completed her first year at headquarters, I left the Chamber."

"To become the founder of the Swigs." Gordy's forehead furrowed. "B.R.E.W.'s enemy." That part didn't make any sense. How did someone go from being a member of the Chamber to the creator of something in open opposition of B.R.E.W.'s guidelines and laws?

Yosuke's eyes twinkled. "Ask me why I did it. Why I abandoned all that I had worked for. My prestige. My reputation. I openly rebelled against B.R.E.W., much like your family did. Why did I do that?"

"I don't know." Gordy shrugged. "Why did you?"

"Because I finally understood that it was *our* doing that brought *our* own pain. B.R.E.W.'s controlling ways, our rules, our harsh punishments, led Mezzarix to us." Yosuke jabbed a thumb into his chest. "Instead of trying to work out our differences, we Banished and ExSponged Elixirists. We created the Scourges, one by one. And when your mother became the Lead Investigator, determined to destroy anyone who thought differently than she did, I knew I could no longer be a part of such a monstrous organization. Wanda was never an evil person. She was kind and thoughtful. Mezzarix may have misled her, but B.R.E.W. transformed her."

The air drained from Gordy's lungs. Could that really be true? Shaking his head, Gordy spoke in a strained voice. "My mom stopped a lot of bad people. They were doing terrible things, and she stopped them."

"Yes, we are safer because of her hard work against the Scourges." Yosuke swirled his spoon in his bowl. "But she also sent a lot of good people away in the process. Ones who were just curious and needed guidance and a place to explore their talents. They needed an institution, not a Forbidden Zone. You've seen the Swigs for yourself. What do you think? Is it bad?"

Gordy swallowed. "Not all bad."

"Precisely!" Yosuke smacked the table.

Gordy thought about B.R.E.W. and what it truly stood for. He thought about the good people trying to do the right thing. Bolter, for sure. And . . . was there anybody else? Sasha's mom had been a corrupt Chamber President, and upon her ExSpongement, the new Chamber had abandoned her. Zelda had been decent up until she joined Mezzarix. And then there was Tobias, who Gordy genuinely liked and respected, but who had been forced to go into hiding by Gordy's mom. Was B.R.E.W., more than Mezzarix, really the enemy?

"B.R.E.W.'s not all bad," Gordy reasoned. They had made advancements in technology and helped with all sorts of important findings that made the world a better place.

"Of course not," Yosuke said. "No organization is all bad. In many ways, the Swigs and B.R.E.W. are brothers in their thinking." He leaned forward, pressing his hands against the table. "If we cannot see past our differences and unite for one great cause, your grandfather will trigger the end of the world as we know it. Nothing should be absolute—neither chaos nor control. True happiness is finding a way to allow both to coexist equally. You've managed to do that in your own life."

"Me?" Gordy breathed.

"You are like your mother and your grandfather in many ways, but you are also different," Yosuke explained. "You are linked to the Community, the outside world, the Swigs, and the Scourges. You are conflicted, but you are also someone with power and influence among many circles."

Gordy snickered. "I don't have any power."

"No?" Yosuke looked surprised. "Have you not fought against and defeated powerful dark Elixirists while also saving and protecting Mezzarix, the Scourge of Nations?"

"Yeah, not exactly. I—"

"Have you not saved B.R.E.W. on more than one occasion?" Yosuke continued, cutting Gordy off. "But also, have you not openly defied the Chamber President and, in the process, become an outlaw?"

"Yes, sort of, but most of that wasn't my fault," Gordy

tried to explain. "I wasn't trying to do any of that. I was just in the wrong place at the wrong time."

"Yet by doing so, you've become rooted in multiple areas of society. You are respected, and you have a good heart and good intentions."

Exhaling slowly, Gordy stared down at his hands, unsure of how to process the information. Despite their unexpected introduction, there was something in Yosuke's manner that Gordy appreciated. Maybe even respected. He liked the strange man and wanted to hear more stories about his mom and the early days of B.R.E.W. Maybe, if he was lucky, Gordy would be able to return another day and share a different conversation with Yosuke.

"What am I supposed to do now?" Maybe it was because it was close to midnight, but he felt exhausted.

Yosuke and Tobias exchanged a glance. "You feel you are too young to be faced with difficult decisions, but there will come a day when you will have to decide on the best choices for our people, and when that day comes, now you will be informed. Perhaps you can help all of us find a middle ground." He raised his spoon and slurped the last of his soup. "Let's retire to the kitchen. I've set up some equipment for us to brew together."

"Really?" Gordy's eyebrows perked up.

"Yes, Tobias tells me you have many secrets," Yosuke said, rising from his seat. "Ones you don't even share with your mother."

Gordy shot a wary glance over at Tobias. "I don't have any secrets."

"Come off it, boy." Tobias grunted. "You didn't really believe I would allow someone to brew in my home without my knowledge of it, did you?"

"What are you talking about?" Gordy felt more than a hint of concern growing in his chest.

Tobias narrowed his eyes. "I have security cameras all throughout my kitchen. It may look like a humble dwelling, but I've never shied away from technology. And I've watched you now, several times, do that weird thing with your finger."

Gordy's concern rapidly morphed into a sinking pit in his stomach. He'd thought he'd been brewing all alone, but Tobias had watched him. He had seen what Gordy could do.

"You look concerned," Yosuke said, gripping the wooden back of the chair.

"Tobias, I'm so sorry!" Gordy blurted. "It won't happen again. I promise!"

Tobias's harsh gaze softened. "I'm not angry with you. On the contrary, it's one reason I brought you here."

"You haven't told my mom yet?" Gordy asked warily.

"Now, why would I do a foolish thing like that?" Tobias replied. "Wanda doesn't do well with secrets, and I've kept my fair share from her." He scooted his chair back from the table and stood next to Yosuke. "But if anyone can help you, it's my friend Yosuke."

14

A blue syringe dangled in place of a sign above the doorway of Wanda and Priss's destination. The door opened, and a bald man wearing an overcoat stepped out. His shoulders filled the width of the doorway, and his hardened expression looked like it had been chiseled from granite. Wanda could see the tips of corked vials poking up from the man's pockets and wondered if there would be any trouble getting past him. But after several tense moments of silence, the guard waved them through.

"He seems friendly," Priss muttered.

"I've seen him before," Wanda answered. "He's one of the Stained Squad's hired muscle."

Through a narrow entryway, Wanda and Priss entered a smallish room that would have made a fortune-teller feel right at home. A modest chandelier hung from the ceiling above a circular table with several chairs tucked beneath it. The air was filled with fragrant incense that coiled and drifted hazily at eye level.

"Hello, Wanda," a woman said. The soft glow of the chandelier cast a faint circle upon her, leaving the rest of the room in shadow. She was of Middle Eastern descent, with thin shoulders, and wore simple, loose fabrics. Her head was covered with a silky wrap.

Wanda scanned the room, clutching her satchel.

"Ah, Priscilla, good to see you as well." Paulina nodded at Priss. "How's Portugal these days?"

"How would I know?" Priss replied. "I've been here for months. My herb garden has shriveled up, and I don't even want to think about my poor goat. Hopefully, someone rescued him from starvation." She slipped next to Wanda, nudging her gently with her shoulder. "Cozy place you have here. I take it you don't entertain many guests."

Paulina smiled pleasantly. "That's not our forte."

Wanda noticed a mirror hanging on each of the four walls. Beneath each mirror, a stick of incense burned in a holder, smoke rising as if drawn to the light. Wanda's true reflection peered back at her, not the one of Akerberg.

Wanda gestured to the sticks of incense. "I suppose anyone could just purchase Unmocita Kara down here in the Swigs. Never mind the fact that prolonged exposure to the smoke has been known to cause irreversible paralysis."

"We won't be here long enough to worry about that," Paulina said. "But there can be no secrets here and no disguises. Certainly not for this meeting. Now, please take a seat."

Wanda and Priss sat, each of them tucking their satchels

in their laps as Paulina drummed her fingers rhythmically on the tabletop.

"Can we finally get down to business?" Wanda asked. "I want to know why you've been withholding information these past weeks. I thought we had a deal."

"Our deal is still intact." The patter of Paulina's fingertips slowed. "I haven't been withholding any information. On the contrary, I've been forthcoming with all that I have learned."

"You know something has happened. You said so on the phone, but you wouldn't give me the details. I need to know what kind of danger my family is in. Starting with the names of the Scourges who have been released from their prisons."

Paulina's eyes flitted between the two sisters before she answered. "Within the last forty-eight hours, anyone worthy of your attention has gone missing from their Forbidden Zones. I've received confirmation from my informants that all high-level areas have been emptied. Upper Siberia. The Southern isles and the arid wastelands. It's the largest organized escape of Scourges in the history of B.R.E.W."

Priss caught her breath. "How many exactly?"

Paulina licked her lower lip. "More than a hundred and fifty."

Falling back in her chair with a thud, Priss whistled. "That's an army."

"A formidable one," Paulina agreed. "Highly skilled

and hungry for a taste of what they've been missing all these years."

Wanda felt a pit open in her stomach. "Forty-eight hours? Why wasn't I told sooner?"

"You're being told now," Paulina answered.

Wanda slapped the table. "This is what I'm talking about. You're withholding information! You have to know they'll be coming here."

"Oh, make no mistake, Wanda, many have already arrived and are even now holed up in their hiding places. We suspect the rest will trickle in by the first of the week. We weren't sure who we could trust with this information. Such is the inconvenience of war. I think you'll agree that traitors can pop up in the oddest of locations." Paulina steepled her fingertips. "Heard much from Zelda these days?"

Like the drifting smoke of the Unmocita Kara, silence hung in the air. Zelda had been Wanda's friend at B.R.E.W. If it hadn't been for Zelda, Wanda's family may have been seriously injured when Esmeralda Faustus first went on the attack. Zelda had been part of Wanda's close-knit circle of trusted associates. And last month, she had turned her back on B.R.E.W.

"You can't pin that on us," Priss said, breaking the silence. "Zelda made her own choices, independent of our wishes."

"To follow *your* father," Paulina added. "And she was

heavily rooted in B.R.E.W. You'll have to forgive me if I don't immediately extend trust to the Stitsers."

"You trust us now, right?" Wanda asked. "I was the one who helped Banish those Scourges." Anxiousness burrowed under her skin. Now, more than ever, she wanted to gather her family and hide them somewhere safe, but they were not together anymore. Gordon, Isaac, and Jessica were far away—perhaps out of danger, perhaps not. She wanted to run to Gordy right away and leave this horrid place. "They'll be coming for revenge."

"Some will," Paulina said, her nose twitching. "The misguided ones. The ones with the shortest tempers and the longest memories. We feel that most, however, haven't come to avenge their Banishments. Not directly at least. They're here by Mezzarix's request."

"To do what?" Priss asked.

Footsteps approached the rear door to the room, and Wanda could hear grumbling voices. It sounded as though there was a struggle happening outside, and she straightened in her chair.

"You will understand better if I show you," Paulina said.

The door opened, and another woman entered. She was dressed in a military uniform lined with pockets and padded armor. Gritting her teeth, the woman dragged in a man wearing a tattered gray business suit, a cloth sack covering his face, and forced him into a kneeling position next to the table.

Green bands glowed around the prisoner's wrists. Wanda recognized them as a modified application of a Ragaszto Ragout formed into handcuffs, something she'd used often in her previous employment. The same glowing substance had been adhered to the man's ankles as well, right above his mud-caked leather shoes. Whoever this person was, Paulina had no intention of allowing his escape.

"Is this really necessary?" the man exclaimed, struggling against his bindings. "I am not a threat to any of you!" His covered head snapped around as though he were trying to gather his bearings.

Wanda narrowed her eyes in suspicion. "I recognize that voice."

"As you should." Paulina nodded at her associate, and the woman yanked away the sack.

The face beneath was nothing special: middle-aged and ordinary. The man was more than a bit overweight, with stocky shoulders and a full head of salt-and-pepper hair. His bushy eyebrows crinkled as he squinted, trying to focus his eyes.

Wanda kept control of the emotions that flared up inside her as she fixed Paulina with a contemptuous glare. "What are you trying to do here?" She massaged the skin beneath her eyes with her fingers. "Just when I thought things couldn't get any worse."

Paulina stared at her prisoner. "You asked for our protection."

"This was not what I had in mind. I assure you, B.R.E.W. is not our enemy!"

"Who are you people?" the man demanded, plump cheeks quivering. "What do you want with me?"

"Who is he?" Priss whispered.

"Straiffe Veddlestone," Wanda answered.

Straiffe straightened his shoulders, puffing out his chest indignantly. "I am the acting president of the Society of Canadian Agro-Healers and one of the senior members of B.R.E.W.'s Chamber. I have been falsely imprisoned and slandered by these mercenaries, and if you wish to . . ." His voice trailed off, eyes widening, as he caught sight of one of the mirrors hanging on the wall. Incense smoke coiled, and Wanda's image reflected back from the glass. "Wanda? Is that really you? Oh, thank goodness! Finally, someone sensible. You would not believe what I've been through. Treated like an animal. Caged and starved and . . ." He held out his hands, bound in glowing shackles, but he kept his eyes on the mirror as though expecting the image to suddenly change. "I assure you this has all been a horrible mistake!"

"This week just keeps getting better and better," Priss said, folding her arms. "Now the two of us are accessories to kidnapping. We were already facing serious punishment. This will end with our lifelong Banishment."

"No, no, it . . . it's quite all right," Straiffe stammered. "These things happen. Accidents. Misunderstandings. I may have been mistreated by these . . . people, but considering the circumstances of Mezzarix's escape, a measure of lunacy is to be expected." He cleared his throat, moistening his lips with his tongue. "I, in no way, hold any of you accountable for these actions. Especially not you, Wanda. Let me go, give me back the personal belongings that you seized from me, and I will be on my way."

Wanda looked at Paulina. "Why *did* you capture him?" Kidnapping a Chamber member was madness, and yet Paulina had always been calculated in her actions. She had to have a good reason.

The woman standing guard over Straiffe removed an object from beneath her vest and placed it on the table. Wooden and cylindrical in shape, with strange markings carved into it, the object was frighteningly familiar.

"Is that what I think it is?" Wanda asked.

"A Decocting Wand," Paulina answered. "Similar to what your good friend Madame Brexil used on her victims. When we discovered this in Mr. Veddlestone's possession a couple of days ago, he had just finished ExSponging four individuals."

"I see," Wanda said, unfazed by Paulina's accusation. "And you wanted to step in and put a stop to it."

The news wasn't that shocking. B.R.E.W.'s Chamber had reintroduced the practice of ExSponging when Talia Brexil became Chamber President. It was harsh and cruel but not out of the ordinary. Naturally, the Stained Squad would be opposed to such an action. Though foolish to go against a Chamber member, it was a noble attempt.

"The Chamber has lost their minds," Priss hissed under her breath. "Who were the poor souls this time?"

Paulina ticked the names off on her fingers. "Davian Jordans, Collette Peterson, Albert Pennyweather, and Josefa Blanco."

Wanda's mouth fell open. "You just named off the other members of the Chamber."

Paulina gazed up grimly. "I did. Straiffe led a group of Scourges into a secret meeting where they proceeded in ExSponging almost every one of the Chamber of Directors."

"I'm not just going to sit here while you accuse me of these hideous crimes. You have no right to keep me and no proof!" Straiffe struggled against his bindings. He almost succeeded in knocking his captor's hands free from his shoulders, but she seized hold and forced him back to the floor.

"We've already obtained a confession from Straiffe using this Axiom Application," Paulina explained, pulling out a jar of glistening white cream. "We know the truth. He was not Blotched by the Scourges. He acted on his own accord as though purposely trying to destroy B.R.E.W."

"You said *almost* every member of the Chamber," Wanda said.

"Iris Glass has gone into hiding, but we are looking for her and hoping to find her before someone else does."

"I don't understand," Priss said. "He ExSponged the members of his own Chamber? That's kind of a backward way of becoming the president."

"I did no such thing!" Straiffe snapped.

Paulina plucked the jar from the table, covered her finger with the cream, and smeared it across Straiffe's forehead.

The portly man's demeanor instantly changed. He no longer struggled, his cheeks ceased quivering, and his pupils dilated.

"Tell them what you told us. Why did you attack the Chamber of Directors?" She twirled the jar of cream with her fingers, regarding Straiffe as one might gaze upon a murderous snake.

"Because I was told to. By Mezzarix," Straiffe answered.

"What did you stand to gain by this action?" Paulina continued.

"The Vessel's powers have been limited because of our Blood Link. Mezzarix's reach is strong but can only stretch so far. By removing all Chamber members, he will have the strength to realize his Manifesto. The Vessel will be destroyed. All prisons emptied. All governments vanquished. All secrets revealed." Straiffe's eyes focused on the Decocting Wand. "And he gave us each a wondrous gift."

Wanda's eyes narrowed. "Are you saying the Scourges he released were given a Decocting Wand to use against us?"

Straiffe nodded, lips morphing into a sadistic smile. "Most of us. The ones he trusted to act on his command. They are in the Swigs. They are in your neighborhoods. They are infiltrating your safe places." The man got to his feet despite the soldier pressing down against his shoulders. It was as though he had secretly ingested a strength potion.

"Rachel," Paulina said, snapping her fingers. "Take control of him."

"Get down!" the woman soldier commanded. "On the ground, now!"

But Straiffe ignored her, splitting his concentration between Wanda and the Decocting Wand resting within his reach. His wrists and ankles were bound, but he had surprising poise for a man of his size.

"None of you are safe!" His voice boomed. "This is the beginning of the end of B.R.E.W. Mezzarix's Manifesto shall be realized. And should you attempt to stop us, your fate will be grim and everlasting." He faced the table, sweat dripping from his furrowed brow. For a moment, he did nothing but gape at the weapon in wonder, his balance wavering. Then he straightened his shoulders and closed his eyes.

"I hereby proclaim myself ExSponged!" Straiffe lunged forward, pulling free of Rachel's grasp. He threw himself across the table, connecting with the Decocting Wand. He gasped sharply, then fell limp. The effects of the Axiom Application faded from Straiffe's eyes as his legs gave out beneath him and he slid to the floor.

"He just Self-ExSponged!" Priss shouted. "Why did he do that?"

"All that stands in the way of our triumph is Iris Glass," Straiffe snickered, his breath wheezing. "She's old and injured. I saw to that, personally. We will find her and ExSponge her. It's only a matter of time."

"You won't be doing anything but rotting in a Forbidden Zone. And now you can no longer brew." Paulina sounded calm, but Wanda suspected the leader of the Stained Squad felt the same anxiousness she did.

Straiffe shook his head. "No Banishment will last under Mezzarix, and once he learns of my faithfulness, he will restore my powers and place me upon a pedestal of prestige and glory. You have lost. I have won."

Rachel wrenched a now-subdued Straiffe from the floor and forced him through the back door, leaving the three women behind in the smoky room.

"Your father's Manifesto, radical as it may seem, has always made sense to me," Paulina said, her scratchy voice deepening. "I don't agree with it, of course, but one could argue his reasoning is rooted in truth. The leaders placed in charge *have* become corrupted just as much as the Scourges. I have no love for B.R.E.W. anymore. Not for many years, but no prisons equals madness. No governments . . . chaos."

"It has always been his wish," Priss said. "Since as far back as I can remember, since we were little girls"—she nodded at Wanda—"our dad has wanted the world to realize his vision."

"'When the truly powerful have control,'" Wanda said, remembering something her father used to say, "'positions won't matter.' Mezzarix sees this as his way of restoring the old breed of Elixirist, with him in the position of the most powerful. The ones we've locked up over the years for their crimes will now be the ones everyone fears. Everyone but our father."

"And B.R.E.W.'s involvement in technology? What becomes of that?" Paulina asked.

Priss sighed. "If he destroys the Vessel, it will all be dissolved."

"But why?" Paulina smacked the table emphatically. "Why take away our advancements as a people? Why not simply take control of the Vessel and use that technology for his own benefit?"

"Because he doesn't need it to be powerful," Wanda said. "And by taking it away from everyone else, Dad will firmly place himself at the top."

Wanda's head was spinning. Though Straiffe had been under the influence of the Axiom Application, he had acted in control of his faculties. He hadn't been Blotched. Whether driven by fear or purpose, it made no difference. The decision to Self-ExSponge had been all his doing. Straiffe had willingly given up his very existence to pave the way for Mezzarix's full return to power. It was terrifying.

And according to the traitorous former member of the Chamber of Directors, the Swigs were now crawling with Scourges just as fanatical as he was.

The ivory cauldron reached a screeching crescendo, announcing the completion of Gordy's potion as he blew out the Amber Wick and thick smoke poured sluggishly over the lip. Silver and nutmeg-colored ribbons swirled about in the bowl.

Yosuke kept silent, his eyes squinting with thoughtful interest, as he selected a wooden spoon from the counter and carefully dipped it into the cauldron, where it instantly crumbled into powder. "Oh my," he said.

Gordy bit his lip, trying not to grin. He had just brewed his first batch of Mureta Mush—a nineteenth-century potion that had been used at Finnish sawmills to pulp entire tree trunks within seconds. Yosuke had pulled the recipe from one of his ancient-looking potion manuals stacked in a footlocker. The yellowish paper, like the wooden spoon, had nearly crumbled to pieces at the slightest touch.

"I daresay your mother couldn't have brewed a finer batch," Yosuke said. "Or even your grandfather."

Gordy hardly knew Yosuke, but receiving praise from the founder of the Swigs seemed like a high honor.

"So what do you make of it?" Tobias asked. "It can't be good for the boy."

"No, it can't," Yosuke agreed.

Gordy swallowed. "What do you mean? I'm just substituting the ingredients."

"In the most unnatural way I've ever seen," Yosuke said.

Gordy had successfully brewed the Mureta Mush without the five black woodpecker bills, one of the essential components of the potion. When the recipe had called for that ingredient, Gordy, like he had done in Tobias's kitchen, had inserted his finger into the cauldron, filling in the gap, much to Tobias's and Yosuke's amazement.

"It's just Blind Batching, right?" Gordy reasoned. Only a handful of Elixirists in the world could Blind Batch, which meant not a lot was known about the mysterious practice.

"All potions have a recipe, even the undiscovered ones, and that recipe requires certain steps and elements. Blind Batching doesn't eliminate any of those steps. It simply works through an alternate recipe. What you're doing is defying the laws of potion-making." Yosuke gazed at Gordy as though seeing him for the first time. "You couldn't always do this, could you?"

Gordy shook his head. This development had only started the past couple of weeks. Before that, Gordy could Blind Batch, but he needed all the ingredients.

"It would seem that after you swallowed the Eternity

Elixir at B.R.E.W., it has taken up permanent residence within you," Yosuke said. "The Elixir is aiding you in supplying the missing ingredients."

"Do you think you can take a stab at Philtering it out of his system?" Tobias asked.

Yosuke shook his head. "I don't dare—not without his mother's permission."

"What's going to happen to me?" Gordy asked.

"There are many mysteries in our world, none more complicated than Mezzarix's prized potion," Yosuke said. "But until we fully understand what is happening inside you, I would avoid giving in to your urges to experiment."

"What if I accidentally do it again in my sleep?" Gordy wondered aloud, fearing the worst.

"I have a feeling you'll be just fine," Yosuke said. "So grim, this one."

"Just like his mother," Tobias added. His phone buzzed in his pocket. "Speak of the devil. Let's see what sort of remarks good ol' Mrs. Stitser has to share now." He tapped on the message.

In an instant, Tobias's snarky expression changed, eyes growing dark. He handed the phone to Yosuke.

Yosuke stood abruptly, grunting with determination.

"What did she say?" Gordy asked.

Tobias showed him his mother's message.

No time to explain. We need to move with phase two of our plan. Get my son out of the Swigs right now!

16

I told you I don't know!" Tobias snapped. "You read the same message I did." Gravel scattered behind the tires of Tobias's pickup truck as he sped out of the parking lot.

Gordy stared through the back window as the school bus shrank behind them. His mom and his aunt were still in the Swigs, somewhere below the road.

"If she's in trouble, we have to go back and help her!" Gordy demanded as he moved to open the door.

"Sit down and fasten your seat belt!" Tobias yanked on Gordy's sleeve, pulling him back into his seat. The truck veered onto the shoulder, mowing through the tall grasses. "We don't go back. We go home," he said, his voice calming. "Your mother will be fine. She's with Priscilla and Paulina, two top-notch Elixirists. If they can't handle themselves, then . . . well, there's nothing we can do to help. Besides, you're leaving in the morning. Packing up your things and cracking off at first light."

"Where are we going?" Gordy wasn't really surprised

by the news. The farmhouse had been a suitable hideout, but his mother had always planned to stay mobile.

"There's a place—west," Tobias said. "The Stained Squad have safe houses dotting the countryside; they'll give you sanctuary. I don't know what your mother did to gain their favor, but that Paulina Hasselbeck certainly feels indebted to her."

Before Mezzarix's attack on B.R.E.W. headquarters, Gordy had never heard of the Stained Squad. He wasn't entirely sure what sort of missions the potion-master mercenaries went on, but he doubted they were legal. Priss had mentioned Black Ops and potion smuggling more than once.

"Blast this fog!" Tobias tugged on a lever next to the steering wheel, activing the windshield wipers across the dry glass. "Must have gone overboard with my last batch of Slosh. Going to have to dial it back. This weather of mine's going to alert someone at B.R.E.W."

"I don't think this is from a storm," Gordy said.

"Of course it is. Look at the rain." Tobias smirked, glancing sideways at Gordy.

"But there isn't any rain," Gordy pointed out.

Tobias looked out the window and frowned. "Then what is this?"

Tapping on the brakes, Tobias slowed the vehicle, and the two of them leaned forward across the dashboard, gazing through the windshield. The truck's headlights barely penetrated the thick fog-like substance gathered around them, and Gordy could smell the acrid scent of wet smoke. What Tobias had initially mistaken as raindrops were actually gray pieces of ash fluttering down and disintegrating against the glass.

"Why would there be smoke?" Tobias muttered more to himself than to Gordy. Then his eyes pulled wide, and he slammed a heavy foot down on the gas pedal. "No, no, no!"

Less than a mile away from the turnoff leading to Tobias's property, the sky had changed from black to a vibrant salmon-colored orange. Gordy spotted the blaze in the distance, rising up above the treetops, at the same time Tobias's bloodcurdling scream rattled the windows.

The truck went off-road, tearing into the trees, a quarter of a mile from the farmhouse.

"They know better!" Tobias shouted, laying all his weight on the horn and jerking the steering wheel from left to right. "They know better than to mess with a McFarland! They'll feel my wrath! Believe you me, they'll feel all of that and more!" His wet eyes glared at Gordy almost as though accusing him of having set the forest ablaze.

"Tobias, slow down. Please!" Gordy kept waiting for the truck to go airborne or crash into a tree. He braced his hands on the dashboard, grateful for his seat belt, as they crested a hill overlooking the meadow outside of Tobias's home.

And then Tobias lost control of the wheel and slammed on the brakes again.

Part of the house, most of the yard, and almost every possible inch of his beloved garden was on fire.

"Tobias, come back!" Gordy tried to project his whisper but he could have shouted at the top of his lungs and Tobias probably would've ignored it.

Several pumpkins exploded, pulp and seeds splattering and sizzling against Gordy's shoes. The effects of Tobias's storm potion churning above the garden hadn't worn off entirely, and a gale of wind whipped through the forest, carrying with it a biting sheet of rain. It was as though the conjured weather mirrored Tobias's infuriated emotions as the rain turned into icy sleet and then back to rain.

Cupping a hand over his eyes, Gordy watched in horror as Tobias sprinted down the hill and into the clearing beyond the trees in front of the house, screaming all the way. Save for a few patches of green, the garden was gone, leaving only a blazing square of scorched earth.

Gordy looked skyward, fearful for all those birds entranced by one of Tobias's concoctions, but they were gone as well. Hopefully the fire had broken their trance and they had flown away. If not . . . He didn't want to think about that.

An ear-piercing cackle filled the air, echoing from just beyond the tree line. The shed Bolter had once used as a temporary laboratory went up in blue flames. Several objects exploded through the walls, whizzing through the air like miniature UFOs in a space battle. It took Gordy a moment to realize they were the hubcaps from Bolter's personal collection.

Then a woman wearing rags for clothing stepped out from the trees, and Gordy felt his spirits plummet.

"Not the mud people!" he groaned.

Gordy had hoped he would never see that woman again, but there was no way he would forget her face. During the attack at B.R.E.W. headquarters, she had doused Bolter's car with a potion that had formed a gigantic octopus that almost drowned everyone.

Several more Scourges emerged from the forest, each with a seemingly endless supply of Pele Punch and Polish Fire Rockets, as well as other combustible concoctions. Crimson potion splashed and ignited, setting everything on fire. Once they pinpointed Tobias's location, they fanned out, forming a perimeter. Gordy counted seven Scourges—too many to handle all at once. Realizing he was standing out in the open, Gordy ducked back behind a tree, but it was too late.

"Spread out!" the woman shrieked. "There's another one here!"

Plunging his hand into his satchel, Gordy pulled out the bracelet Bolter had made him and slipped it over his wrist. All four chambers had been previously loaded with Ghost Glass vials, making the bracelet look like a gaudy piece of costume jewelry, complete with colorful rhinestones. Wiping rain and sweat from his eyes, he heard footsteps racing toward his tree.

The vial nocked in the first chamber was bright blue.

As the Scourge closed in, Gordy leaped from his hiding place, shattering the glass with his thumb. A wire-thin beam of Torpor Tonic shot out like a laser, striking the mud-covered Scourge right between the eyes. Liquid splashed. The man's head snapped back. He didn't even have time to shout before dropping to the ground with a thud.

"Holy cow!" Gordy whispered breathlessly. "That was awesome!" Terrifying, but awesome. Hands shaking, he twisted the bracelet counterclockwise, loading the next vial into position.

Two more Scourges, both men with long hair and beards, charged up the hill. They hurled bottles that smashed on either side of Gordy's feet.

The one to his left ignited into a pillar of fire that singed Gordy's eyebrows as he turned away, shielding his face and coughing from the billowing smoke.

He whirled back around, aiming his wrist, but then stumbled in surprise as a three-foot-long centipede funneled out from a pool of black liquid splattered on his right.

The insect continued to grow by the second. Its bulbous, yellow eyes scanned the area, and dagger-like claws stabbed at the ground, kicking up dirt and leaves as it found its footing. When it stopped growing, it was the size of a twelve-foot python.

Massive insects weren't uncommon in the potion-making community. Gordy had used Essence of Ampliar before on mealworms and maggots down in the family lab, but none of those insects had ever grown as large as this centipede.

A chittering noise, like the sound of a rotary lawn sprinkler, rose from the insect's throat. The centipede lunged, snapping with its pincer-like jaws. Dodging beneath its strike, Gordy fired the next potion from his bracelet, a Vintreet Trap, which zapped a branch a few feet above the creature's head. Vines appeared, squirming and snatching, but the centipede easily plucked them out of the air, gobbling them up with its mandibles.

"Get on with it!" one of the Scourges shouted, prodding the creature from behind with a large, flaming stick.

Gordy didn't have time to check which potion was loaded next in the chamber. As he looked up to take aim, the centipede reared back, towering at least eight feet above his head. He shrieked, jabbing the vial with his thumb, and orange liquid blurred through the air. The spray, however, arced to the right, completely missing its target. Gordy felt a whimper rising in his throat, but then the potion doused one of the Scourges in the chest.

The man expelled a grunt before transforming into a mini tornado, instantly pulling the other Scourge into the funnel as well. Both men blurred together, their arms and legs whipping around like the Tasmanian Devil from the cartoons Gordy's dad liked to watch on Saturday mornings.

The funnel reached the centipede, drawing in several of its rear segments. Stabbing at the ground with its claws and trying to free itself, the creature chittered and squealed.

Gordy clung to a tree trunk, fighting against the pull of the raging wind as the tornado whipped both Scourges down the hill. Though the centipede fought violently, the funnel firmly caught the bug, and it careened into the burning trees and brush, drowning out all other sounds of the storm above.

When the tornado finally stopped, one of the Scourges lay on the roof of Tobias's farmhouse while the other had been propelled straight through the front door of the house. Neither man was moving much. Gordy had no idea where the centipede had ended up, but judging by the puddles of green-and-black sludge everywhere, he doubted it had survived.

"Did you cause all this rigmarole?" Tobias shouted from the roof as he stood over the man Gordy had zapped with the Funnel Formula.

"Technically, not *all* of it," Gordy replied. Stepping out from behind the tree, he traipsed down toward the house.

Two of the Scourges who had tried to surround Tobias were out on the lawn near the front hedges, buried up to their chests in the ground. A pair of glowing watering cans hovered above their heads, dousing them with a constant deluge of water.

"How did you make those?" Gordy asked once he'd slid down to the bottom of the hill and reached the clearing around Tobias's home.

Tobias stood up and dusted off his knees. "Those are my Potable Penyirams. I can fashion them to look like just about anything I want. Say, you didn't happen to see where that—"

A bottle smashed against Tobias's chest, cutting him off midsentence.

"No!" Gordy shouted.

Before the shards of glass had dropped to the rooftop, the potion had tangled Tobias in a cocoon of thick spiderwebs. Gordy hadn't seen where the vial had been thrown from, but then the mud-covered woman emerged from her hiding place, stepping out of the front door of the house, her lone companion following behind. Neither one of them said a word as they both suddenly took off in a run, charging straight toward Gordy.

Twigs tore at Gordy's clothing as he sprinted through the forest. Trees and thorn-riddled bushes hedged up the way. Lungs aching as he held his breath and peered into the darkness, Gordy stopped to listen for the sound of crunching branches. Aside from the low hum of insects, he heard nothing out of the ordinary. But then a mess of tangled hair emerged from behind a tree less than fifty yards away, and Gordy felt his hopes shatter.

The grinning, wild-eyed woman never spoke but tossed a bottle a few feet from where she stood. There was a sudden whoosh, like the sound of air being sucked into a tube, and the ground at Gordy's feet split open. One moment he was standing on solid earth, the next he was clambering for low-hanging tree branches, his feet cracking the dirt as though he were standing on eggshells.

"Careful now!" the woman called out in a singsong tone. "Mind your footing."

There was nothing to stand on, and Gordy began to

sink. Clinging to a thick root, he managed to stop his fall, but it wouldn't last. The weight of his body and the tug of his satchel draped over his shoulder, bogged down by dozens of potions, was too heavy for his fingers to hold.

"All right, Dergus, he's had his fun," the woman said, turning to the Scourge standing behind her. "Get him out before he suffocates."

Gordy felt like an insect sinking in the sands of an hourglass as Dergus trudged along the edge of the mini cavern the Terramoto Tonic had opened, heading toward him.

The root suddenly slipped from Gordy's fingers, and he began to sink once more. He would be buried ten feet beneath the ground by the time the Scourge reached the hole! Lashing out, Gordy seized hold of something with one free hand. Something cold and firm and made of metal. He didn't take time to question it but hurriedly wriggled his fingers around the smooth tube.

"Hey, Joette," Dergus called, skittering to a halt. "You ain't gonna believe this, but look what's sitting out here in the middle of the woods."

Blinking the dirt out of his eyes, Gordy swung his other arm out of the hole, hefting his satchel along with it as he clasped the piece of metal.

Dergus chuckled. "It's one of those . . . you know?" He snapped his fingers. "Minibikes or something."

"A what?" Joette demanded.

"Like a motorcycle, only wimpier and not as noisy." Dergus sniffed. "A moped. That's it! Seems to be in fine condition, too, like it's just been washed and waxed. What kind of moron goes and parks it out here?"

Gordy swiveled his head to get a good look at what the man was fussing about and realized he was holding on to the polished muffler of a motorized scooter. Moonlight illuminated the orange paint of its steering column, and Gordy could see a key inserted in the ignition as well as a rabbit's-foot keychain fluttering in the breeze.

"I'm heading back," Joette announced. "See to the boy. Make sure he's bound tightly."

"Reckon this moped's mine now," Dergus muttered under his breath as Joette trudged away. "It's my lucky day. Yours?" He grinned down at Gordy. "Not so much."

"What do you want?" Gordy asked.

"What do you want?" the man mocked. "Took us a whole month to find you. Joette's Cepha Slop can be tracked, but we had to wait until they were done dredging the lake. By now, that ol' octopus is fat and happy down at the bottom. Imagine the looks on their faces when some-one decides to take a swim there for a holiday!" He burst out laughing. "Now, hold still and don't thrash about." In an instant, Dergus turned serious and jabbed a sharp fin-gernail into Gordy's back. "And if you so much as make a move toward that bag of yours, even a twitch, I'll wop you right on your stupid noggin."

A sudden vibration traveled through Gordy's hands, the cool metal under his fingers beginning to warm.

"What did I say?" Dergus smacked Gordy's shoulder.

"I didn't do anything!" Gordy said.

"Yes, you did. You—"

The odd vibration transformed into a low rumble as the scooter's engine sparked into life. Exhaust belched out from the muffler right into Gordy's face. He coughed, blinking away the smoke. He tried releasing his grip but realized his fingers were stuck to the metal!

"How are you doing that?" Dergus stood up.

"I'm not doing anything." He wasn't, was he? And why couldn't he let go? Something weird was happening, and Gordy wasn't sure he wanted to be anywhere near the scooter once it figured out whatever it wanted to do.

Dergus stepped on Gordy's wrists and tried to kick him free from the muffler. The scooter's engine roared louder and louder, dark-gray exhaust billowing out in another suffocating cloud. Using a nearby tree for leverage, Dergus tried standing on both of Gordy's forearms as though they were a balance beam and he a poorly dressed gymnast.

Gordy squirmed, trying to knock him off before his arms were broken.

Dergus grunted but never got the chance to speak as the scooter suddenly shot forward, flipping him backward.

And then Gordy could no longer see Dergus anymore, or the enormous crack in the earth made by the Terramoto Tonic, or the trees, or anything at all for that matter. His eyes had forced themselves shut as the scooter exploded through the forest with Gordy clinging helplessly to its muffler, unable to let go and screaming at the top of his lungs.

19

The possessed scooter traversed several miles of dense forest before finally stopping by the side of the road. Gordy had tried pleading with it to slow down, but every time he opened his mouth, he ate grass and dirt and at least half a dozen small rocks. Gordy could feel the grime coating his teeth and taste the bugs he'd inadvertently swallowed. The key in the ignition magically turned over again, and with one final burst of exhaust from the tailpipe, the engine sputtered out. The magnetic hold on Gordy's fingers released, and he dropped to the ground with a thud.

Gordy tried not to move too much. His jeans had been ripped at the knees, and both legs were scraped and bleeding. His abdomen was bruised, and his hands and wrists throbbed. All the twisting and slogging through the woods and being dragged behind the scooter like a wakeboarder with his hands glued to the rope had done a serious number on his body.

"That was ridiculous!" He moaned and sat up.

Nothing seemed broken or dislocated, though a couple ribs felt tender to the touch. Remembering he had brought along a container of Boiler's Balm, a healing cream that could alleviate almost any pain, Gordy carefully opened one of the pockets of his satchel.

"Thank goodness for Sasha!" Gordy never thought he would say that, but because of the high-quality bag she had given him as a present at a potion-making party, not one of the vials had shattered.

Gordy walked to the edge of the road and slathered a generous portion of Boiler's Balm onto his hands, wrists, and legs. After that, he emptied the remaining contents of the jar onto his chest and stomach, massaging handfuls of the opaque goop into his skin.

All things considered, it had been a miracle he had managed to survive the journey. He had escaped the clutches of multiple Scourges and a giant centipede and now found himself right on the main strip of highway that could take him anywhere he needed to go.

Gordy debated heading back to the Swigs. He still knew the way to the broken-down bus, though he doubted Spider would let him in. Not without his Scheel disguise.

Or he could try to contact his mom. If only he had his phone.

Gordy faced the scooter. "How did you do that?" He wondered if it had been started remotely, which would explain how it had turned on, but not how it had navigated the forest. Come to think of it, they hadn't crashed into any trees—just the dirt and rocks kicked out by the back tires and straight into Gordy's mouth. Could a remote-operated scooter do that? Then there was the issue with him being unable to let go of the muffler.

The scooter made a sudden rumbling sound, snapping Gordy from his pondering. The headlamp turned on, a beam of golden light blinding his eyes, and it inched forward, the rumbling increasing in volume.

"Now, hold on a second." Gordy stepped back, not wanting to repeat his last adventure through the woods.

Was someone trying to help him, or was it an enemy toying with him? Had he escaped one group of psychopaths only to land in the clutches of another? And why did this situation feel oddly familiar? He had never owned a scooter before, and yet this particular vehicle, with its strange behavior and orange paint and silver stripes, triggered a memory. That rumbling in the engine seemed familiar. It sounded like purring.

"Estelle?" Gordy asked, gawking in disbelief.

In response, the headlamp blinked, like an enormous eyeball the size of a grapefruit. The light brightened, and the scooter leaped forward, pressing against Gordy's leg, warmth radiating from the metal.

Gordy ran his fingers through his hair. "You're Estelle? But how?" Then he remembered Bolter mentioning a special gift he'd intended on leaving behind. This was that gift. "This is crazy!" Even more so than when Bolter had infused his car with the essence of Estelle, his cat. This scooter was operating on its own accord, as though it could make its own choices.

Gordy straightened. "Can you drive me somewhere?"

He had taken several rides in Estelle when she had been an old, refurbished Buick. At first she had acted aggressivly toward Gordy, as though she would sooner have run him over than allow him to ride as a passenger. Eventually though, she had grown less hostile.

"I'm going to climb on you now, okay?" Gordy cautiously lifted a leg over the seat and gently gripped the handlebars. When the scooter remained calm, he fitted his satchel into the metal basket at the rear and latched it in place. Estelle's motor hummed as she crept forward until her front wheel moved off the shoulder and onto the asphalted highway.

It was decision time. Should Gordy travel back to the Swigs? Head for the gas station and a phone? With Estelle cruising down the highway, he could be at either location in less than twenty minutes.

There was, however, a third option. One he had just thought of and felt certain could land him in a heap of trouble, possibly with B.R.E.W., and definitely with his mom once she found out. But at the moment, Gordy needed to get away from danger and go somewhere he could lie low and sort things out.

"All right, Estelle," Gordy whispered, gripping the handlebars tightly. "Let's head for Max's."

The five ingredients needed for the Moholi Mixture
lay out on the concrete porch behind Adilene's house.
Her mom was still out at book group and her dad was
snoring on the couch. If her parents found out Adilene had
snuck out of her room, she would be in so much trouble, but
she couldn't help herself. This was her chance to brew, and
her mom and dad weren't ready to understand this just yet.

Igniting the kerosene for her portable camping stove,
she turned on her flashlight and unfolded the recipe. Sasha
had neatly printed the instructions, along with her com-
mentary in parentheses. Despite the condescending tone in
the notes, Adilene found Sasha's observations rather helpful, and, fortunately for her, Sasha had written everything
in a slightly larger font. Adilene could read them without
having to strain too much.

MOHOLI MIXTURE
Step 1—Fill container with twelve ounces of melted
ice and turn up heat. (It has to be melted ice, not

just water from the tap. Unless you want Moholi Mixture in your hair for weeks.)

Step 2—Dice one stalk of bronze fennel into evenly shaped triangles. Add to the mixture.

Step 3—Sprinkle in powdered shells of three flower chafer beetles, making sure to completely coat the surface of the liquid in a thin layer. (The gold baggie.)

Step 4—With a copper spoon, rhythmically scrape the side of the cauldron as you stir counterclockwise until liquid becomes the consistency of molasses. (Think of some dumb tune you like to sing to your-self when you daydream about Gordy and keep that pace. It doesn't matter the song as long as the rhythm is consistent during the mixing process.)

Adilene stopped reading and growled. *Oh, that girl!* If this potion actually worked, she was tempted to pour it into Sasha's school locker.

Step 5—Drop one wadded piece of aluminum foil into the center of the cauldron.

Step 6—Add four petals from the proteas flower, drop-ping them from above your head to allow petals to flutter into the cauldron. (Second baggie—read the label. And if you miss the bowl on the first try, you can pick them up and do it again.)

Step 7—Light the Amber Wick and blow out after six seconds. Then silently count to one hundred and fifty before turning off the heat to the cauldron. (Use a stopwatch for the Amber Wick, but you can

*count at whatever pace you want for the next part.
Has to be silent, though. Don't botch this at the
very end.)*

Seven steps. Five ingredients. Just as Sasha had promised. If it worked, the potion would end up being rose-
colored and glisten with a metallic shimmer.

"Here goes nothing," Adilene muttered, rubbing her
fingers together.

The first three steps only took Adilene ten minutes to
complete. Dicing the fennel proved tricky, but her triangles
ended up geometrically sound, like tiny pyramids waiting
to be dunked into the cauldron. Step four took longer.
Adilene struggled to keep a steady beat in her mind. She
kept rereading Sasha's comment on daydreaming about
Gordy, and her rhythm broke every time.

Why did she have to put that in the notes? Adilene didn't
daydream about Gordy. Grinding her teeth, she tried to
concentrate. After another couple of minutes of scraping,
the potion became as thick as maple syrup.

She dropped in the aluminum foil and the flower petals
and then lit the Amber Wick, letting it burn for exactly six
seconds. Blowing it out, she began to count silently to one
hundred and fifty, not even moving her lips. Her excitement
grew as she sped through the numbers, watching the potion
settling in the pot. Would the mixture actually do what
Sasha said it would? Would it melt metal? And if so, would
this prove to everyone that Adilene was indeed a Dram?

Though dark outside save for the reddish glow of the

camping stove beneath the cooking pot, Adilene still noticed a shadow pass over her workstation. Cold air gathered around her as the crunching of footsteps arose a few feet away from the porch. Hastily stopping her count at one hundred and thirty-six, Adilene looked up, blinking away the light. Blobs of unfocused darkness clouded her vision, but when they dispersed, she saw a figure standing in front of her.

Adilene screamed as the figure lunged for her, the pot of what might have become a batch of Moholi Mixture overturning. Of course, that no longer mattered because a skeletal hand clamped over her mouth. Adilene's heartbeat throbbed in her ears, and her stomach churned, forcing her dinner back up into her throat.

This couldn't be happening. How could there be a skeleton in her backyard? Because that's what it was, or at least what it looked like. Felt like. Maybe the potion she had been brewing had unleashed some sort of mind-altering vapor. Was she hallucinating? No, this vision had definite substance. The creature's knobby legs pinned her to the ground. Adilene desperately tried to claw her way backward, but the skeleton held firm. Its clammy fingers pressed against her lips.

She braced herself, waiting for the creature to strike, but it only stared back at her, never speaking or hissing or doing whatever skeletons did right before they attacked. The skeleton held up a skinless finger, and Adilene squealed, the sound muffled beneath the pressure of its palm. The thin finger tapped against its mouth, as if telling her to keep quiet. Then it removed its hand from her mouth.

Adilene opened her mouth to scream for help but stopped short. There was something about the skeleton's eyes. They were nothing but . . . no, wait! They weren't actually eyes at all. There weren't even sockets where the eyes should have been. Instead of a nose hole and chattering teeth, the skeleton had a crudely drawn face on a head made from a large, egg-shaped stone.

"You're Doll, aren't you?" she asked, her voice shaking.

The skeleton nodded.

"Are you going to hurt me?"

Doll shook his head, a random joint making a hollow-sounding pop.

"Then can you get off me, please?" Adilene felt her courage returning.

Doll scanned the ground at his knees, his shoulders noticeably slumping. Then he climbed off and sidestepped a few feet away. Adilene stood up and brushed the dirt from her jeans. She saw the coagulating mess of goop on the ground and moaned in disappointment.

Another cool breeze licked at her skin, and she hugged her arms. "Look, I have to go inside. If my parents see you . . ." Adilene puffed out her cheeks and laughed nervously. "So maybe you could tell me what you want and then leave." The sooner the better, she thought to herself.

Doll's face creeped her out. Adilene dropped her gaze and stared at his chest. When she realized she could see the outline of her tire swing in the gap between his ribs, she glanced away entirely, but not before seeing Doll reach for something over his shoulder. She flinched, fearing it was a weapon, but then Doll grasped the object in his hand and offered it to Adilene.

"Is that for me?" Adilene asked. The object looked like a stick, or maybe a tent spike, the pointed end glowing with a soft light.

Doll nodded.

"What is it?" She approached Doll, and he gently dropped the stick into her hands.

The edge of a piece of paper tied with string around the object crinkled in the breeze. Instructions, maybe, or perhaps a message. But from whom? The symbols etched into the wood suddenly grew warm, energy radiating from the item.

Adilene untied the thread fastening the message to the wooden rod. Quite a bit had been penned upon the musty paper with long, flowing strokes, but she couldn't read it. Not in the dark, and certainly not with her crummy eyesight. However, as she squinted, straining to decipher anything, she did manage to make out three words.

My Dearest Gordy,

This gift wasn't for her. It was meant for Gordy! "So, what am I supposed to . . ." Adilene's words hung in the air.

Doll no longer stood in front of her. The skeleton had

moved halfway across the lawn, his bony feet crackling as he lumbered away.

"Hey, wait!" she called out, but he never looked back, and before she could muster up the courage to race after him, he was gone.

"Crazy, creepy . . . monster," Adilene muttered. Though relieved to be rid of the skeleton, she was puzzled by the creature's strange gift.

Adilene gazed down at the overturned cauldron, the potion seeping into the soil. She looked inside the bowl, noting that a decent amount of the liquid remained. Using a spoon, Adilene carefully extracted the syrupy substance and poured it into an empty test tube. Wedging a piece of cork into the opening, she held the vial next to Sasha's actual dose of perfectly brewed Moholi Mixture.

The two potions looked nothing alike. Sasha's was pink with a metallic sheen; Adilene's was auburn-colored and gave off absolutely no sparkle. Adilene had wanted so badly to succeed. Maybe Gordy could help her work out the kinks. Cushioning the test tube in soft cloth, Adilene slipped her potion into her front pocket and checked the time on her phone. It was way past her bedtime, and if her parents found out where she was, Adilene would be grounded for sure.

She sighed heavily. Adilene doubted Doll's late-night visit could mean anything good for her—and certainly not for Gordy.

CHAPTER

21

The fragrant scents of cranberry bushes permeated the air as Estelle pulled onto Maddux Avenue. Gordy kept his head down, trying his best to look inconspicuous, though the neighborhood seemed empty and quiet.

"Good girl." Gordy patted the console. "Pull up over there."

After swooshing up the driveway, Estelle skidded to a halt on the edge of the Pinkermans' backyard. The engine died to a soft putter, and Gordy climbed down from the seat. Then Estelle started purring again. At least that's what the hum sounded like. The cushion trembled as Estelle nestled up next to Gordy's leg, digging a handlebar sharply into his thigh. Gordy winced but patted her affectionately, and after about a dozen vibrations, the purring stopped.

"I need you to stay out here and lie low." Gordy's eyes darted to Max's bedroom window. Estelle's single headlight dimmed slightly, and the handlebars tilted at an angle. As he started to walk away, her front tire clipped his heels, nearly tripping him.

"No, Estelle. Wait. Here." Gordy jabbed his finger at the driveway. The handlebars tilted to the opposite angle as though she were confused. "Do you understand what I'm saying? Stay outside and keep an eye out for enemies. Please!"

The headlight suddenly brightened, and Estelle's handlebars swiveled from left to right as though searching for danger.

"Exactly!" Gordy nodded. He didn't dare pet her in case it caused another purring eruption.

Estelle reversed into the shadows beneath the Pinkermans' massive pine tree and dimmed her headlight.

Crouching beneath Max's window, Gordy opened his satchel. The Pinkermans owned a really dumb dog named Corn Chip; Max had named her, of course. Once Corn Chip started barking, it was nearly impossible to shut her up, so knocking on the front door was out of the question.

Gordy uncorked a caramel-colored vial of Certe Syrup and drizzled the liquid along the windowsill. The wood produced a pop as wisps of steam rose from the crack. He opened the window with hardly any effort and hoisted his body up, dropping catlike through the opening with a muted thud.

Max lounged in his pajamas in a black leather gaming chair facing the television in the corner of his room. A flurry of images flashed across the screen, but the only sound was the wild clacking of Max's fingers on his controller.

"Take cover in that bush and wait for me," Max hissed into his gaming headset. "You're going to get us all killed!"

The images on the television were of armed soldiers stalking the perimeter of a building. Max's video game handle, Stinkerman0909, was displayed above his character.

"That's how it's done, son!" Max whooped, pumping a jubilant fist in the air. "Oh, yeah, you think you can hide over there in those boxes? Not!" His character tossed a grenade into the corner of an underground parking lot, and the boxes exploded.

Gordy knew Max's bedtime was ten o'clock during the school year and eleven on the weekends. Max's bedside alarm clock displayed the current time of 1:15 a.m. There was no way his mom would've permitted him to be playing video games this far past midnight.

Carefully approaching Max from the rear, Gordy scanned the room in search of Corn Chip. With no sign of the dog, he reached out and tapped Max on the shoulder.

Max flew out of his chair, screaming. His headphones pulled free from the gaming console, and the blaring sounds of machine-gun fire filled the room. Several cans of soda dropped from the television stand, covering the floor with dark liquid. Gordy covered his ears. The volume on the game had been turned all the way up. Corn Chip attacked from outside Max's door, barking like a shrieking banshee.

Still screaming, Max spun around, eyes wide as dinner plates.

"Whoa, calm down! Max, it's me." Gordy tried to keep his voice at a whisper, but there wasn't any need. His plan to avoid waking Max's parents had failed spectacularly.

Grabbing the television remote from a puddle of soda on the floor, Max muted the cacophony of sound. "Gordy? What the heck, man?" He puffed out his cheeks and collapsed back into his chair. "Do you even realize how close I came to choking you out?"

Gordy shrugged apologetically. "I didn't mean to scare you."

"Yeah, well, how did you get past Corn Chip? She hates you." Max glanced at the door. Corn Chip's shrieking barks had quieted, but Gordy could still see the tips of her paws tearing at the carpet beneath the door.

"I came through your window." Gordy pointed to the smoke still hanging in the air around the opening.

Max's alarmed expression turned to curiosity. "Potion?"

"Certe Syrup," Gordy answered. "Popped the window free from the latch."

"Wicked." He nodded, scratching the edge of one of his nostrils. "Stupid name, but effective. And you came here tonight because . . ."

"I needed a place to stay," Gordy started to explain. "And I was hoping that . . . Hey, where are your parents?" He realized that aside from Corn Chip snuffling beyond the door, the rest of the house was silent. The eruption most certainly would have woken them, but neither Max's mom or dad had charged into the bedroom demanding an explanation.

"Gone," Max answered casually. "Their marriage counselor suggested they take a trip to work out some of their *differences*." He made air quotes with his fingers. "They headed out yesterday afternoon. My mom wants to do a couples' massage, but I'm pretty sure my dad bought tickets to the Twisted Sister concert in Bixby. Anyway, they won't be back until tomorrow night." Max rubbed his hands together. "This is perfect, dude! We're going to have the most epic sleepover ever! First things first, we're going to need a crowbar and some safety goggles. My dad locked down the kitchen before he left, and my snack stash is getting dangerously low."

Max's father was a locksmith by trade and loved junk food as much as his son did. If he didn't secure the pantry after bedtime, Max would sneak out and hoard cupcakes and sugary treats all night. An enormous bag of potato chips lay crumpled next to Max's chair, and discarded candy-bar wrappers littered the floor. How his best friend had managed to live this long without weighing a thousand pounds was a miracle.

"You can use my beanbag chair. I'm sorry if it smells like sardines." Max snagged an extra game controller from the television stand and offered it to Gordy. "These losers I keep getting paired up with have no finesse when it comes to dominating in battle."

"Max, I can't play this," Gordy said, staring down at the sticky controller.

"Sure you can. You know the drill. Just stay hidden until I need you to flank someone, and make sure you feed me all your heavy ammo."

Gordy placed the controller on Max's bed. "You don't understand. I didn't come here for a sleepover. I was attacked."

The air seemed to fizzle out of Max's lungs. "What do you mean 'attacked'?"

It took awhile for Gordy to bring Max up to speed on everything that had happened. The meeting in the Swigs with Yosuke while his mom met with the leader of the Stained Squad. The showdown with the mud people at Tobias's farmhouse. Knowing how Max felt about bugs, he opted to leave out the part about the giant centipede.

He wasn't sure how Max was handling all the information. Throughout the story, his best friend hardly made more than a grunt and never asked any questions. Max rarely had the ability to keep quiet, so his strange silence was worrisome.

"Do you see why we can't play games right now?" Gordy asked, warily studying Max's impassive expression. "We need to be on our guard, just in case."

It took a moment for the words to elicit a response. Then spit blubbered from Max's lips as he blew an exasperated raspberry. "Just in case of what?"

"I don't know. Just in case someone shows up."

"Here?" Max's eyes widened in panic. "Were you followed?"

Gordy retreated a step. "I don't think so." He felt confident he had escaped the Scourges, but there was a possibility one might have followed him.

"Have you lost your mind?" Max bellowed. "Of all the nights to get yourself mixed up with the nutters, you choose tonight? My parents are gone! We don't own a weapon, unless you count my mom's glue gun." He dragged his fingers down his face, stretching his lower eyelids until all Gordy could see were the whites of his eyes.

"It's going to be all right. I mean, we're probably fine. I just need to use your phone."

"My phone?" Max blinked. "Check under the . . ." He sputtered, his face turning pale as he pointed at the window. "What is that?"

Gordy followed his finger and reared back, shielding his eyes as the whole room filled with light.

"We're under attack!" Max shouted.

Gordy realized what he was seeing. A glass bulb. Handlebars. A silver-and-orange metal console. "That's Estelle," he explained. "She's, uh . . . she's my ride."

Max backed into the wall so abruptly that one of his two participation medals from little league soccer dislodged from its hooks and jangled to the floor. "What do you mean 'she'? Who's driving that thing?"

Estelle must have been leaning up on her back wheel in order to peer through the window. The headlight blinked, the light flicking on and off in a feverish pattern, almost like Morse code.

"What is it, girl?" Gordy asked, approaching the window.

"Dude." Max covered his eyes with his palm. "You've finally snapped."

"I hear voices," Gordy whispered.

"Yeah, you hear voices," Max agreed.

"No, actual voices," Gordy explained. "Estelle, get down! Lights off!"

The scooter instantly dimmed her headlight and vanished from the opening. Gordy heard the soft whir of her tires as she zipped to the backyard and out of sight.

"How are you doing that?" Max asked. "Is it like artificial intelligence?"

"Be quiet!" Gordy hissed.

Max clamped his mouth shut, and the two of them strained to listen. Someone was approaching the driveway, and Gordy could hear the low grumble of discussion. The voices grew louder, closer, until he could make out some of their argument.

"That's not my problem," one of the voices said. She sounded annoyed and wasn't trying to keep her voice low.

Max scrunched his face up and mouthed "Sasha."

"What's she doing here?" Gordy asked. The Brexils lived out on Harper Hood Lane, which was pretty far from Max's home.

"But it almost worked," the other voice said. "I brewed

everything as the recipe said, but then I was interrupted. I just need more ingredients. I'll pay for them!"

That was Adilene, which meant something was definitely wrong. Sasha may have been a rule breaker, but not Adilene. If her parents instituted a curfew, she followed it precisely.

"Again, not my problem," Sasha replied. "I never said you brewed the potion incorrectly. On the contrary, you're the type of person who would never miss a step. But like I've said a million times before, it doesn't matter. You're not a Dram, and you never will be."

"Maybe they'll just keep walking." Max's tone was hopeful. "Maybe they're not even coming here."

"Yeah, right," Gordy said.

Moaning in annoyance, Max's eyes flitted over to the television as his avatar, Stinkerman0909, who had been standing idle in the middle of the field, was suddenly mowed down by a spray of bullets. The character blipped from the screen and returned to the starting menu. "I don't have enough video game controllers for everyone," he said. "So much for the perfect sleepover."

"We might want to meet them at the door," Gordy suggested as the girls' voices moved from the front lawn onto the porch.

"Why would we do that?" Max asked.

And then the doorbell rang, and Corn Chip practically imploded.

"Do you have any idea what time it is?" Max demanded, swinging open the front door and glaring down at the girls standing on the porch. He flipped on the outside light, and Adilene yelped. Sasha started in surprise but then regarded Max with a pathetic gaze.

Gordy stood back, shielded by Max's body. So far, neither one of the girls had noticed him standing in the darkness. They were too distracted by the Yorkshire terrier yapping and figure-eighting between their legs.

"Sensible people have bedtimes, you know?" Max had brought a bag of potato chips from his bedroom and crammed a handful into his mouth, chomping obnoxiously. "And my dad is looking for his shotgun as we speak. We don't grant late-night prowlers any mercy."

Security lights snapped on in a few of the neighbors' yards as other dogs began to respond to Corn Chip's ceaseless barking. It was almost two o'clock in the morning.

Adilene stooped down to try to calm Corn Chip. "I

told Sasha not to ring the doorbell, but she doesn't listen to anybody. Easy, girl, easy," she cooed, tending to the pooch. "How did Max ever get such an adorable puppy?" Corn Chip's tail started wagging as she leaped up and buried her wet nose into Adilene's knees.

"A shotgun?" Sasha folded her arms, refusing to yield to Max's threats.

"We're sorry, Mr. and Mrs. Pinkerman!" Adilene called out, cupping her hand around her mouth. "This was all just a mistake."

"They're not home," Gordy said, shouldering past Max and onto the porch. "It's only the two of us."

"Gordy!" Adilene exclaimed. She threw her arms around him, bear-hugging him so tightly he thought he might lose consciousness.

"It's good to see you too," Gordy wheezed. In that moment, having his two best friends with him made everything seem normal again. Even if Sasha had invaded their trio of friendship, Gordy didn't mind.

"Whoa, Rivera, give the man his space." Max eyeballed Adilene in disgust. "You're cutting off the circulation to his brain. He's turning blue."

"Shut up, Maxwell," Adilene said, sniffling.

"Are you crying?" Max asked.

Adilene shoved him in the arm. "I'm just happy and surprised."

"Yeah, this is awkward," Sasha added. "Hello, Gordy." Then she too gave Gordy a hug.

Gordy couldn't remember a time when two girls had hugged him simultaneously. Though Sasha's hug felt more like a formality than Adilene's, it was impressive nevertheless.

"So I guess I'm chopped liver," Max grumbled. "It's not like Gordy's been deployed overseas. He's only been gone a month."

"This is so crazy that you're here," Adilene beamed, ignoring Max. "I was actually coming over to try to contact you."

"We both were," Sasha corrected.

"Maybe we should talk in private," Gordy suggested as several of the neighborhood dogs took to howling.

"This is where you live?" Sasha asked Max once the four of them were inside. She gazed at the walls and the furniture, her eyes lingering upon the Pinkermans' grand piano.

"No, this where we keep the bodies hidden," Max answered. "Does it not meet your standards?"

"Actually, it's the opposite," Sasha said, her lip curling. "I was half expecting a pigsty."

"Yeah, that's actually in Max's bedroom," Gordy said.

"Which none of you are allowed to see, so don't even ask," Max added.

They moved to the living room, where Gordy sat in one of the wingback chairs. Adilene and Sasha took spots on the couch, while Max turned on the ceiling fan and plopped onto the carpet, wrestling with an unopened bag of pretzels. Corn Chip leaped onto the couch, snuggling down in Adilene's lap. That dog had yet to let Gordy within a few feet of her without growling, but there she was cuddling with Adilene, who stroked her ears affectionately.

"I'm pretty sure I've found him," Sasha said, folding her arms.

"Found who?" Gordy asked.

"Your grandfather," she said. "I think I know where he is."

"You didn't tell me that!" Adilene's long black hair whipped around as she gaped at Sasha.

Sasha shrugged. "You were too busy trying to buy ingredients for another failed potion-making attempt."

"What are you yapping about?" Max snapped his fingers, trying to convince Corn Chip to join him on the floor, but the dog ignored him.

"I found a tracking potion online, and I won't go into details"—Sasha cast a sidelong look at Adilene before returning her focus to Gordy—"but I was able to pinpoint his general location."

"Where is he?" Gordy's heart thudded with excitement. This was huge information! Of course, he wasn't exactly sure how to stop his psychopath grandfather, but pinpointing Mezzarix's hideout was a definite step in the right direction.

"He's within three hundred miles off the coast of Florida," Sasha answered, her voice carrying a slight tremor, like she was just barely holding her emotions together. "At least that's where the signal went cold. The tracking potion uses GPS and triangulation and a bunch of other stuff, but that was the reading." She dropped her eyes and fidgeted with the straps of her satchel.

Frowning, Gordy glanced at Max, who was wearing the same expression. "You know that doesn't really tell us anything, right? Three hundred miles could be anywhere. And if the signal went cold—"

"Don't you think I know that?" Sasha's eyes snapped up, puffy and red. "The tracking potion didn't work the way it was supposed to. I think it has something to do with the magical properties of the Silt or maybe the island itself. It's like it doesn't want to be found. I don't know why, but I can't find it. Without the keystone, the place might as well be invisible!"

"What are you laughing about?" Adilene demanded as Max snickered under his breath.

"Just how she wasted all that time brewing with your blood," Max said.

"It's not funny!" Sasha shouted, leaping up from the couch. "My mom's a shell of the person she once was because of his grandfather." She jabbed an accusatory finger in Gordy's direction. "And none of you are doing anything about it!"

"That's not true," Gordy said.

"You were supposed to come back to help me. And now my mom just wanders around the house, muttering to herself. My dad lost his job." Adilene gasped, but Sasha clenched her hands at her sides. "I'm running out of ideas!

Maybe I should ask the Scourges for help. Maybe they could find a cure for my mother. I certainly can't trust my friends."

"Sasha," Adilene whispered. "We're going to help you. We're doing all that we can, and Gordy's here now." She frowned, confused. "How is it that you're here, Gordy? Is your family okay?"

Gordy swallowed, suddenly dizzy. "Max, can I please use your phone?" he asked, his voice cracking.

Max seemed like he was about to protest, but one look at Gordy's worried expression and he hurried out of the room. He returned a few moments later and tossed his phone into Gordy's outstretched hands.

No one spoke as Gordy typed in the number and waited. After three rings, his mom's answering service kicked on. He didn't want to leave a recording, but he owed it to her to let her know he was safe. Partway through his message though, Gordy choked up and barely finished without crying.

"Something bad happened, didn't it?" Adilene asked once he'd set the phone aside.

Gordy nodded.

"And your mom?" She leaned forward on the couch. "What happened to her?"

"I think she's okay. I mean, I hope she is." Gordy told Adilene and Sasha everything he had shared with Max, but when he got to the part about the fire at Tobias's property, he had to look away. Until that moment, Gordy hadn't given much thought to what had happened. There had been too much adrenaline coursing through his veins. There, sitting in Max's living room with everyone listening, it all finally sunk in.

"Your mom's fine." Adilene nodded. "I know it."

"Yeah, and she's got your crazy Aunt Priss on her side," Max agreed.

Gordy wiped his nose with the back of his hand, then jumped when Max's phone rang. His mom's number appeared on the screen, and he exhaled in relief.

"Mom?" he asked into the receiver.

"Oh, thank goodness!" she replied. "Don't say anything about your location. I know where you are, and we'll be on our way soon."

"You're okay?"

She sighed. "Yes, we're fine. I didn't mean to alarm you, but it was time for you to leave the Swigs."

"What's happening?" Gordy asked.

"It's hard to explain, but you need to know there are Scourges on the loose, and I have reason to believe they may be in the vicinity."

Gordy groaned. "But I am at . . ." He caught himself in time. "I mean, the place where I'm at is not necessarily . . . guarded."

"That's okay," she insisted. "Your location should work as a hiding place until we arrive. Just stay inside and keep away from the windows."

"When will you get here?" Gordy asked.

"We're planning a strategy now, and we're waiting for

more of Paulina's squad to arrive. When I leave, I'm coming directly to you, so it's imperative you stay put. We can't waste time wandering all over town trying to find you. Do you understand?"

"I understand," Gordy said. "But, Mom, Tobias was captured. And his house—"

"We know," his mom answered. "Don't worry about Tobias. We got him back."

Gordy closed his eyes and leaned his head back into the chair cushion.

His mom sighed. "Tobias is naturally upset, but we'll help him replace what was—" The end of her sentence cut out as the line went dead.

Gordy pulled the phone back from his ear and stared at the screen.

"Did you lose the signal?" Adilene asked. All three friends had moved to the edge of their seats, watching Gordy as he shared his conversation with his mother.

Gordy pressed the power button, but the phone didn't respond. "I think the battery is dead."

Overhead, the whirling blades of the ceiling fan slowed and then stopped. The outside porch light had suddenly gone dark as well.

"Power must have gone out," Max said, staring out the window. "Everyone's lights are off."

Gordy gazed through the glass, searching for storm clouds, but the sky was mostly clear. There was no thunder or lightning. No reason for the power in the neighborhood to suddenly shut off. Thankfully, the moon was peeking out from behind the few clouds in the sky, otherwise it would have been impossible to see anything on the street. Gordy could hear dogs howling and barking again. Corn Chip scampered toward the front door, growling deep in her throat.

"Check your phone," Sasha whispered to Adilene. "Mine stopped working as well."

Adilene dug in her pocket and pressed the button a few times. "Dead," she muttered. "What kind of power outage could do that to all of our phones at the same time?"

A car rolled past Max's driveway, the headlights dark, the engine silent. It traveled a few feet beyond the Pinkermans' mailbox before coming to a complete stop. The driver stepped out and stared at his vehicle, confused. He popped the hood and leaned over the engine.

Some of Max's neighbors emerged from their houses, a few carrying candles that emitted a soft, eerie glow from their doorsteps. The driver called out, looking over his shoulder at someone farther up the street. Gordy assumed he was speaking to one of the neighbors, but as the man straightened, Gordy heard the distinct crack of glass breaking on the asphalt. His eyes pulled wide as he saw the spray of liquid splash up.

"Get down!" Gordy commanded to the others.

Snatching Adilene by her sleeve, he pulled her to the floor just as the man outside collapsed beneath a thick, sticky covering of spiderwebs.

Streaks of light illuminated the living room as mini explosions ignited outside the window. Gordy heard shouts of anguish and screams of alarm and confusion all coming from Max's neighbors.

"What's going on?" Max lay on the floor, cradling a yapping Corn Chip in his arms. He tried pinching the dog's mouth shut with his fingers, but the terrier wriggled free, nipping and snarling.

Sasha had taken cover beneath one of the chairs, her hands clamped over her ears, eyes darting about the room with every jolt of magical light. It was like having a private fireworks show, but the rockets weren't being blasted a thousand feet into the air. They were leveling fence posts and demolishing cars out on the street. And then everything fell silent as an unsettling calm spread over the outside world.

Max waited a minute before poking his head up and casting an anxious glance out the window. Almost immediately he ducked for cover. "There's a whole bunch of freaks out there!"

Keeping his chin level with the windowsill, Gordy knelt and peered outside. The smell of noxious chemicals filled the smokey haze. He could Decipher barberry seeds and axle grease, both commonly found in Polish Fire Rockets and Latvian Dunka Draughts.

A dozen strangers stood beyond the edge of Max's yard, glowing objects in their hands. One of them stood over the poor motorist now lying in the street like a limp, rolled-up rug. All of Max's neighbors had vanished from their porches. At least that's what Gordy assumed, until he noticed several heaps of vines and spiderwebs squirming on the concrete and struggling beneath hedges.

"Scourges!" Sasha crawled from underneath the chair, keeping below the window as she crowded next to the others.

"Really?" Adilene whimpered. "Couldn't they be from B.R.E.W.?"

Gordy wasn't sure that was a better alternative. Anyone hunting for his family was a threat. And although Scourges tended to attack first and ask questions later, the B.R.E.W. Investigators now shared the same dangerous tendencies.

"Definitely not from B.R.E.W." Sasha went into a crouch and slid her satchel beneath her. "That man with the ratted hair and the eye patch is Steffan Musk, also known as Steffan the Seventh."

"Steffan the Seventh?" Max asked. He had discarded his potato chips on the floor where Corn Chip immediately scarfed them down. "What does that mean? Is he like royalty?"

"Kind of," Sasha said. "Steffan was once considered the Dr. Frankenstein of the potion community. My mom helped Banish him back when she was Lead Investigator. She used to tell me bedtime stories about how he kept body parts in jars all around his house."

"Yeesh," Max muttered. "You didn't sleep much, did you?"

Sasha glared at him. "Point is, I've seen pictures of Steffan in my mom's photo albums. His eye patch covers an empty socket, and back in the day, he carried his most deadly potions concealed behind the patch."

"In his head?" Max blurted.

"Oh, you've got to be kidding me!" Sasha gripped the windowsill and nudged Gordy with her elbow. "Recognize that woman?" She pointed to the Scourge standing in the middle of the group.

Gordy narrowed his eyes, trying to make out the individual from the motley lineup. It was too dark to see, until she raised some sort of glowing staff and her face came into focus.

"Zelda!" Gordy gasped, recognizing the squat, green-haired traitor.

"The crazy Oompa Loompa?" Max cradled Corn Chip in the crook of his elbow. "Forget it. This whole neighborhood is about to go up in flames!"

"What are they all doing here?" Adilene demanded. "And what are they holding? Are those bottles?"

Gordy stared at the items many of the Scourges were holding. Long rods that radiated with a soft, incandescent glow, the objects didn't look like any container Gordy had used with brewing before.

Zelda waddled over to the broken-down car and climbed up on the hood. She held something up to her mouth. "Attention, good citizens of Maddux Avenue!" Her shrill, magnified voice echoed through the neighborhood. "We will be searching your premises. Each home must be inspected, as we believe one of you may be harboring a fugitive. Attempt to obstruct our search, and you shall be engaged aggressively. Help us find her, and you shall be rewarded. Please remain calm. We should be on our way and out of your lives in just a few moments. Thank you for your immediate cooperation."

Zelda lowered the device from her mouth and then vanished.

Gordy gasped. "Silt!" he hissed, gaping at Adilene.

Adilene bit her lip as one by one, several more Scourges disappeared, winking out of existence.

"What are we supposed to do now?" Adilene demanded.

The remaining Scourges moved forward, stepping onto lawns and over bushes, hunched like a band of prowlers. Gordy cringed as several moved stealthily toward the home next to the Pinkermans'. He wasn't sure where Zelda had gone, or the others for that matter, but if they had Silt in their systems, they could easily slip right inside Max's house and no one would know until it was too late. Wordlessly, Gordy backed away from the window, and the others followed.

Moonlight lit the hallway faintly, but once they were in the kitchen, Gordy had trouble seeing a few feet in front of his face.

"Nothing electronic is working. Not even my flashlight," Sasha muttered. "I've never heard of anything like this."

"Don't you have potions that could light our way?" Adilene asked.

"Not with me," Sasha said.

Max nearly knocked Adilene over as he suddenly pushed past her.

"Where are you going?" Adilene reached for his arm, but her fingers only grazed his shirtsleeve.

Thudding against the wall, the terrier yelping in surprise, Max vanished into the hallway. A couple minutes later, a soft light emerged from his bedroom as he returned, no longer toting Corn Chip in his arms but instead carrying two dozen glow sticks, several of which had already been cracked open.

"Why do you have so many of those?" Sasha asked.

"For trick-or-treating," he answered matter-of-factly. "Duh." He turned to Gordy. "I had to lock Corn Chip in her kennel; she bit me." Max rubbed the back of his fist where the tiny pinpricks of Corn Chip's insignificant fangs had barely dented his skin.

Max cracked another stick, and a luminous yellow glow lit up the kitchen. The artificial lights bubbled as Gordy and the others vigorously shook their glow sticks and then slipped the elastic loops attached to the ends over their heads, wearing them as necklaces.

"Now what do we do?" Max asked.

In response, Gordy handed him a Booming Ball, freshly selected from his satchel. Max stared down at the glass bauble, which was the size of a baseball and oozed an iridescent light, uncertain of how to hold it. Gordy passed a Torpor Tonic to Adilene and was reaching for another bottle to offer Sasha, but she held up her palm.

"I've got my own weapon," she said, brandishing a container of fluorescent blue liquid with red blobs swirling inside like a miniature lava lamp.

Something heavy hit the front door, and Gordy tightened his grip on his satchel. The knock rang out again and again, the wood splintering from each blow until the door fell off its hinges.

Steffan the Seventh entered the house. Dressed in loose-fitting clothing, he was tall and angular, as if he possessed a few extra elbows and knees. His patch bulged over his right eye—a patch that could be concealing a deadly potion.

Steffan immediately spotted Gordy, and he hurled a bottle through the air toward the four of them. The vial swooshed over Gordy's shoulder, striking the far kitchen wall. The liquid splashed into a web, and deadly thorns sprouted, the tips glistening with poison. The thorns punctured the cabinets, shattering Mrs. Pinkerman's floral dishware.

"My mom's going to flip out when she sees that!" Shouting a war cry, Max turned and fired his Booming Ball. The bauble struck the floor a few feet from Steffan, sending a rushing wave of air in all directions. The force of the Booming Ball uprooted Mrs. Pinkerman's couch, which became lodged in the wall.

"Drams?" Steffan inquired dryly, one eyebrow rising above his eye patch. "This should be fun." But before he could select another weapon from his arsenal, Gordy sprang into action.

Selecting a new concoction from his satchel, Gordy threw a triangular-shaped bottle at Steffan's abdomen. The glass shattered, and the Scourge cried out, only to have his voice instantly quieted as a column of smoke enveloped his body. Gordy and the others shielded their eyes until the smoke dissipated.

"What did you do?" Max gaped into the living room, laughing in surprise.

Steffan the Seventh was enveloped within a human-sized glass bottle, complete with a corked lid, like an enormous action figure trapped within its packaging. After several seconds of confusion, Steffan finally realized what had happened and pressed his splayed fingers against the glass.

"Did you make that one up yourself?" Sasha asked, impressed.

Gordy nodded, flashing Max a smile. "I've been waiting to test it out. It needs a name, though."

"Already got you covered," Max replied, winking at Gordy. "The Aladdiner."

"The Aladdiner?" Adilene asked dryly.

"You know? Aladdin? Genie in a bottle?" Max looked at the others for confirmation. "It's perfect."

Gordy knew the potion would last for at least fifteen minutes. That was if the Scourge didn't shatter the glass first, which he seemed determined to do. Steffan started shifting his weight back and forth, trying to tip the bottle over.

Peering into his satchel, Gordy grabbed two more potions. "Okay," he whispered. "We'll go to the neighbors first. We'll have to slip in the back door to surprise them, but I think I have enough to take those creeps down. They definitely aren't expecting anyone to fight back."

Sasha made a disapproving cluck with her tongue. "You're not seriously thinking of taking these guys on right now, are you?"

Gordy's brow creased. "Why not? They don't scare me."

"And here I thought I was the arrogant one. You got lucky with *one* Scourge." She nodded at Steffan, who was still rocking his body against his glass prison. "There's no way you'll have the same success going up against a dozen of the world's worst with a handful of Torpor Tonics and—no offense, guys—but these two at your side." She nodded at Max and Adilene. "They're not trained."

"You know, I'm not all that excited about this either, but I can at least throw a bottle!" Max proclaimed defensively.

"Oh, really?" Sasha gestured to the webwork stretching across the kitchen wall. "What kind of thorns are those?"

Max shrugged. "Uh . . . don't know, don't care."

"Well, you should. That's called Tickling Tinik. It's from the Philippines, but don't believe its funny name. It's not a good time. One prick from a single Tickling Tinik thorn and your skin will start to stretch and threaten to fall off."

"Serious?" Adilene eyed the thorns in horror. Max inched away from the wall as well.

"Luckily for you, I happen to have ampalaya rind in my satchel. That's the cure," Sasha said. "But what if we get separated in the fight? Do you know the first thing about concocting antidotes with a limited supply of ingredients to counteract deadly poisons?"

Max opened his mouth as if to challenge her, but then looked dismally over at Gordy. "I don't want my skin to fall off."

"Me neither," Adilene whispered.

A huge chunk of Gordy and Sasha's Dram training had been about what to do during battles with Scourges. Max and Adilene had never been present for those lessons.

Gordy could feel his desire to fight leaving him. She was right. They didn't stand a chance against the Scourges. It was time to run.

"We're clearly outmatched," Sasha went on. "And they have Silt, remember? How can you surprise anyone if you can't see them? They'll alert the others, and we'll get caught. But if we leave right now, we may have the upper hand."

"How so?" Gordy could see shadows dancing across the floor back in the living room and wondered when another Scourge would appear in the window.

"Did you not hear Zelda just now? She said they were looking for a 'her.' Unless you know something I don't, they're not searching for you." Sasha moved to the back door.

Out beyond the kitchen, the whole world seemed to have drifted into complete darkness. No lights shone from any of the homes, but Gordy could see blips of artificial illumination as potion smoke blossomed up from rooftops. Dread and hopelessness settled in his chest. The Scourges were everywhere. Where had they all come from? And why were they attacking the city?

"Thoughts on where to go?" Max closed the back door behind him, eyes darting around in panic.

Gordy knew his mom was coming to rescue them, but they could no longer wait in the neighborhood.

"I think we should go back to Tobias's," he suggested.

Max groaned. "Are you kidding me? That's like forever

away from here. And didn't you say it burned to the ground?"

"Yes, but that's where my mom will be, at least for the next little while."

"None of the cars are working," Max said. "There's no way I'm going to be able to run that far. It'll take us at least two days. Probably longer."

"Maybe not." It was a long shot, but Gordy had a hunch. He looked apologetically over at Adilene. "Try not to freak out, okay?"

Then he called out for Estelle.

CHAPTER

24

Gordy didn't know if the scooter had a weight limit, but he felt certain the four of them well exceeded the maximum capacity.

Sitting on the padded seat and holding on to the handlebars, Gordy muttered instructions to Estelle. Adilene sat snuggly behind him, one arm wrapped around his waist, her hand digging into his abdomen, while her other hand held a wad of Sasha's shirt.

Sasha sat on the metal basket facing the road, potions ready to throw at anyone trying to follow them. Gordy couldn't see where they were driving because Max's reddening face blocked all visibility. Straddling the handlebars and hanging on for dear life, Max was trying to keep his feet from being accidentally pulled under the front tire.

"You can slow down a little," Gordy said to the scooter, squeezing Estelle's handlebars.

Her headlight seemed dimmer than usual, and she took to the road with a herky-jerky movement, as if trying to buck one of them off. After half a mile, Gordy warned Max to stop complaining, because he sensed Estelle getting annoyed. The scooter passed a couple of people walking along the shoulder of the road, having abandoned their inoperable vehicles.

"Everyone's stranded," Adilene said. "What happened?"

Gordy had been trying to wrap his brain around how the Scourges had knocked out the entire city's power along with their cars and everything else electronic. No potion he had ever read about could cause that much damage.

Estelle suddenly began to purr, and both Gordy and Adilene jumped in surprise.

"What does that mean?" Adilene asked.

"She does that from time to time," Gordy replied.

Estelle's front wheel stuttered as though skidding on gravel, and Max's head poked up, trying to peer over Gordy's shoulder. "Do you know how uncomfortable this is?" he griped. "Are we out of gas or something?"

Gordy tapped the gauge to see if it was working. "We still have a quarter of a tank."

The wheel jerked again, the whole vehicle wobbling to one side, and Sasha shouted, "Stop goofing around!"

"I'm not doing anything," Gordy insisted. Estelle didn't require actual steering. Holding the handlebars was just for balance.

Her speed dropping drastically, Estelle suddenly stopped in the middle of the road. Her headlight still flickered, but she wasn't moving anymore. Not even an inch.

"We haven't even gone five miles yet." Grimacing, Max hopped down from the handlebars, giving Gordy a clear view of the road up ahead and with it, rows of city lights brightening the sky less than a mile away.

"That must be where the outage ends," Adilene said. "Maybe we can get a taxi to drive us the rest of the way."

"Please tell me you're not complaining," Max groaned. "You got to sit on the cushion for the ride."

Adilene shrugged. "I didn't think you wanted to hug Gordy the whole time."

"I would've hugged Gordy," Max grumbled as he started walking toward the lights.

"All right, Estelle, we just have a little way to go, and then maybe you can follow us to Tobias's." Gordy waited for the scooter to lurch forward, but she only sputtered exhaust.

Sasha pointed. "Can you see that?"

Gordy followed her finger. He could see a ripple in the air, but the images on the other side of it were distorted. The haze continued up at least a thousand feet into the sky and arced overhead.

"It looks like some sort of gas," Sasha said.

"I . . . can't . . . move . . ." Max grunted from a short distance away. His left foot was raised off the ground but appeared to be frozen. He gasped, finally dropping his foot behind him, his breath rushing out unsteadily as he looked back at Gordy. "There's something blocking me from walking any farther."

None of them could move more than a few feet past

the point where Estelle had stopped. The air there felt solid and reeked of potion ingredients. The almost invisible haze stretched for miles in every direction as though a massive, magical dome had been dropped over the city.

Gordy heard voices from behind him and looked back, noticing the small group of people who had been walking along the road before gathering around Estelle.

"How did you get this to work?" a man wearing hospital scrubs asked. "Our cars all stopped running."

Gordy looked at the others. "I'm not sure, really. She just . . . um . . . I mean, it just started up fine." He hadn't considered why Estelle continued to work when every other machine in the area had been rendered incapacitated, but then again, Bolter's scooter operated on Fusion potions. Every moving part within Estelle functioned due to the magical properties of Bolter's bizarre concoction.

"What is this?" asked a woman, who, like Max, stopped abruptly once she hit the invisible wall. "Why can't I move?"

At first, everyone marveled at the strange force field hedging up the way, but then they started to panic.

"We need to get out of here," Adilene whispered into Gordy's ear. "We can't be out on the street with everyone else. What if we draw the attention of the Scourges?"

Gordy nodded in agreement, but where could they go? Tobias's home made the most sense, but that path was blocked.

"Hey!" the man wearing scrubs announced. "There we go. Someone's coming."

A vehicle approached, headlights shining, from the area unaffected by the power outage. Just before the car reached the point where the dome began, it braked and came to a stop.

"Can I get a ride?" a young woman behind him called. "I have an early shift in the morning, and I'm exhausted."

Gordy saw a shadow moving behind the windshield, but no one stepped out. After about a minute, the car suddenly reversed and made a U-turn. Gordy just assumed the large group gathered in the road had probably weirded out the driver, but when another car approached and did the exact same thing, he realized what was happening.

"Distractor potions," Gordy whispered. "There's a gigantic ward covering us."

"Impossible," Sasha said. "Wards can't get this big."

"How else can you explain it?" Gordy asked. "Those drivers can't see us. They probably can't even see the road."

"Uh, we may have another problem." Max pointed toward Estelle and the heavyset man now straddling her seat. He was wearing a white, button-up shirt and black slacks and held a piece of luggage in his lap.

"Hey, that's mine!" Gordy blurted.

The man held up a finger. "No need to shout. I'm just going to borrow this. I can even pay you." He dug in his pocket for a wallet and waved the leather billfold in the air. "I have to get to the airport. I can't miss my flight."

"How are you going to get there?" Max scoffed. "This force field is blocking us from getting through."

The man shook his head. "That doesn't make any sense. There must be a perfectly good explanation. I just can't wait around with you people. There has to be another way through."

"Sir . . ." Adilene started, casting a cautious gaze at Gordy. "I think you need to get off Estelle."

"Here's fifty dollars." The man extended a folded bill in his fingers. "I'll give you my number, and we can work out a way to get this vehicle back to you from the airport. You just don't understand. I cannot miss my flight. I cannot—"

And then the man was gone.

Well, not gone.

Launched.

Estelle's engine fired up to maximum intensity, and the man hollered as he was catapulted into the treetops above them. Everyone gasped, including Gordy. He had expected something would happen just by the sound of Estelle's angry motor, but he never suspected she could eject someone like that. That poor fellow had been large and heavy, and now he dangled from a branch twenty feet in the air, calling out for help.

Not wanting to wait around and try to explain himself to the strangers, Gordy raced toward Estelle, the others right behind him; they climbed aboard. The onlookers watched in shocked silence as Gordy and his friends took off on Estelle, back in the opposite direction.

Back toward the Scourges.

O f all the amazing potion effects Wanda had seen throughout her life as an Elixirist, this one took the cake. No longer disguised as Akerberg, Mrs. Stitser stood in a lightweight jacket, shoulder to shoulder with Priscilla. Several yards away, a gargantuan crater easily the size of the Grand Canyon, spread out in front of them.

In fact, it *was* the Grand Canyon.

The Stitsers had once taken a road trip to Arizona, and Wanda could still remember the expansive, magnificent views of the natural wonder. The thin, snaking line of the Colorado River glimmered at the base of the canyon, and she could smell sand wafting in the hot breeze.

Only they were currently standing in Ohio, not Arizona, and had been just a few miles from the Pinkermans' home, driving Tobias's pickup truck on their way to rescue Gordy when they'd nearly plowed through the visitors' center and plummeted to their deaths.

"Dad's really outdone himself with his distractor potions," Wanda said, her fists planted on her hips.

It was still early morning, but the sky had started making its change to gray, the sunlight just above the majestic plateaus out on the horizon.

Priss's nose twitched. "Why the Grand Canyon?"

"Some wards play on memories. I think this was intended for just us. Dad's way of trying to send a message."

"What sort of message?"

"That there's no point in trying anymore," Wanda said. "That the gap between us and stopping him has widened to the level of impossibility."

When they first hit where the ward's powerful effects took hold, Tobias had casually turned the truck around, whistling all the while, and headed back the opposite direction. No one had argued, and it wasn't until several miles down the road when Wanda realized they were going the wrong way. The bizarre experience happened three more times, one right after another, before she took control of the situation and forced Tobias to stop driving. They approached the dome on foot, testing the strength of the distractor potion, until they found the spot where the ward began diverting their attention.

"We have reason to believe this ward completely surrounds the city," Paulina announced, crunching through the leaves as she and a few of her Stained Squad appeared on the road. "I've made some phone calls, and the report is the same on the other side, coming in from the east."

Tobias stooped over a portable camping stove at a closed service station nearby. Neon lights announced gas prices and illuminated his hunched frame as he tossed herbs into a cauldron. The fumes from his potion circled into the air, and raindrops began to fall in a concentrated torrent above the others. A microburst of wind whooshed toward the invisible barrier, but broke against it, dispersing with a soft roll of thunder.

"That didn't work either." Tobias chucked a rock toward the dome. The rock instantly looped back like a boomerang, and he barely had time to duck as it whizzed past.

Wanda turned to Paulina. "What means do you have of snapping this?"

Paulina shivered. The older woman had her head wrap cinched close, trying to stay dry from Tobias's manufactured rainstorm. "We could punch a hole, perhaps. We'd need a lot of wardbreakers for something this complex. It could take several hours."

"Several hours?" Wanda snapped. "My son is trapped in there, surrounded by an army of Scourges!"

"Yes, I know, but my insect wranglers are still on their way. I've called them several times, but they keep turning around and finding themselves lost and confused."

"Well, bring them here." Wanda angrily jabbed her finger at the ground. "We'll punch a hole from this spot."

Paulina nodded, and she and her soldiers headed back into the woods.

Wanda's phone rang. Cocking her head, she gazed

down in amazement at the name on the screen. Wanda showed the phone to her sister before she answered it gruffly. "Finally decided to check in on your friends, have you?" Wanda asked.

On the other end of the receiver, Bolter fell silent, though Wanda could hear him fretting about what to say.

"Do you even know what has happened back here?" Wanda demanded.

"I . . . um . . . I heard," Bolter replied feebly. "How is everyone?"

"We're not good, Bolter," Wanda said. "Gordy is trapped inside the city, and all but one of the Chamber members have been ExSponged."

"Oh, my," Bolter muttered. "And I suppose you harbor some ill feelings toward my abrupt departure?"

"You could say that," Wanda answered. Bolter didn't work for her. He was free to make his own decisions, but they certainly could have used his help throughout the whole ordeal.

"Where is Gordy now?" Bolter asked.

Wanda heard violent clanging in the background, followed by an earsplitting shriek. It sounded as though Bolter was calling from some auto mechanic's workshop, though she had no idea what had made that awful screeching noise.

"We don't know." Wanda bit her lower lip. "I hope somewhere safe and hidden."

"Perhaps I can help. I should be ready to leave within the hour. I'll try to find—"

"You can't enter the city," Wanda said, cutting Bolter off. "No one can. There's a force field blocking all entry." More shrieking rose in the background, and Wanda held the phone away from her ear.

"Hmm," Bolter mumbled to himself. "Well, I can at least make my way to you and, oh yes!" His voice squealed with excitement. "I'll just call Gordy and pinpoint his exact location!"

"Call him?" Wanda shook her head. "Nothing works inside the force field. No electronics. No phones. There's no way of reaching him."

Bolter giggled. He may have also dropped the phone, because Wanda heard a thunderous clatter as though the receiver had been kicked across concrete.

"Bolter?" Wanda asked. "Hello?"

"Yes, hello! How are you?" Bolter's voice returned, and Wanda sighed in frustration. "Sorry about that. It's a madhouse here. A productive madhouse but insanely distracting. You let me worry about finding Gordy and getting him to safety. It's the least I can do."

Before Wanda could protest further, the line went dead. When he wanted to, Bolter could be the most stubborn Elixirist she knew, but it was good to hear his voice again.

"I can't believe Dad did this," she muttered, returning

her attention to the canyon. "He's really going through with his plan this time."

"And he's far more equipped to outlast his enemies than he was thirteen years ago," Priss said. "Dad was always ambitious, but this is taking it to another level."

"There has to be a way through." Wanda squeezed the straps of her satchel, the leather twisting in her grip. "Something he missed."

Someone cleared his throat from behind, and Wanda spun around. Standing next to the gas station, surrounded by more than two dozen strangers, was a man Wanda hadn't seen in more than a decade. His hair was longer than she remembered, and he had lost some weight, but she recognized him almost instantly.

"What are you doing here, Yosuke?" she demanded.

"Perhaps we can help."

The founder of the Swigs, an individual highly wanted by B.R.E.W., was standing less than ten yards away, and she no longer had the authority to arrest him. And yet seeing Yosuke after all these years ignited a glimmer of happiness within her. Yosuke had been her friend and her trainer. Because of his intervention, she and Priss had avoided Banishment for the part they had played in their father's first attempt to overthrow B.R.E.W. Wanda owed Yosuke her life—a life she had been able to share with her family. But that didn't change what he had become.

Wanda plunged her hand into her satchel, and Yosuke flinched in surprise. "Already wanting to fight?" he asked, appalled. "I've come to offer you the assistance of the Swigs."

"I don't need your assistance," Wanda snapped. Yosuke's people were a ragtag mess of shady Elixirists, and Wanda didn't have time to entertain them.

Yosuke bowed slightly. "But maybe Gordy does."

Wanda's eyes narrowed, and she whirled on Tobias. "Is that where you went during my meeting? You took my son to *him*?"

Tobias looked appalled. "Did I not mention I love a good cup of creamed ham?"

"You're in on this, too, aren't you?" Wanda growled at Priss.

Priss shrugged, smirking. "This is all on Tobias."

"My dear, foolish Wanda," Tobias said. "Are you really refusing help? If what you say is true, then we're about to square off with a massive Scourge army. We need reinforcements."

"Yes, but not from criminals," Wanda insisted.

The group standing behind Yosuke grumbled at the comment, and their leader held up his hand to calm them. "From what I hear, you are all criminals now, and the institution that has named you as such is about to be no more. Can we not put aside our differences and unite for the betterment of society? We are equal in our hatred of Scourges. None of us wishes to experience a world where the Manifesto is our guiding government. It would certainly be bad for my business." Yosuke sighed. "And it doesn't matter anyway. I have met your son. He is a wonderful boy, and I intend to do all that I can to rescue him, with or without your permission."

Though it pained Wanda to admit it, she needed help. Without B.R.E.W. as her support, she and her friends were severely outnumbered. And before he had moved to the Swigs, Yosuke had been one of the most amazing Elixirists Wanda had ever met. With him on their side, they stood a fighting chance.

"You might as well make yourself comfortable," Wanda conceded. "We have a long wait ahead of us before Paulina's insect wranglers arrive."

Yosuke clicked his tongue. "If we needed bugs, we could've brought some from my restaurant. I have plenty scurrying about the floor. But perhaps there is another way—one not requiring a long wait."

"That ward has created a dome over the town," Priss explained. "There's no going through it."

"Agreed," Yosuke said. "Masterful work. An unprecedented display of power. But what if we didn't need to go *through* it?"

"How else do you intend to bypass the ward?" Wanda raised an uncertain eyebrow, glancing sideways at Priss and Tobias.

"My dear, isn't it as plain as day?" Yosuke asked. "You're talking to the founder of the Swigs, after all, with miles and miles of established tunnels at my disposal." He folded his arms confidently. "We simply travel under."

This is a bad idea," Gordy whispered.

"I agree," Adilene and Sasha said in unison.

"I'm telling you, no one's in there," Max answered.

The four of them crouched behind the dumpster in the driveway of Gordy's old house. The overflowing garbage smelled of rotted banana peels and something deeper than normal decay. The bin had been resting against the side of the house, untouched, for more than a month.

Estelle's headlamp dimmed as the scooter, no doubt relieved to be free of the heavy load, reversed into the backyard and parked beneath Jessica and Isaac's jungle gym.

"It just feels too easy." Gordy could see a pile of junk mail heaped on the doormat. "What if it's a trap?"

"Then they've already waited a long time to spring it," Sasha said. "My guess is they've moved on by now."

"Exactly." Max nodded. "I snuck in a couple of days ago, and it was just fine."

"Why did you go in there again?" Gordy still couldn't get over how Max had barged in without checking with him first.

"For snacks," Max replied. "And potions and stuff. But I think your wards have kept everyone way."

"If the wards are still working, how did Max get in?" Adilene asked.

Max looked baffled for a moment, then shrugged. "I must be impervious to magic spells."

"Big word, smarty-pants," Sasha said, snickering.

Max smiled as if he considered Sasha's jab a compliment.

"My home wards allow certain people in. They always have," Gordy explained. "Bolter, Grandma and Grandpa Stitser, people from my dad's work—they're allowed through. Adilene and Max can come and go whenever they want because they're friends of the family."

"There's that," Max agreed. "But also my imperviousness."

"Do you think he's right, then?" Adilene asked. "Have your wards kept other people away?"

Gordy gnawed on his lip. "I don't think they can prevent anyone from B.R.E.W. from coming in, unless my mom specifically altered the wards, which I don't think she did. But they should keep Scourges away." In theory, at least. Nothing felt certain anymore. Gordy had once believed the home wards to be impenetrable. Boy, had he been wrong. Since Esmeralda's attack on his house, he had seen wards consumed by bugs more times than he could count.

"And B.R.E.W. would have already gone in by now to perform a search," Sasha reasoned. "We probably don't have anything to fear at the moment."

"That's what I've been saying," Max blurted. "It's the safest place around!"

Going to Gordy's house hadn't been their first choice, despite Max's suggestion.

Sasha's neighborhood had been overrun with Scourges; they couldn't even drive on the road for fear of being spotted and had to get close to Sasha's house by climbing over fences. Sasha's parents had been standing out on the front lawn, acting as if everything was normal. Sasha tried to help them, but her mom told her they were waiting for a taxi because they were going to a big meeting at Kipland Middle, where her father would be getting his job back in a wonderful ceremony. Never mind the fact it was four o'clock in the morning.

Adilene's neighborhood was no different. She spotted her parents filing into a line of people walking casually down the street. Her dad held a Tupperware container filled with papusas he intended on selling at a school function. Both he and Mrs. Rivera were in their pajamas. They had been Blotched. Gordy had to drag Adilene away before they were caught and Blotched as well.

Steeling his nerves, Gordy crept onto the porch. He checked through the windows, saw that it was empty, and then tested the doorknob. The door was unlocked, just as Max had said. After a scan through the living room to make sure the coast was clear, Gordy beckoned to the others, and they slipped into the kitchen without incident.

"Brilliant!" Max repeated. He whipped open the refrigerator door and then frowned with disappointment. "You guys don't have anything to eat." Opening a carton of orange juice, Max sniffed the lid and, though looking somewhat repulsed, took a sip.

"We haven't exactly been home, you know," Gordy said.

"Gordy, can you come here for a second?" Adilene called out. She sat in one of the chairs around the kitchen table. "You need to see this." Lying upon a piece of cloth in front of her was a rod-like object. The tip glowed with a haunting, off-white light, and there were strange markings carved along the exterior. Adilene ran her fingers along the edge of the cloth, not daring to touch the wand. "This was given to me." She cleared her throat. "By Doll."

Gordy blinked, trying to process the information.

"Wait," Max said. "Are you telling me that Slim visited you?" His voice cracked with uneasiness. "The skeleton?"

Adilene nodded.

"Are you sure it wasn't just someone dressed up in a skeleton costume?" Max asked.

Gordy's head snapped up. "Did he know who you were?"

"I . . . I don't know. I think, maybe." Adilene winced, pressing two fingers against her left temple and gasping in pain.

"What's wrong?" Gordy asked. Adilene hadn't said much all evening, and he'd assumed it was because they had been running for their lives. Now he suspected something else was wrong.

"I have a splitting headache," she said. "I've had one all week."

"Why didn't you say something?" Gordy opened his satchel, but his jar of Boiler's Balm was empty.

"It's okay. It's just my eyesight," she said.

"What about your eyesight?" Max asked between gulps of rancid orange juice. He wiped his mouth with the back of his hand and belched.

"You're disgusting," Sasha said.

"I need glasses, I think, or at least an eye exam. It doesn't matter right now," she said testily. "Doll wasn't there for me, not directly anyway. He was looking for you. Maybe he couldn't find you, but for whatever reason, he came to my house and dropped off the wand. Along with this." She handed a piece of paper to Gordy. "I didn't read it."

Gordy unfolded the paper and saw his grandfather's name inked at the bottom.

My Dearest Gordy,

I hope you took the necessary steps before opening this letter. Normally, I would have implored you to deliver this message directly to your mother for inspection. One can't be too careful these days, especially when all manner of creatures can be employed by the darkest of means.

Gordy gasped and tossed the paper onto the table as though it had burned him. Max dribbled orange juice down the front of his shirt.

"What's wrong?" Adilene asked.

How could he have been so stupid? That letter had come from Mezzarix, the Scourge of Nations, and Gordy hadn't thought to test it out for Dire Substances. What if he had been Blotched? What if Adilene had been Blotched this entire night?

"Sasha, hurry! Spray this." Gordy scooted back from the table, giving his grandfather's letter a wide berth. He didn't feel like he was under the influential spell of a Scourge, but he also had no idea what that actually felt like. Would his mind be clear enough to notice a difference?

Rolling her eyes, Sasha brought out her bottle of Detection Spray. "We're all doomed," she murmured, spritzing the paper.

Clenching his hands into fists, Gordy waited for something to pop or fizzle, but after a solid minute of nothing, he felt able to breathe. He picked up the letter and continued reading.

> *As I'm sure you've heard by now, I am constructing an army. B.R.E.W. will be dissolved within the week, and the secrets our Community has kept hidden for three hundred years will be brought into the light. After the annihilation of B.R.E.W., I intend to continue my removal of governments everywhere. Humans are the*

only species who place limitations on power. It isn't natural. My plan will not find success without casualties, and for that I feel a hint of sorrow. But only a hint.

Now, Gordy, you must heed my warning. I know my Scourges will be ruthless as they tear apart that little town of yours on a mission. In order to protect you, I am entrusting this weapon in your very capable hands. I care not about anyone other than you, my precious grandson. I urge you not to show restraint. When it comes to protecting your well-being and your potion-making abilities, you must be vigilant. The world cannot lose such a gift.

Once this war begins, it will take many months to complete, but eventually the dust will settle and there will be peace. Then you and I will find each other, and we will live the life we always should have. The mightiest of Elixirists. The ones destined to stand atop the pillar.

I look forward to the day where we might brew together. Oh, the things we shall concoct! But until then, take care.

> *Your loving grandfather,*
> *Mezzarix Rook*

Gordy finished reading the letter and set it down. He looked at the others, uncertain of what to say.

Adilene carefully picked up the paper and, with Sasha and Max crowded behind her, perused Mezzarix's words in silence.

"Why do I need this weapon?" Gordy asked once they had finished.

"Isn't it obvious?" Sasha replied. "We're going to be attacked. We already have been attacked. You saw what they did to my parents. That's what your grandfather wants. I think he intends to Blotch the whole city."

"But why go to all that trouble?" Max plopped into a chair, running a hand through his hair so it stood on end like a fauxhawk.

"Because he's looking for somebody." Adilene smoothed the crinkles of the letter. "That's what Zelda said earlier, and Mezzarix said so just now." She ran her finger along the words until she found what she was looking for. "'I know my Scourges will be ruthless as they tear apart that little town of yours on a mission,'" she read. "That's the mission."

"But who could they want who's that special?" Max asked.

"Me." The announcement came from behind, just outside the kitchen.

Gordy spun around, his chair falling back with a thud.

A sallow-skinned, middle-aged woman stood in the kitchen doorway. Clearing her throat, she smiled at Gordy. "They're looking for me."

CHAPTER

27

Calm down, children. I'm not here to harm you," the woman said with a strong Southern accent. Dressed in dark clothing, she displayed her empty palms to the four of them.

Shoving away from the table, Max stood up, his chair immediately crashing to the floor. Gordy and Sasha grabbed potions while Adilene snatched up the letter and held it behind her as though concealing a piece of evidence.

"I heard your voices, and I thought the ghost had finally decided to speak to me," the stranger said. "Then I feared the Scourges had somehow broken in. Your wards are quite strong, I must say. Someone went to great lengths to keep this house a secret." Eyes flickering toward the stairs, the woman sighed. "Believe me, I hadn't planned on taking shelter here. I'd much rather be home, but I had no time. The streets were crawling with criminals, and I was not operating at full strength."

She leaned against the doorway, and Gordy noticed her

right leg was heavily wrapped in some sort of splint, down along her shin.

"I gathered linens and made myself a little space in your laboratory," she continued. "Though the only things left in the lab are empty bottles and the faintest hint of residue on the countertops. That would be my fault, of course."

Sasha raised her bottle of Torpor Tonic higher. "You're Iris Glass."

The woman gave a strained smile. "It is a pleasure to meet you, Sasha. How's your mother fairing these days?"

"She's been Blotched." Sasha's tone darkened. "Along with my dad and everyone else in this stupid town."

Iris nodded. "That's what I was afraid of."

Sasha moved around to the front of the table, next to Gordy and Adilene. "You should take that weapon and use it on this woman right now!"

Gordy blinked rapidly. "Um . . . do what?"

"Iris Glass is a Chamber member," Sasha said, raising her voice. "She's the enemy!"

Gordy remembered having heard that name before. A few weeks ago, his mom had made him memorize the names of all the Chamber members. She had wanted to prepare him should he ever come across one. The Stitsers were wanted criminals, and right now, standing in his kitchen, was one of B.R.E.W.'s leaders. Was this what Mezzarix had been talking about in his letter? Was it already time for him to defend himself against an enemy?

Gordy touched the rod and instantly felt heat and pressure trembling beneath his skin.

"I'd be careful with that. Wouldn't want an accidental ExSpongement to happen, now would you?" Iris's eyes locked on the weapon at Gordy's side.

"ExSpongement?" Gordy repeated in confusion.

Iris nodded. "That's a Decocting Wand."

"A what?"

Iris looked disappointed. "How is it the son of Wanda Stitser doesn't know what a Decocting Wand is? B.R.E.W. uses them to ExSponge Elixirists."

"That's not what this is," Sasha said confidently. "My mom had one, and it didn't look anything like this."

"Well, it's been modified, now hasn't it, child?" Iris explained. "The Scourge of Nations has littered the city with these horrific tools of destruction."

Gordy gaped in shock at his grandfather's gift. That was the weapon? Something that could take away someone's potion-making abilities? The tingling in Gordy's fingers made him want to chuck the wand into the garbage. Images of Sasha's mom being ExSponged flooded his memory. He saw Madame Brexil dropping to the floor in the basement laboratory, her arms falling limp as though her very soul had been snapped away.

"Passing judgment upon some poor soul is not for the faint of heart," Iris said. "Besides, I'm not here to harm any of you."

"Don't listen to her," Sasha hissed. "She was at my

house, right after it happened. Right after they kicked my mom out of B.R.E.W. Iris signed off on the order to have you captured."

"I did," Iris admitted, bowing her head and pressing a hand to her chest. "We made that decision together, but that was before we realized the magnitude of Mezzarix's escape. And now I regret my mistakes."

"Where are the others?" Sasha squeezed the bottle in her hand. "Are they all upstairs hiding?"

"The other Chamber members?" Iris looked perplexed. "My dear, the entire Board has fallen at the hands of the enemy. I am the only one left."

Gordy suddenly felt boxed in with the table behind him and the enigmatic Iris Glass standing in the doorway.

"You see," Iris said. "ExSponging me would be a horrible idea. Once I'm eliminated, there will be nothing standing in the way of Mezzarix's global, chaotic reign. The beginning of the end. The full realization of his Manifesto."

"The what?" Adilene stood closer to Gordy, her shoulders shaking.

"No more prisons. No more government," Iris began, her voice smooth like a batch of roiling Certe Syrup.

"And no more secrets," Gordy finished, remembering Yosuke's words.

"What, is that a song?" Max snapped his fingers next to Gordy's ear. "Are you under her spell?"

Gordy swatted away his hand. "It's my grandfather's plan of chaos."

"Indeed," Iris said. "We've had to deal with Mezzarix before, but now that he possesses the Vessel, he's far more equipped to see his plan through to the end. Of course, your grandfather did experience a slight hiccup. After Esmeralda's attack on B.R.E.W., the Chamber realized we lacked certain safeguards. We added an extra element into the Vessel, further linking the seven Chamber members to its power and ensuring it could not be transferred without our unanimous consent. Never in three centuries has such a bold addition been necessary, but then B.R.E.W. has never seen the likes of your family before."

"But Mezzarix has the Vessel," Max said. "He's using it."

"Mezzarix can cause mayhem even with the instrument's limited capacity, as you can see," Iris said. "To fully take control of the Vessel, however, and therefore ultimately destroy it, he needs all seven Chamber members to willingly pass off on that decision."

"Or have you all ExSponged," Sasha added.

Iris winced, her eyelids tightening. "Your mother was the first to go, and then Straiffe Veddlestone received a mysterious gift. A promise of power and wealth—and a Decocting Wand like the one beneath your hand." She pointed to Gordy's weapon. "Straiffe had always been the weakest of our Chamber. Easily persuaded. He led a group of Scourges to our secret Board meeting and ExSponged the lot of them. I barely made it away, but not without injury." She glanced at her wounded leg and suddenly laughed. "The scoundrel hit me with a Mangle Potion.

Ironic, don't you think? A member of the Chamber using an outlawed potion to disable me."

"I could make you some Boiler's Balm," Gordy offered.

"I've used plenty of that already, but thank you, Gordy." Iris bowed politely. "Numbing tonics will only ease my suffering for a short time. I'm sorry to use your house as my hideout, but I honestly didn't have anywhere else to go. Like you said, Sasha, everyone's been rounded up and Blotched. It's only a matter of time before I'm found."

As if on cue, a sharp whistling arose outside, like the sound of a bottle rocket streaking down the road. Gordy heard an explosion erupt close to the house, and he rushed into the living room, Max right behind him.

"I'd avoid looking out that window," Iris warned.

But Gordy had to see for himself. After removing the glow sticks from around his neck and burying them beneath the couch cushions to dim the light, he pulled back the curtain an inch and cautiously looked out. There were people crowded in the street at the end of the cul-de-sac. Adults and children, too many to count, walking shoulder to shoulder. They moved silently and lethargically, like a herd of ambling zombies.

"Where are they going?" Max whispered.

Gordy heard another whistle and saw the outline of two figures standing less than fifteen yards from his mailbox launching potions at the front door of the home three houses down. They were both holding sticks in their hands, ones with glowing tips. After the third explosion, the door opened, and three of Gordy's neighbors emerged. They didn't even try to run away; they simply walked over and joined the horde.

The two figures suddenly vanished, just as Zelda had done earlier. More enemies equipped with Silt. Whatever hope he had of escaping the city was fading fast.

Gordy allowed the curtain to fall back into place and backed away from the window. "That's how they're Blotching them. They hit the house with a potion, and everyone just comes right out."

"It's called a Perplexity Projectile." Sasha stood in the living room next to Adilene. "B.R.E.W. uses them to put large groups of non-Elixirists into a sort of stupor. Makes people easier to manipulate in an emergency."

"What sort of emergency?" Adilene asked.

"Imagine there was an explosion," Iris said, standing in the doorway, her injured leg bent awkwardly behind her. "Some Elixirist's laboratory goes up in smoke, or some foolish man creates a hurricane in a public swimming pool. Folks start asking questions. Simply round them all up and erase that memory at once."

"Where are they taking them?" Max demanded.

"To the school, I think," Iris said.

"Kipland Middle?" Adilene asked.

Iris nodded. "They're filing them into the gymnasium for further inspection."

"Why?" Gordy asked. The whole scenario was becoming weirder by the minute.

"I suspect they have no idea who they're looking for," Iris replied. "Perhaps a few of the Scourges remember me from their Banishments years ago, but the Chamber members are typically away from the action. We issue punishments while someone else, like your mother, carries out the orders. These criminals may have a photo to refer to, but they don't have the patience to go door-to-door matching up a picture with my face, like Cinderella's prince and her shiny glass slipper."

"What if one of those Scourges throws something at this house?" Max asked. "Could we be Blotched?"

Iris shrugged. "It may not do anything. Not with these wards protecting us. But, like I said, it's only a matter of time. They won't stop until they've found me."

"How do they even know where you are?" Adilene rubbed her forehead with one hand, eyes squinting from pain. "You could be anywhere by now. We drove to where the force field ended. It's not far."

"They're tracking me, and they've pinpointed my location to this general area," Iris explained. "They don't know the exact address of the house I'm hiding in yet, but they know I haven't left."

"How are they tracking you?" Sasha asked.

"With a potion, of course. Straiffe had plenty of my possessions. They raided my home before they sprung their trap. I suppose they did that to all the Chamber members, just in case one of us, like myself, got away. All they needed

was something with enough of my DNA to add to the concoction."

Sasha stood stiffly for a moment, eyes darting about
the room. Then she gasped excitedly and sat on the floor,
pulling items from her satchel, ingredients contained in
baggies and clay jars.

"We can do it as well!" Sasha withdrew a porcelain
cauldron no bigger than a soup bowl, and a hot pad with a
coiling black cord. "No electricity," she mumbled to herself.
"We'll need a heat source." Her head snapped up, focusing
on Gordy. "What could we burn here?"

Gordy frowned. "What potion are you—"

Sasha cut him off, pointing to Iris. "The Scourges are
tracking her, and they've narrowed her location to within
maybe five to ten miles. That's pretty accurate, don't you
think?" She continued to lay out ingredients on the floor,
stalks and stems, a container of black beetles.

"Yeah, it's accurate," Gordy said. "That's why we need
to keep moving."

Sasha snapped her fingers in annoyance. "Come on,
Stitser, think about it. What if we could pinpoint your
grandfather's location to within five or ten miles? Wouldn't
that be worth trying?"

"But you need something with his DNA," Max said.
"Where are we going to find that?"

Gordy's eyes suddenly widened, and he looked at the
folded piece of paper clutched in Adilene's fingers. The letter from Mezzarix.

ordy tore open his satchel and dropped to the floor alongside Sasha. "I've got matches and iskry powder. That should start a pretty good fire." He pointed at the end table next to the couch. "Max, bring me all those magazines."

"Okay, I guess." Max looked grumpily at Adilene as he carried over a dozen past-issues of Mr. Stitser's subscription to *Royal Dishwasher Magazine* and dropped them next to Gordy.

Sasha had her face almost buried between the pages of her notebook, flipping rapidly from recipe to recipe. "It's called the Seeking Serum," she said. "With the right ingredients, it's supposed to be foolproof." She looked at Gordy, lips pressed together, breathing rapidly. "I think we have the right ingredients now."

Sitting down and crossing her legs, Adilene gaped at the assortment of ingredients. "Why didn't my blood work?"

"It did work, but just not good enough. I suppose the amount of Silt in your blood was too faint to narrow down the location," Sasha said distractedly.

"Perhaps you should do this in the lab," Iris suggested. "You'll burn straight through the carpet."

Realizing how much trouble he would be in if his mom found out he had set fire to the living room, Gordy and the others hastily gathered up the items and charged up the stairs.

Where it had been dark earlier, morning had announced its arrival, and the laboratory had taken on a grayish hue. The glow sticks had finally run out of juice, making them look like yellowed fangs dangling around Sasha's neck. A handful of empty vials and pieces of cork had settled into the grooves between the wooden floorboards. Gordy spotted a blanket and a pillow nestled in one corner of the room where Iris had been hiding. How long had she been sleeping there?

The lab was almost completely empty, and Gordy felt a twinge of anger. This was his mother's second laboratory that had been demolished, and the person doing it stood in the doorway, regarding the barrenness with indifference. Though she had treated him cordially, Gordy didn't trust Iris. But for now they needed to work together if any of them wanted to survive.

Sasha ignited the iskry powder, and the stack of magazines instantly burst into cream-colored flames. The pungent scents of vanilla bean and scorched horsehair filled the room. Adilene coughed as she fed blank pages from her notebook into the fire, stoking the heat beneath the porcelain cauldron.

Lips pulled into a taut line, Sasha began to brew, scraping the bark from a forked branch into the mixture.

"What is that?" Gordy asked, curious.

"Dowsing rod," she answered tersely.

"What does it do?" Max peeked over Gordy's shoulder.

"Locates water in the ground. Please, stop talking," Sasha instructed.

She smashed several shark's teeth with a mortar and pestle and dropped the misshapen pieces into the tumbling liquid. She added pickled piranha scales swimming in a clouded mason jar and wiggled her hands above the bowl. The potion began to smoke, responding to her rhythmic thumb twitches. Once the contents inside the cauldron resembled the consistency of stale oatmeal, Sasha tore Gordy's letter from Mezzarix in half and rested it lightly on top.

After several seconds, the ripped section of paper liquified, sinking into the mixture, and steam rose from the cauldron. Sasha hurriedly gathered the steam into a glass container and screwed on a lid. Then she brought out a world atlas from her satchel and a magnifying glass. The map of the islands off the coast of Florida had been dog-eared.

"How do you know for sure he's close to Florida?" Max asked. "Maybe he's somewhere—"

Sasha's eyes whipped up, glaring at Max, and he stopped talking.

"He's there," she said. "I know he is."

Nostrils flaring, Sasha opened the container and poured the steam onto the map. Separating, the steam drew several lines on the thick paper as though they were tiny bloodhounds tracking a scent. The vaporous fingers moved away from the cluster of islands off Florida, heading purposefully to a spot intersected by a longitude line out in the ocean. Then, all at once, the smoky tendrils reformed into one solid stripe and shrunk to the size of a pinprick on the map.

Sasha released a shaky breath. Taking the magnifying glass, she held it over the pinprick of steam. A minute ticked by in silence before she finally pulled away, eyes reddening with tears.

"It didn't work." She wiped her nose with the back of her hand. "The search area is probably five hundred miles."

"How's that possible?" Max blurted. "That's just a dot!"

"It's a map, you idiot!" Sasha shouted. "A dot in the ocean could be even a thousand miles."

"May I see?" Adilene asked, reaching for the magnifying glass. Bending over, she scanned the map and then grumbled. "I think I'm going blind. I don't see anything at all."

"Maybe you do need glasses," Gordy said. He could see the steam circling around a small search area, with enough space in between that could have contained Rhode Island.

"Yeah, probably," Adilene said. "But it just happened all of a sudden."

"After you met Cadence?" Gordy asked, suddenly remembering Ms. Bimini's warning.

Adilene nodded. "I'm not turning old, am I?"

"You're going to need a walker soon," Max said, snickering. "And orthopedic shoes."

Adilene whimpered. "Really?"

Gordy shook his head. "Ms. Bimini said there would be some subtle changes because we drank the Silt. And you drank more than any of us."

"I don't want to go blind."

"You're not going blind," Gordy promised. At least he hoped she wouldn't. What if Adilene's eyesight never improved? What if her consumption of the Silt had caused irreversible damages?

"Can you two stop flirting with each other for one second and focus on the real problem?" Sasha snapped. "We're never going to find Mezzarix."

"You need his blood, child," Iris announced. "It was a valiant effort, a worthy idea, but unless you can procure that, the Seeking Serum won't find him. For all we know, he didn't even write that letter. He could have dictated it to one of his servants."

A fresh streak of tears dribbled from Sasha's eyes, her lips quivering.

Gordy didn't know what to say. He felt irritated at how well his grandfather had covered his tracks, but it was different for Sasha. Finding Mezzarix meant saving her mother, and this last attempt had left her with nothing.

Sasha slammed a fist on the countertop, disrupting the liquid in the cooling cauldron, and stormed out of the room. She left behind her satchel and her ingredients but didn't seem to care.

Adilene sighed as though already regretting what she was about to do, then followed Sasha. With all the ruckus being made, Gordy feared the Scourges outside would hear them and grow suspicious. But there was no way he was going to tell Sasha and Adilene to quiet down.

"My, my, my," Iris purred, gazing into the hallway as Adilene and Sasha thundered down the stairs. "We've made a royal mess, haven't we?" Then she too disappeared from the doorway, hobbling off to some private corner of the house.

Gordy and Max were left in the empty laboratory.

"Women." Max picked up a vial of liquid from the counter. "What are you going to do?" He squinted at the wording printed on the label and whistled, jiggling the bottle. "It's Adilene's blood. Maybe we could mix it with an insect. Make a little Adilene cockroach for a pet."

"Give me that." Gordy wrestled the bottle from Max's grip. There was only about half an ounce of blood left inside the vial. No more than a couple of drops.

"I was just kidding," Max said, playfully elbowing Gordy in his side. "It's too bad all we have is a bottle of *her* blood, right? If only you had taken some from Mezzarix when you visited him in Greenland. Asked him to donate to the cause. That would have been helpful."

Gordy nodded. *If only*, he thought. All his problems would have been solved. Well, not all of them. They still had to find a way out of the city, break through the force field, and travel the long distance to Florida. And there was still the issue of what he would do once he found his grandfather somewhere out in the ocean. He wasn't looking forward to that. But if he had a bottle of his blood, they would be one step closer.

Glancing around the ransacked room, Gordy tried to remember how it used to look. In his memory he could see flasks and vials and where they had been stored. Pieces of masking tape were still stuck to the various drawers of the apothecary table, listing their contents. Gordy's focus drifted down to the bottom drawer marked "Volatile."

And then the idea struck him right between the eyes.

"Max! You are a genius!" Gordy moved over to the apothecary drawer and wrenched it open.

"I've been telling you that for years," Max said.

Gordy cradled a vial in his hand, no bigger than his pinkie finger. The cork had been removed, the bottle discarded among several other empty glass jars as though forgotten. But Gordy remembered.

"We do have a bottle of his blood," he said, holding up the vial for Max to see. The same bottle his mom had brought home from Greenland the previous year after Mezzarix had agreed to destroy it. The one that had once contained the Eternity Elixir. "We've had it all along."

For the first time since Gordy could remember, Max acted like a legitimate lab partner. He tucked in his shirt, rolled up his sleeves, and nodded at Gordy with grim determination.

"Just tell me what to do," Max said. "I won't let you down."

With the door closed, and the others elsewhere in the house, Gordy and Max went to work. Most of the ingredients Sasha had used to brew the Seeking Serum had been wiped out. Despite not having the necessary materials, Gordy began thinking up alternative solutions. Images of substances and ingredients formed in his head, cycling through as though his brain was a computer and he had access to elite potion-making software.

"Keep the heat steady if you can," Gordy whispered.

Max grunted as he heated the fire beneath the cauldron and kept the temperature smoldering within the bowl. He combined the iskry powder and ogon oil, per Gordy's instruction, into a sparkling paste, and fanned the flames with one of the ripped magazines.

Closing his eyes and blocking out all other sounds and distractions, Gordy began to Blind Batch.

Every potion needed at least one form of the four main elements: liquid, mineral, chemical, and herb. In Sasha's mixture, she'd used the pickling solution of the piranha scales, but they still had half a jar of the pale-green liquid dappled with bits of fish. She'd used all of the shark teeth for the mineral; not a single piece remained. While Gordy stirred the liquid with the dousing rod—providing the necessary herbal component—he asked Max for the container of smashed quartz to use as substitute. Three of the four elements were done, but Gordy wasn't finished yet.

Though he knew it was risky, he didn't have much of a choice. Sucking in a breath, he inserted his finger into the boiling liquid in the cauldron. He heard Max gasp in surprise, but Gordy ignored him.

A minute passed and then two, and Gordy sensed an approving tingle under his skin. He immediately removed his finger and dabbed a couple of drops of Oighear Ointment on the flames to extinguish the heat. Gordy then funneled a ladle of the potion into the empty Eternity Elixir vial. The mixture smelled like rotten eggs and instantly transformed into smoke. Before any of it could escape, Gordy plugged the opening with a piece of cork and placed the bottle on the counter.

"Are you feeling okay?" Max asked, his voice unsteady.

Gordy grinned, his cheeks flushing with embarrassment. He knew how it must have looked. "I'm fine." He held up his finger. Not even the tip looked red or burned. "It doesn't hurt, I promise."

"That's not what I'm talking about. You . . . uh . . . you looked different just now. Weird." Max averted his eyes. "Really weird."

"I was Blind Batching," Gordy explained.

"Yeah, I know, but I've seen you Blind Batch. I was there when you nearly blew up B.R.E.W. headquarters, and you've never looked like that before. Did you even open your eyes once this whole time?"

The question caught Gordy off guard, and he laughed. "Of course I did." He had paid careful attention during the whole brewing procedure. Judging by Max's look of awe, however, Gordy wondered if he actually had. Maybe that was why the skill was called Blind Batching.

The smoke within the vial swirled. Gordy reached for the atlas, glancing at the closed laboratory door. "Should we call the others?"

Max considered it for a second. "Let's see if it worked. Just the two of us. *Mono e mono.*"

Gordy didn't think that was the right way to say that phrase, but he agreed. It should just be the two of them testing it out.

"Just don't do that again, okay?" Max smiled at Gordy awkwardly. "I've seen enough stuff to give me a lifetime of nightmares already. I'd rather not see anything more."

F ive miles." Gordy tossed the atlas on the downstairs
coffee table.

Both girls sat on the carpet, Sasha with her face
buried in her knees and Adilene next to her, consoling her.

"What are you talking about?" Adilene asked, squeezing Sasha's shoulder.

"I know where Mezzarix is hiding, and I've narrowed
it down to a five-mile area." The last of the smoke had
dissipated, but not before Gordy had circled the spot on
the map with a pencil. He had also written down the coordinates of the exact location of his grandfather's hideout,
less than sixty miles from the coast of Miami and just ten
miles north of a little place called South Bimini Island.
That wasn't a coincidence.

Sasha looked up, her face wet and glistening. "How?"

"Your potion worked," Gordy replied. "We just needed
the right ingredient. The letter didn't have enough of
Mezzarix's DNA, but I knew where to find some."

"Reap it, losers!" Max cheered. "We're the dynamic duo!"

After hurriedly returning to the lab to gather her possessions and snagging a few tissues to clean her face, Sasha was back to her old self again. "We'll need a flight to Florida. And then a boat," she said, poring over the map and plotting a course to the island. "Something inconspicuous, but with enough fuel for the sixty-mile journey there and then the return home. We can stop at my place to pick up my mom's credit cards. I doubt any of you have enough cash to even get us to airport."

Max smirked. "Airport? Boat? Since when are we the ones going?"

Sasha stared at Max in disbelief. "This is our chance to take back the Vessel. Mezzarix won't suspect us coming to the island."

"But we're just kids, remember?" Adilene said. "You said it yourself, we don't have training."

Sasha turned to Adilene as if sizing her up and then shrugged. "Then stay. What do I care? Gordy and I can handle it."

"Uh, I think we need to get this information to my mom first," Gordy said. It had always been his intention to hand off the assignment to the professionals. His mom, Aunt Priss, and Tobias were way better equipped to take on Mezzarix than they were.

Sasha huffed. "We can't do that! They won't bring us along."

"That's the whole point," Max said.

"But then I'll never be able to help my mom!" Sasha shouted. Gordy and the others eased back out of range, just in case she started swinging. "They will go there and maybe find a way to defeat Mezzarix, but do you think they'll pause for one second to return my mom's abilities to her?"

"Of course they will," Gordy said.

"To the person who threatened to ExSponge all of you? To 'crazy Madame Brexil'? Not a chance!" Sasha buried her fists under her arms and looked down at the map. "I'll go by myself if I have to."

"Not to change the subject," Max said. "But it's not like we can even leave the city if we wanted to. There's still no way out of this weird invisible dome."

The four of them fell silent. Max was right. They were trapped.

"This potion—it's like a ward, right?" Adilene asked. "How do you get rid of those?"

"With wardbreakers," Sasha said. "With bugs."

"Oh, yeah, the bugs," Max groaned. He had been at the Stitsers when Esmeralda had attacked the home wards with more insects than they could possibly count. They had swarmed through the front door and devoured the protective potions. By the end, the floor had been completely covered with their quivering husks oozing with goo.

"Do you know how to brew a wardbreaker potion?" Adilene asked Sasha.

Sasha thought for a moment. "It's illegal for anyone not approved by B.R.E.W. to make one. If you're caught concocting a wardbreaker, they'll arrest you."

"But your mom could have done it, right?" Adilene looked hopeful. "As Chamber President, she would have been allowed—"

"My mom's no longer the Chamber President!" Sasha snapped. "And she's been ExSponged. She wouldn't know the first step of how to brew one of those anymore. Oh, and she's been Blotched and kidnapped by Scourges!"

Gordy clenched his jaw. "Could we please stop overreacting?"

"Yeah, Sasha, it's not like you're trying out for the school play," Max added. "How about you dial it back, like, two hundred notches?"

"I don't like being trapped in your house or being reminded about what happened to my mom," Sasha apologized through gritted teeth.

"What I was trying to say," Adilene offered, "is that if your mom could have brewed a wardbreaker as Chamber President, wouldn't Iris Glass also know how to do it?"

"Maybe," Sasha said, her tone easing. "I mean, yeah, I suppose she would."

"Do you think she'd help us?" Gordy asked.

"She wants to get out of here as much as we do, and she's been somewhat helpful," Adilene said.

"You're forgetting something," Sasha said. "We don't have any bugs."

Gordy sighed with frustration. He had imagined busting a hole through the force field, but now they were back to square one.

"Why do they have to be bugs again?" Max asked.

"Because they can be easily manipulated," Sasha explained. "But you need a lot of them. I read that to break the ward for a small house, you need at least two hundred thousand cockroaches."

Max's nose crinkled with disgust. "Fat chance of finding that many." Then his eyebrows rose. He looked at Gordy with a grin.

"Before you say it, no, I don't have any bugs," Gordy replied. They used to have a few terrariums in the family lab back before B.R.E.W. wiped it clean, but even then they had no more than a hundred insects at one time.

"No, but maybe you could lure them here with a potion." Max waggled his eyebrows. "With something like Rat Magnet."

Gordy grinned at his friend. Max was full of ideas tonight.

31

It took Gordy and Sasha the whole morning to whip up the right potion. Pooling their supplies, they had enough ingredients. Iris, who agreed to help, estimated they would need close to fifty million insects to destroy the ward surrounding the town, possibly more. Referring to his potion journal, Gordy modified his Rat Magnet recipe and put the final touches on a newer version. The potion filled a two-liter bottle with a vibrant-pink liquid fizzing with carbonation.

They ate a lunch of stale crackers and overcooked spaghetti noodles Adilene heated up on the stove using the last of Gordy's iskry powder. Despite not having any sauce for the noodles, they scarfed down the food.

A massive swarm of insects would definitely draw the attention of the Scourges, so they decided to wait until evening. Then they would head to the forest by the edge of the barrier to lay out the lure and hope there were enough insects in the area to wipe out the ward.

It was starting to get dark outside when Gordy was startled awake. He hadn't realized he'd fallen asleep; Adilene, Max, and Sasha were still dozing on blankets or sprawled out on the couches. Gordy wanted just five more minutes of rest when he heard the movement upstairs. Something was shuffling from one end of a room to another.

Sitting up, he strained his ears to listen. Iris Glass had certainly made herself at home, but this was getting ridiculous. It sounded as though she was moving around in his parents' bedroom. Hadn't she and B.R.E.W. ransacked enough already?

"Ah, you're awake," Iris asked from the kitchen. She leaned on a crutch to help with her injured leg. "I hope you don't mind, but I found this in the master bedroom earlier this afternoon, and I borrowed it. My leg is growing worse by the minute, and the less stress I place on it, the better."

"Yeah, sure," Gordy said.

"I suspect you know this, but I don't intend to go with you when you head to the barrier," Iris said. "Should there be any trouble, I would only get in the way, and my ExSpongement would escalate things in the wrong direction. You understand, don't you?"

Gordy had been wondering what they would do with Iris when the time came to make their move, and he started to nod in agreement. Then he heard another floorboard creaking upstairs, and his pulse quickened as he shot to his feet. "Did you hear that?" he asked.

"Hear what?" Iris glanced around the room.

Max's snoring sounded like static from a walkie-talkie, but Gordy knew it wasn't that.

Iris smiled. "From time to time, I hear it too. Your ghost, walking across the floor."

"My house isn't haunted," Gordy said. If there was walking, it meant someone else was there.

"Then it's a critter. Or poorly constructed floorboards. We found a snake in one of the compartments in your lab a few weeks ago. Big fellow with an uneasy temperament. Perhaps he had a brother we missed."

Gordy's mom had only ever had one snake; she used his shed skin for potions. The thought of a rogue python slinking through the rooms while everyone slept gave him the shivers.

"There's no one up there," she insisted. "I was there earlier, and I assure you, we are alone."

Gordy needed to see for himself. Taking one of his last remaining Torpor Tonics from his satchel, he ascended the steps and peered down the dark hallway.

"If you see the snake," Iris called out in a hushed whisper from the foot of the stairs, "I'd leave it be."

First, Gordy checked his bedroom and found it in the same condition as it had been when he'd left a month ago. A search through each of the twins' rooms came up mostly empty, though Gordy discovered a pillowcase stuffed with last year's Halloween candy crammed under Jessica's bed. Gordy figured Max would find something edible amid the rock-hard taffies. There was no one in the bathroom or hiding in the hall closet.

Then, heart pounding in his ears, Gordy pulled off the comforter from his parents' bed and threw open their closet doors. He found more blankets and photo albums, a box full of his dad's spare refrigerator filters, but no snake, no intruder, and certainly no ghost.

Gordy was about to return to the living room when something tucked in the back of the closet, hidden behind his mother's shoe caddy, caught his attention. The uneven edges of crinkled paper poked out from the leather binding, and Gordy recognized it at once. It was his grandfather's potion journal.

The last time Gordy had handled the journal had been months ago when Max and Adilene had come for a brewing session during dinner. They had spent the evening in the lab trying to see if Gordy's friends could make potions on their own. The journal had been on the top shelf next to a collection of his mother's various recipe manuals. Gordy had assumed it had been taken by B.R.E.W. along with everything else, but it would seem his mother had wanted to keep it safe.

Gordy thumbed it open to the middle page and scanned the ingredients for a potion his grandfather had named Pitter-Patter. There were drawings of skulls and bones and creepy puppets with marionette strings scribbled on the paper. Suspecting this potion had led to Doll's creation and not wanting to think about the skeleton while alone in his possibly haunted house, Gordy snapped the journal closed and tucked it into the bottom of his satchel.

"Did you find it?" Iris was sitting on the couch when Gordy returned, her crutch leaning against the armrest. Both Adilene and Sasha were awake as well and seated on the carpet, laying out Sasha's potions in a row.

"Find what?" Max asked, yawning.

"Nothing," Gordy answered. He tossed the pillowcase of candy at Max. The bag struck his friend across the face before landing in his lap.

"Ouch!" Max rubbed his cheek. "Why did you do that?" Then he noticed the Tootsie Rolls spilling from the opening, and his mouth dropped open with excitement. "Dude, it's the mother lode!"

"We should probably go," Gordy announced.

"I have three Fire Rockets, two Torpor Tonics, a Vintreet Trap," Sasha said, listing off her inventory, "a Dunka Draught, some Heliudrops, a Spinnerak Net, and a handful of Blitzen Beads. I'd say this, along with whatever you have left in your satchel, should be enough to fend off a small army."

"'Blitzen Beads'?" Max asked through a mouthful of stale gummy bears. "Sounds like reindeer droppings."

"Far from it," Sasha said. "When you throw them, they explode with blinding light. If you don't shield your eyes, you won't be able to see for at least three minutes."

"Sweet!" Max said enthusiastically. "Make sure that goes in my grab bag."

"Will Estelle drive us there?" Adilene asked, standing up.

"That's the plan," Gordy said. "But we can't all go."

Sasha's head snapped up from counting potions. "Going alone is a dumb idea, even for you, Stitser."

"I know," Gordy said. "That's why we should split up."

"This is how it starts," Max muttered while chomping on his candy. "The beginning of the end for everyone."

Gordy held up his hands. "Just hear me out. We can't leave Mrs. Glass by herself, and she's in no shape to ride on Estelle."

"I'm afraid he's right. I'll only slow you down." Iris reached over and, with one snapping motion, yanked the pillowcase from Max's grip. He dove for the candy, but despite her injury, Mrs. Glass had impressive speed. "You're going to make yourself sick, young man. Show some restraint."

Max licked his fingers. "It's not like it's the good candy anyways. What are the teams?" he asked. "Or is it obvious? Gordy and me—and Tweedledum and Tweedledee."

"Actually, I think it needs to be Sasha and me," Gordy said.

Adilene's head cocked to one side, eyebrows knitting into a stern expression.

"My thought exactly." Sasha gathered up her potions and snapped them into the compartments of her satchel. Then she moved over to stand by Gordy.

"Why does it have to be you two?" Adilene asked, looking noticeably unhappy.

"We need to lure the insects to our location and infect them with the wardbreaker solution," Gordy explained. "There are a few steps remaining to the potion, and if something goes wrong, we need to be able to brew a backup." He looked apologetically at Adilene, hoping she would understand. There was no easy way to say this, and he worried it would hurt her feelings. "It has to be done by Elixirists."

"And we're not." Adilene folded her arms and nodded. "I get it. So Max and I will stay here and keep Mrs. Glass company."

"I'm eager to get to know you better," Iris said. "We'll hunker down and be ready for when our two heroes come back to rescue us."

This seemed to agitate Adilene even more. "That's great! What do you think, Maxwell? Are you okay with being a damsel in distress?"

Max, too busy smacking his lips and staring longingly at the candy sack, didn't seem to be paying any attention.

CHAPTER
32

Sasha squeezed her arms around Gordy's waist as Estelle darted down the road. This section of the city looked completely deserted, and the scooter whizzed along the empty streets, undeterred. Estelle started purring again about a mile away from their destination.

Gordy couldn't tell if Estelle was happy or agitated. The purring happened sporadically, making it difficult to figure out her mood. Twelve sharp bursts, then she fell silent once more.

"Hey, I think you made the right choice," Sasha said. "Picking me to come with you, I mean. I know it was hard to break it to Adilene, but she just doesn't know when to quit. She doesn't understand what it's like to be different, you know? Special."

Estelle began to slow, sputtering as she neared the force field. Gordy clung to the handlebars, digging his knees into the side of the scooter as they came to a complete stop in the identical spot as the previous evening.

"We're not special," Gordy said once Estelle's engine died down to a low rumble. Up ahead, the haze of Mezzarix's Distractor ward shimmered in the air, distorting the images beyond. "No more special than Adilene or Max." He glanced back at Sasha. "And every time you say something like that, you just sound mean."

Sasha batted her long eyelashes, feigning innocence. "Oh, please," she scoffed. "I'm just trying to be realistic. You're not doing them any favors by stringing them along. Sooner or later you're going to have to cut them loose."

Gordy climbed off Estelle. "They're my best friends, and they've helped me more than any Elixirist. Definitely more than you."

Sasha curled her lower lip and pouted. "You don't like it when I tease your girlfriend?"

"She's not my girlfriend!" Gordy raised his voice. "Why do you keeping saying that?"

"Come on," Sasha groaned. "Maybe you don't think it, but she sure does. I mean, you *are* a highly-skilled Dram. You can do things she can only dream of."

"Let's just get this over with and get back to the house."

With Estelle rooted to the asphalt, facing the glowing lights beyond the barrier, Gordy poured an ampoule of ogon oil into a pile of brush gathered in the gravel. The oil instantly gave off heat, and Gordy held the vial of Bug Magnet—it was the best name he and Max could come up with on such short notice—over the rising fumes with a pair of metal tongs. Within a few seconds, the mixture began to sizzle. When steam started to build beneath the cork, Gordy tossed the bottle a short distance away between two crooked trees just off the highway. A tiny plume of smoke drifted up from where the potion landed and dissipated in the cool night air.

"How long do we have to wait before we know it—" Sasha started, but Gordy held up a finger to silence her.

He could already hear scurrying noises coming from the woods. Like millions of chattering teeth, the sound grew louder, and the taller weeds began to dip and sway. A black mass, chittering with the calls of crickets and beetles and who knew what other sorts of insects, convened upon the syrupy goop puddled on the ground.

Sasha yelped as a colony of ants—black ones and red ones and enormous silver ones—marched past her feet. Gordy could see the glinting of wings on the backs of flies and locusts and could smell the sour scent of earthworms burrowing up from beneath the ground, which seemed to shift beneath their scuttling feet as a tremendous screeching filled Gordy's ears.

"What kind of insects are those?" Sasha shrieked, pointing at the large black things circling above them.

Gordy had never seen bugs that big before and doubted they were indigenous to Ohio. And then, as the winged creatures began dive-bombing the insects gathered around the potion, he realized they weren't bugs at all.

"Crows!" Gordy exclaimed as an enormous bird whizzed past his shoulder and scooped up a mouthful of bugs. Several more followed, enjoying an easy meal. There were at least a dozen crows flying close, their dislodged feathers landing on his sleeves. Gordy grabbed his satchel and swung it at the crows like a mace.

Shielding her hair from both the kamikaze birds and the bugs showering down from their beaks, Sasha dove to her knees and opened her satchel. She scanned through a few potions as Gordy continued to swing wildly at the crows, missing by a wide margin each time.

"Cover your eyes!" Sasha commanded.

"Do what?" Gordy asked. But before he could obey, Sasha smashed something on the ground, and he was blinded by the brightest light he had ever seen.

Gordy stumbled backward, his eyes watering. "I can't see anything!"

Wind blew against the back of his neck as the cawing crows flapped their wings. Gordy buried his face in the crook of his elbow. The shrieking grew distant as they flew away from Sasha's Blitzen Bead.

"I told you to cover your eyes!" Sasha shouted over the still-chittering mass of insects.

"Well, maybe next time you'll give me two seconds to think about it first." Gordy didn't have anything in his satchel that could restore his eyesight, which meant he'd be blind for the next three minutes. All he could see was a painfully bright, white backdrop. "You're going to have to do the next step by yourself," he instructed.

"Already on it," Sasha said. "I'm going to assume the

bugs are done gathering. In any case, this looks like more than enough for the job."

Gordy heard her move off the road, gagging and groaning as insects crunched beneath her feet.

"I'm going to pour the wardbreaker potion next to the Bug Magnet," she called out. "Just hang tight. There's a lot in this bottle."

Gordy wasn't going anywhere. The Blitzen Bead had disoriented him, and he didn't want to accidentally trip and fall into a pile of fire ants.

The sound of clicking insects suddenly grew quiet as Sasha emptied the potion. Gordy heard liquid splashing from the bottle, and then the unmistakable sound of slurping. The crickets and the ants and the beetles and the worms were lapping up the potion as though it were maple syrup glistening on a pile of pancakes.

"It's working!" Sasha shouted. "They're taking turns and waiting in line. It's seriously weird."

"Do you know what to do next?" Gordy asked. He had never concocted a wardbreaker before. Come to think of it, he had never made a Blitzen Bead either. He would have to swap recipes with Sasha after they got back.

"Yeah, Iris wrote it down for me in my notebook. I just have to—" She grunted and fell silent.

"Just have to what?" Gordy asked.

Sasha didn't respond.

"What are the bugs doing?"

Gordy felt a wave of heat in front of him as though

he had approached a blazing oven, and he could smell an awful stench, like burning hair. The strobing white wall began to dissipate from behind his eyelids. As he blinked, splotches of gray began to take shape, and he could make out the trees up ahead. Stumbling forward, he brushed past something metal and bulky and growling.

"What is it?" Gordy asked, putting his hand on Estelle. "What's wrong?"

As his vision returned, Gordy discovered the reason for the scooter's irritation. The bugs they had lured from the forest had all been set on fire. Orange flames danced across the millions upon millions of crackling insect carcasses.

"What happened?" Gordy demanded, turning toward Sasha.

And then he realized why she had gone silent.

Zelda Morphata stood next to Sasha, a hand covering her mouth.

Sasha looked like she was hardly breathing.

Zelda was at least a foot and a half shorter than Sasha, but Gordy knew why his friend wasn't moving. The traitor held a Decocting Wand to Sasha's throat.

"Sorry about your bugs. I do hope they weren't pets." Zelda peered over her shoulder at the bonfire of beetles. All Gordy and Sasha's work had literally gone up in smoke. There was no way they could lure more bugs now.

"Lucky for me, I was taking a stroll when I saw the light. Though I wasn't expecting to come across the likes of Gordy Stitser and Sasha Brexil. Very convenient, I must say. Ah, don't move, please." Zelda raised the wand closer to Sasha's forehead, and she stiffened.

Gordy had accidently taken a step toward her. His eyesight had returned, and it threw off his balance.

"Please don't ExSponge me," Sasha pleaded.

"So you know what this is, then?" Zelda swished the wand through the air with a flourish. "You must have had

an excellent trainer. Do you know what happens to someone when they're ExSponged?"

Sasha began to whimper.

"Of course you do, dear Sasha. Your poor mother."
Zelda tipped her head. "Let me guess—it's as though she's
numb to the world now." She gazed upon the wand, relishing its power. "The ExSpongement removes the portion of
your brain that controls your potion-making ability."

Gordy didn't know what to do. He couldn't reach for
his satchel or make a run for it. Any sudden movement and
Sasha could end up ExSponged. "Let us go, and we'll disappear," he said. "You've burned up all our bugs. You don't
have to do this."

"Oh, I know. In fact, I suspect should any harm come
to you specifically, your grandfather might lose his mind.
But Mezzarix put me in charge here. And he knew the
risks of such a choice. I warned him of what could happen.
To you and your family. To your friends." Zelda's green
hair jiggled as she nodded toward Sasha.

"Please!" Sasha begged.

Zelda's eyes snapped open wider. "I hated your mother.
Talia Brexil was a tyrant. Unsympathetic to anyone with
an opinion different from hers. And you are just like her,
Sasha. You think position gives you the right to make de-
cisions. But you're wrong." Zelda raised the wand toward
Sasha. "Power gives you the right. And this is true power."

"I know where the final Chamber member is hiding!"

Gordy blurted. "And you need all of them to make Mezzarix's plan work."

It took a second for Zelda to respond. Then she snickered, lowering her hand from her target. "Come now, Gordy, that's nonsense. You're clever, but unfortunately, lying doesn't fit you very well. You wear it like a poorly measured suit jacket."

"Iris Glass is hiding in my house," Gordy said. "I can take you there."

"Take me there?" Zelda scoffed. "I've had tea in your home on a number of occasions. I know the way."

"But you can't get in without me," Gordy reasoned. "You're not part of B.R.E.W. anymore. The wards will turn you away. Guaranteed."

"If you can wrangle a million bugs, what do you think I can do?" Zelda chuckled, her voice squeaking hideously. "So desperate. It's quite amusing. I think I will allow you to go free, unscathed. I'd like to keep my status with Mezzarix as long as he is in power, and ExSponging his precious grandson might end up being a poor decision." She winked at Gordy and then raised the Decocting Wand, touching it to Sasha's forehead. "But I cannot offer her the same deal."

"No!" Gordy shouted.

Sasha fell to her knees, sobbing uncontrollably, but Zelda kept the wand pressed against her.

Dropping to the ground, Gordy yanked opened his satchel. He felt nauseous and dizzy, which may have been from the lingering effects of the Blitzen Bead, but that wasn't all. His next move would determine Sasha's fate. He only had a handful of potions, and though effective if thrown, he knew they wouldn't work in time.

"Sasha Brexil," Zelda announced, her voice increasing with determination. "By the power granted me through the Vessel, I hereby declare you—"

Gordy thrust his hand through the loop of his bracelet, the one remaining vial of Ghost Glass nocked in the chamber, and not taking any time to aim, fired from his hip like a gunfighter. The bulb smashed beneath his thumb, and he closed his eyes, afraid to watch as the potion shot out from his bracelet like lightning.

Sasha screamed once, then fell silent.

Gordy peeled one eye open and gasped. Both Sasha and Zelda had disappeared. Running to the spot where they had been only moments before, Gordy began frantically searching for Sasha. He gaped at the empty bracelet, trying to recall what had been loaded in the chamber. He thought it had been either a Torpor Tonic or another Vintreet Trap, but neither of those potions made someone vanish. Then Gordy heard muffled cries coming from the woods a short distance away.

Sasha's arms and legs protruded from the trunk of a large tree. She squirmed desperately, pawing at the bark over where her mouth would be. Racing over, Gordy started breaking off pieces of wood, which crumbled away under his touch. And then Sasha was spitting out wood pulp, coughing and retching and . . . laughing.

"What was that?" she asked between wheezy gasps.

"My mom's Sumi Sauce." Gordy had followed the recipe from her manual one evening back at Tobias's. This was the first time he had ever seen it in action, and it did not disappoint.

"That was the weirdest feeling," Sasha said. "I couldn't catch my breath at all."

Gordy pulled away more chunks of the tree. "I didn't have time to pick a better potion."

Finally stepping out of the hole, Sasha brushed splinters out of her hair. "Don't apologize. That was perfect!"

"And you're okay? You're not ExSponged?" Gordy asked warily.

"I'm fine, thanks to you," she said. "Now, where's that traitor?"

They found Zelda three trees over, struggling to free herself from a knotted tangle of branches, but she was too embedded in the trunk to move. Unlike Sasha, Zelda's face had been left unconvered. However, every other part of her was trapped in the wood. At the base of the tree, resting upon an exposed root, was Zelda's Decocting Wand.

Gordy leveled his gaze on Zelda, his anger boiling under his skin. This woman deserved whatever was coming to her. She was an evil Elixirist now. A Scourge who had been less than a second away from ExSponging Sasha.

"Now, Gordy, I understand you're upset." Zelda swallowed. "You have a right to be, but hear me out first."

Before Gordy could reply, Sasha spritzed Zelda in the face with a spray bottle. The woman's lips sealed together, and no matter how hard she tried, nothing but garbled moans escaped her throat.

Gordy picked up the Decocting Wand. "Do you think it works the same when I use it?" he asked, studying the etchings. "That I just have to say the words and I could ExSponge her like she was about to do to you?" So simple and yet so permanent. What if Zelda had been mere heartbeats away from ExSponging Tobias? Or Aunt Priss? Or even Gordy's own mother?

"Might as well test it out," Sasha said. "What did she say again? Oh yes, 'By the power granted me through the Vessel, I hereby declare you'—I'm assuming it's 'ExSponged.'" Her eyes twinkled. "And then it's done."

Zelda's cheeks puffed out in desperation, but with no way to escape her lips, the air whistled out through her nostrils.

"Think of it as an act of mercy," Sasha urged. "After what she did to all those bugs." She hissed with agitation. "We'll never be able to gather enough wardbreakers in time!"

But Gordy no longer felt the desire to pass judgment upon Zelda. He didn't want to see someone else ExSponged and certainly not by his own hand. Instead,

Gordy opened his satchel and gently placed Zelda's weapon inside, next to his own Decocting Wand.

Sasha scoffed. "I'll do it if you're too scared. Why should she be allowed to brew when my mom can't?"

"She shouldn't be allowed to," Gordy agreed. "But B.R.E.W. should make that decision."

"There is no B.R.E.W.," Sasha snapped. "They're all gone."

"For now, but hopefully once we stop my grandfather, they can be restored."

Sasha hesitated, then nodded at Zelda. "We can't just leave her here. Someone will eventually show up and pull her out of the tree."

"I know," Gordy said. "We're going to have to take her with us."

"As a hostage? How do you suggest we do that?"

"Do you still have your Spinnerak Net and Heliudrops?" Gordy asked.

Sasha scrunched her nose in confusion. "Yeah. Why?"

Glancing at Estelle still lightly puttering on the side of the road, Gordy shrugged innocently. "I think I may have an idea."

Adilene felt sick knowing Gordy and Sasha were headed into danger and there was nothing she could do to help. Just like Iris, she and Max would only be in the way. But unlike the Chamber member, Adilene couldn't brew a potion, no matter how hard she tried.

Max had fallen asleep on the couch, covered in a pile of blankets, the corners of his mouth stained brown from all the chocolate he had eaten out of Jessica's pillowcase. Lying at the edge of the couch was Iris's satchel, a few corked bottles poking out of the unzipped pocket.

"Here you go, dear," Iris announced from the kitchen. "Dinner's ready." She had heated up macaroni and cheese over a pot of ogon oil and sat at the table, blowing across a spoon. "Has a bit of a gamey flavor. I hope you don't mind."

Adilene joined her and eyed her noodles with little interest. A chartreuse-colored orb Mrs. Glass had called a Jarqil Candle rested at the center of the table. The orange cheese in her bowl clumped together in unappealing glops, and Adilene's hunger vanished, her thoughts too preoccupied with worry.

"What if they get caught?" Adilene asked.

"Don't think that," Iris said. "Optimism is a much stronger attitude."

Adilene's head bobbled. "I wish I could have gone with them."

"And leave me behind, all by my lonesome? What would happen if I was discovered and no one was here to protect me?"

"We would've left Max," Adilene reasoned.

As if in response, Max mumbled in his sleep and kicked off one of his blankets.

Iris held a finger to her lips. "Do you hear that?" she whispered.

Adilene jutted her chin forward. "What am I listening for?"

"I called it a ghost, but it's a probably a snake or a rodent. A big one at that. When you least expect it, a floorboard will creak. Typically, when the conversation settles a bit." Iris took a bite and grimaced, swallowing with some effort. "I know your heart was set on accompanying your friends, but how could you have helped them? If I'm not mistaken, you can't brew, and you certainly ask a lot of questions, which could be a distraction."

Adilene looked away, her cheeks reddening with embarrassment.

"Don't look so sad." Iris touched Adilene's elbow.

"With my injury, I'm no different than you are. We're in the same boat, you and me. That's not so bad, now, is it?"

The same boat? That meant that on her best day, Adilene was no better than an injured Elixirist. Whether she was trying to be insulting or not, Iris was coming across as flat-out rude.

"I can help," Adilene muttered. "I was at B.R.E.W. when it was attacked."

"Yes, I know," Iris admitted. "You were captured by Scourges, were you not?"

Adilene bit down on her lip. "I also helped him catch Ms. Bimini!"

Iris waved her spoon like a baton. "You did—after you were snookered into believing she was a thirteen-year-old girl named Cadence and then led her straight to the Stitser's lab. You practically gift-wrapped Gordy's deepest secrets and gave them to her on a silver platter."

It took all Adilene's strength not to slam her hands down on the table. No matter how angry Iris made her, Adilene couldn't deny the truth in her words. Maybe she was more trouble than she was worth. Maybe if Adilene hadn't been around, none of these problems would have happened to Gordy.

"We just need to play to our strengths," Iris said. "That's all I'm saying. People like you just need to not get in the way. That's the best you can hope for and the best help you can provide." Iris pushed away her bowl of ogon-oil-infused mac and cheese. "Why did you become friends with Gordy?"

"What?" Adilene asked.

"Did you get paired up on a school project? Sit next to each other in a classroom?"

"Gordy used to live across the street from me," Adilene said.

Iris's eyes twinkled with understanding. "That makes sense."

"Why does that make sense?" Adilene rested her elbows on the table and leaned toward Iris. She wasn't sure where the woman was headed with this conversation, but felt certain she wouldn't end up liking it.

"Most Drams befriend other Drams when they're younger. Their parents see to it they have appropriate companions to play with. Makes it easier to practice potion making. At least, that's how a normal Elixirist family functions."

Adilene pursed her lips, squeezing her fingers into fists. "I guess the Stitsers aren't normal Elixirists, then."

"Oh, I know." Iris sighed. "Believe me, my dear, I know."

A large black beetle with two sets of translucent wings suddenly dropped from the ceiling into Iris's bowl. Orange cheese spilled onto the table, and both Iris and Adilene moved back in surprise, out of the way of the splattering liquid.

Iris looked up at the ceiling. Adilene followed her gaze, but nothing else scuttled out.

The bug made a clicking sound, wings beating wildly, then it fell silent.

Adilene peered over the lip of the bowl. The insect lay on its back, floating in the sauce, tiny antennae twitching.

It was dead.

But something was off about the creature. Emerald-green liquid seeped from the bug's shell, mixing with the macaroni.

Adilene's eyes widened. "That's a potion!"

"What do you mean?" Iris climbed awkwardly to her feet, grappling for the crutch, as the distant scurrying of insects sounded from upstairs. Another beetle flew drunkenly into the room, only to drop dead on the floor with a splat.

Iris pointed toward the living room. "Fetch me my satchel!"

There was a clop of heels on the tile, and someone cleared a throat.

"I knew I saw you," Esmeralda Faustus exclaimed, stepping into the kitchen and wielding a Decocting Wand as though it were a battle-ax. "I heard that machine leaving the Pinkermans' yard the other night and saw that clever trap you sprung on Steffan. It wasn't difficult picking up your trail and following you here."

Esmeralda's hair had grown long and discolored. Her sunburned skin was peeling, the corners of her mouth pinched and cracked, but she looked as confident and de-termined as when she had sat across from Gordy in the Vessel room almost a year ago, on the verge of ending B.R.E.W. with the Eternity Elixir.

Iris wobbled, her eyes flickering between Esmeralda and Adilene. "Mrs. Faustus, you have broken so many laws already. Don't make another mistake. The punishment would be—"

"Punishment?" Esmeralda laughed. "I've already been Banished and ExSponged. My life taken from me. My parents taken from me. What could B.R.E.W. possibly do to me now?"

Adilene tried to challenge Esmeralda as she strode into the room, but the woman simply cast her aside with a harsh shove.

"When I finish with you, there will be no more B.R.E.W., and I will be rewarded. My powers restored. My family released from their Forbidden Zones."

"Max!" Adilene shouted. "Wake up!"

A bottle containing white liquid shot through the air, shattering against an empty chair in the kitchen. The metal legs buckled as though made of rubber. Max had launched the potion from a seated position on the couch.

"Careful, Maxwell," Esmerald warned. "If you strike me with Jackjoint Juice, I will squash you like a beetle."

Adilene heard Max struggling and saw Yeltzin diving over the couch, grappling for the satchel. The burley

Russian was too large for Max to fight, and within seconds, Yeltzin had Max in a headlock.

"Now, where was I?" Esmeralda continued. "Oh, yes. Iris Glass, by the power granted me by the Vessel, I hereby proclaim you ExSponged." Esmeralda swung the Decocting Wand toward Iris in a wide arc.

The older woman, hobbled by her injured leg, could do nothing to stop it.

The weapon whooshed through the air, and Adilene stepped in front of it, the end of the wand slamming against her shoulder. She felt a wave of heat coursing through her chest and heard screams—one from Iris, and one that felt like it had bubbled up from her own lungs—as she collapsed back into the fallen Chamber member.

Adilene felt her heart beating in her throat and Iris sobbing beneath her as they fell to the floor together. And then, through her blurry vision, she saw someone else charging into the room. Assuming the wards had been broken and the rest of the Scourges had arrived to finish them off, Adilene cried out in horror.

Then, to Adilene's surprise, the mystery figure took flight, vaulted the kitchen table, and plowed into Esmeralda Faustus like a torpedo.

CHAPTER

35

A few miles away, Wanda ascended a rusted wrought-iron ladder and scrambled out of the hole. Pulse quickening at the sight of more than two dozen figures encircling her, Wanda reached for a weapon, but a hand closed around her wrist.

"It's all right," Priss whispered, helping her sister to her feet. "They're mannequins." She pointed to one of the rigid figures nearby.

Most of the dummies stood with their plastic hands upon their thighs, while a few knelt or waved. Others were contorted into bizarre positions, and many had additional limbs or heads sprouting from their lifeless bodies. Wanda shivered at the display.

They had traveled for several hours underground, weaving their way through damp corridors. Electric lamps had been rigged every twenty feet along the tunnel walls, interconnected by wires, casting flickering light overhead. However, once they arrived at the area controlled by Mezzarix's massive potion, the lights ceased to work. Fortunately, the concoction had only disrupted the electricity; the Distractor wards had no impact on Wanda and the others, and their journey beneath the ground was uneventful.

"There may be people outside," Priss instructed, her voice low. "We have to be careful."

Yosuke had warned that the entryway into the Swigs might be guarded. Most of the Scourges released by Mezzarix had been Banished years before the entrance had been relocated in the city, but there could be a few still aware of its existence. That was why Paulina and her Stained Squad, along with several of Yosuke's followers, had headed toward a secondary entrance into the Swigs.

"What is this place?" Wanda asked.

"This is Spider's home." Yosuke's head poked up from the hole as though disembodied.

"Spider—from the school bus?" Wanda asked.

"The very one." Yosuke pressed his palms against the floor and hoisted his body the rest of the way up the ladder. "And he wanted me to instruct you not to touch any of his belongings. They are precious to him, and he will know if something has been tampered with."

Several of Yosuke's followers clambered out next, and Tobias brought up the rear, wriggling through the opening and immediately recoiling at the sight of the misshapen mannequins.

"What sort of twisted department store is this?" Tobias

barked. Priss flashed him a warning glare, and he softened his tone. "Remind me never to talk crossly with Spider again. He's one crooked cookie!"

"Now, now, no need to judge," Yosuke said. "Spider assured me this room is used for training. The mannequins are his targets."

"And the ones with the extra heads?" The creases in Tobias's forehead deepened.

Yosuke hesitated. "Best not to dwell on it, but if you happen to see a small creature walking around on two legs," he said. "That is simply Nipsy strolling about."

Wanda remembered hearing Spider mention his pet to Gordy. She scanned the floor, hoping she wouldn't spot the humanoid cat.

"Where exactly are we in relation to B.R.E.W. head-quarters?" Wanda asked.

Yosuke squinted in the darkness. "It's within two miles of our location."

Wanda faced the direction Yosuke was pointing and gasped. "Spider has a house within two miles of B.R.E.W.?"

"Yes, and you have a house within six," Yosuke said, smiling. "As far as I know, Spider is not a wanted criminal. You, on the other hand . . ."

"But this home has an opening into the Swigs?" Wanda was dumbfounded. How could she have not known about its existence?

"Try to keep some perspective, Wanda," Priss said. "Now's not the time for bickering."

"Indeed," Yosuke agreed, holding a finger to his lips. "Now is the time for stealth."

Wanda held her tongue as they moved out of Spider's training room and into a hallway reeking of kitty litter. As they entered the living room, lights flashed from outside, and shadows danced beyond the glass of an exterior window. Carefully peeking behind the curtain, Wanda's eyes narrowed. Jarqil Candles adhered to lampposts illuminated a procession of people ambling through the street. She saw mostly strangers, but there were a few familiar faces amid the crowd, Elixirists from B.R.E.W. falling in line with the others.

"It would appear they have all been Blotched," Yosuke whispered, joining her at the window, "and are being transported to some central location."

"Why?" Wanda asked.

"They haven't found her yet," Tobias said. "Iris Glass. That's who they're looking for, right? My guess is they're emptying the homes in order to better search for her." Tobias withdrew some ingredients from his satchel. "They're getting desperate."

"Or they're closing in," Priss suggested.

Wanda scanned the roads, taking in the faces of the Blotched prisoners, searching for Gordy. If she saw him, she would need to control her emotions. That was the only way she would be in the right mind to save him.

"If he has been taken," Yosuke said, prying the curtain from Wanda's fingers, "we'll get him back. I promise."

"Unless he's already been ExSponged," Wanda replied, her voice cracking. She didn't want to think about it, but the possibility existed. If something horrible had happened to Gordy . . .

"Dad wouldn't do that," Priss said. "He would never hurt Gordy."

"Do you think he can control these Scourges?" Wanda looked away from the window. "There's a reason we Banished them all. They did horrible things."

"Yes, and they deserved their punishment," Yosuke agreed. "But they have not found Gordy yet."

"How can you be certain?" Wanda demanded, gazing into her old trainer's eyes.

Yosuke sighed. "He is a skilled boy, Wanda. I spoke with him, and I could tell he is sharp enough to avoid capture. Do you not feel that too?"

"I do," Wanda finally conceded.

"Me too," Priss added.

Tobias grunted from the floor. "A lot of good we'll do if we don't take down that ward and bring the fight to these nasties. Help me get a fire going, Priss. It's time to forecast some weather."

Wisps of smoke drifted away from Tobias's cauldron as he began concocting. Tobias had worn a permanent scowl since the Scourges had burned his property to ash. He was out for vengeance, and Wanda was glad he was on her side.

The Jarqil Candles outside the house flickered and

then went out all at once, blanketing the room in darkness. Yosuke reached for the blinds, but Priss stopped him.

"Back away from the window," Priss whispered, shoulders tense.

Clumsy footsteps rushed up to the opposite side of the front door, followed by the sound of heavy breathing.

"Keep me covered as best as you can," Tobias whispered. He removed the cork from a bottle with his teeth and dumped an amber-colored syrup into his cauldron, releasing the potent fragrances of rainwater and ozone. Everyone in the room held a weapon, their sights aimed at the target.

The knob twisted, and the door opened.

The poor man didn't stand a chance.

Wanda's Spinnerak Net struck him first, splattering against his collarbone. The man yelped and then released a whooshing gasp as the webs whirled him round and round like a top spinning out of control. When he finally collapsed in a heap, liquid from half a dozen concoctions from thrown bottles stained the doorway. Vines wriggled and snapped, and blue Torpor Tonic pooled on the floor by the welcome mat.

Wanda's eyes narrowed. The intruder certainly hadn't acted like a stealthy Scourge creeping into Spider's house. He'd been nervous and uncertain, and he wasn't clutching a single potion for combat. Sensing a trap, Wanda nudged the unconscious man with her shoe, and her fears were confirmed when she saw the message inked across his forehead.

Welcome home, Spider!

The man wasn't a Scourge; he probably wasn't even an Elixirist. Just some poor Blotched citizen sent to check the house.

"Decoy!" Wanda shouted. "Get back!"

A Polish Fire Rocket screeched, and a blinding orb of orange flames flew over Wanda's shoulder, smashing against the far wall of the living room. Several of Spider's paintings went up in a blaze of scorching heat.

Wanda saw figures cloaked in shadows approaching the house. She barely had time to leap back before another barrage of vials shot through the doorway. Two of Yosuke's men shouted as they were both thrown through the back wall of flames and into the next room.

The remaining Elixirists dove behind the couch, while Yosuke heaved an end table through the front window and sprayed Funnel Formula out the opening. Cyclone winds erupted in the front yard, and several Scourges shouted in surprise.

"This party has certainly attracted a fine group of visitors! Don't think I don't see you, Cedman Oldricker!" Yosuke announced, throwing another handful of potions at the enemy. "The Antipodes will be welcoming you back by the end of this night! Ah, and there's my good friend, Steffan Musk! What sort of goodies have you brought in that wretched eye socket of yours?"

"He's having too much fun," Priss said to Wanda, nodding at Yosuke before flinging a Vintreet Trap out the front door. The bottle struck a wild-haired female Scourge in the back as she ran for cover, gobbling her up in a mass of green vines.

The ground split like overripe fruit, swallowing sections of the tattered carpet into the cracks and shifting the walls.

"Terramoto Tonic!" Wanda warned, leaping over the expanding crevice.

Tobias muttered something under his breath and shattered a test tube next to his workstation. A wall of fluorescent-yellow slime emerged from the broken glass, filling up the cracks beneath his cauldron and expanding to shield him. Several more bottles bounced harmlessly off the rubbery substance. Wanda and Priss leaped to the ground and took cover behind Tobias's homemade barrier.

"This particular draught needs time to percolate, my friends!" Tobias huffed in exasperation, gesturing to his cauldron. "One misstep and she'll turn nuclear!" Judging by the array of ingredients next to the smoldering concoction, it appeared Tobias still had multiple steps remaining to his masterpiece.

"What exactly do you want us to do about it?" Wanda fired back. They were under attack by a dozen heavily armed Scourges. Word would reach the others fast, and soon everyone in the city would know that more than just Spider had returned home for the evening.

Tobias rolled his eyes. "Weren't you once B.R.E.W.'s Lead Investigator? Hmm? And you—" He whirled on Priss. "Aren't you, oh, I don't know, Priscilla Rook? Take care of them and give me time to brew!"

Wanda smirked at Priss. Tobias had a point. She had taken down plenty of hardened criminals in her day, and Priss's reputation in battle was legendary.

"Any ideas?" Wanda asked her sister.

Priss poked her head above Tobias's barricade to check the perimeter. "I have a few," she said, ducking as a Booming Ball struck the outer wall, carving out a beach-ball-sized hole in the ceiling and raining insulation down upon their heads.

Wanda's eyes widened as a two-foot-tall creature suddenly barreled down the stairs, hissing as it hightailed past her and into the kitchen like a miniature, fur-covered man in a footrace. "That must be Nipsy."

"Yeah, Spider's never going to forgive us," Priss said. A smile suddenly cracked her hardened façade, and she winked at Wanda. "Do you remember Uzbekistan?"

Wanda shook her head fondly. "No way I could ever forget that." She dug into one of the compartments of her satchel and found the vials hidden beneath a smattering of packaged ingredients. "It just so happens I brought along a couple tubes of Purista and a hearty dose of Miedo Tonic."

"Just like old times, eh?" Priss asked, grinning.

Wanda cupped a hand over her mouth and shouted, "Hey, Master Nakamura!"

"Yes, my dear?" Yosuke replied. Sweat covered the old man's face, and he was breathing heavily, but he looked to be having the time of his life.

"Care to lay down some covering fire for a couple of old friends?"

"It would be my pleasure!" Yosuke said, offering her a quick bow. "I must warn you, though—a few of our enemies have suddenly vanished."

"It's the Silt," Wanda said. "That's not going to make this easy."

"No, it will not, but we will do our best to keep their attention averted." Yosuke barked orders to the remaining Elixirists, and they joined him at the window.

Eyes locked on Priscilla and grasping bottles in both hands, Wanda readied herself to lunge. Then, as Yosuke and his followers unleashed chaos upon the Scourges, the two sisters raced for the front door and out into battle.

At one point in her life, Zelda had been one of the most revered Elixirists in all of B.R.E.W. Now, thanks to Gordy, she was nothing more than a poorly constructed kite flapping in the wind behind Estelle.

After stunning her with a Torpor Tonic and breaking her out of her tree prison, Gordy had wrapped Zelda with a Spinnerak Net and doused her with Heliudrops. Being exposed to so many potions at once was dangerous, but Gordy figured it was better than being ExSponged.

As Estelle puttered along the main road less than a mile from Gordy's cul-de-sac, she began to purr for the fiftieth time.

"Seriously," Sasha said. "What's wrong with her?"

Before he could answer, the scooter suddenly bucked off both Gordy and Sasha, and they tumbled through the air, landing roughly on the asphalt.

"Is she trying to kill us?" Sasha snapped, rubbing her elbow.

Estelle reared back on her wheel like a wild stallion. Above her, still floating like a blimp from the Heliudrops, Zelda struggled against her bindings.

Gordy approached Estelle cautiously, trying not to startle the spooked machine. "Calm down! What's wrong?"

A latch broke free on the underside of Estelle's seat, and the cushion opened, revealing a secret compartment. Inside was Bolter's specially modified telephone. The one that could make phone calls underwater and into Forbidden Zones. The one now vibrating, the ringtone sounding like a purring cat.

On the twelfth ring, Gordy plucked the phone from the compartment and answered it. "Hello?"

"Oh, for Pete's sake!" Bolter's voice echoed through the receiver as though the speaker mode had been engaged. "It's about time you answered!"

"Bolter? Where are you?" Gordy asked.

"Up," Bolter answered matter-of-factly.

Gordy looked up. "Where?" All he could see were clouds and the faint, quivering haze of the force field.

"About nine thousand feet above the town."

"In a helicopter?"

Bolter hummed to himself. "More or less."

"How are you calling me?" Gordy shook his head. "The ward has shut off all power."

"My boy, that phone will always ring no matter what.

But it's a worthless feature if someone, namely you, refuses to pick up."

"I didn't know there was a phone," Gordy explained. "It just sounded like purring."

Bolter chuckled. "And how has Estelle been treating you? No, no, no! No time for chitchat. Don't distract me, Gordy. I need to know your exact location."

Gordy frowned. How was he the one distracting Bolter? "I'm at the house."

"Who's house?"

"My house."

Garbled static filled the receiver.

"Bolter?" Gordy feared he had lost him.

"You've been hiding out in your own home?" Bolter clarified. "I must say, that's ingenious. No one would think to look for you there. It's too obvious! Now, listen carefully. A nasty war is about to begin. Your mother and the Stained Squad have entered the infected area and are about to engage the Scourges. They should have the ward down in no time. More Elixirists will pour in, the battle will ensue, and it will become very hazardous in and around your neighborhood."

Gordy had a lot of questions about his mother, but he didn't have time to ask any of them because Bolter kept spewing out information. There was the sound of whirring turbines, and Bolter suddenly screamed at the top of his lungs.

Gordy pulled the phone away from his ear. "What was that?"

Bolter cleared his throat. "No reason to be alarmed. Just a 747, I think. They banked wide and to the right. Barely missed me. I'm quite fine, but I suspect I will now be labeled as a UFO. As I was saying, trust no one. There are Scourges everywhere. They are searching for someone of great importance, but they will attack you without hesitation."

"I know," Gordy said. "They're looking for Iris Glass. She's with us at my house."

"She's what? How did you . . ." Bolter grumbled something under his breath. "Never mind. Who's this *us* you speak of?"

"Max, Adilene, and Sasha," Gordy answered.

"Sasha Brexil?" Bolter chirped. "That horrible girl?"

Gordy glanced at Sasha, who scowled, and he shrugged an apology.

"Well, I'm certainly impressed, and I should have room for all of you. I definitely don't want to leave anyone behind. Now, be out on the front lawn in exactly forty-five minutes or as soon as you see your mother's signal."

"Okay," Gordy agreed. "What signal?"

"The power surge, of course," Bolter answered with a laugh.

"Where are you taking us?" Gordy asked.

Static, followed by more awkward humming. "I'm taking you to be with your father and siblings. You can stay with them until the Stained Squad mops up these infernal Scourges." Bolter grunted and then gasped. "I've got to go! Evasive maneuvering!"

The line went dead, and Gordy examined the special phone in amazement. No matter how oddly the Elixirist acted, Bolter made wonderful tools. Latching down the seat, Gordy climbed onto Estelle. "Come on. Bolter's coming to pick us up and take us somewhere safe."

Sasha stood her ground. "What about Mezzarix and the Vessel?"

Gordy knew how she felt. All he really wanted to do was stand by his mother's side in battle. Those Scourges didn't stand a chance now that Gordy's mom was in charge. "Right now, we need to get Mrs. Glass out of the city. That's the most important thing." The two of them had to look past their own desires and do what was right. Gordy patted the seat. "I promise—we'll help your mom once we rescue the Vessel."

Reluctantly, Sasha climbed on the scooter and gripped Gordy's waist as Estelle lurched forward, speeding toward the house.

ead insects littered the driveway, crunching under Estelle's wheels. Gordy could see where bugs had gobbled a path straight through the protective ward. Leaving the engine running, he leaped from the scooter and ran into the house.

The first body Gordy found belonged to Yeltzin. The enormous Russian was sprawled unconscious next to the couch, his rubbery legs stretched out in a full-on split as though his knees and hips had been magically removed. Gordy glanced worriedly at Sasha and then raced into the kitchen.

Sitting on the floor, Adilene had her back pressed against the wall, a wet rag held to her forehead. Iris Glass sat in a chair, sobbing softly, while Max stood in the corner, a potion vial in his hand. His eyes were locked upon the two figures at his feet: Esmeralda Faustus, lying on her back, and Carlisle Bimini, squatting on top of her.

"Max?" Gordy blurted.

"Dude!" Max shouted, looking up. "I just poured Giraffe Guts into Esmeralda's mouth." He held up the bottle. "It's not going to kill her, is it? She looks pretty messed up."

Gordy shook his head in bafflement as he sidestepped Carlisle. Esmeralda lay deathly still, arms and legs stretched out, as rigid as if she had been made of wood. Only her face moved, contorting into a variety of odd expressions one right after another, some of them funny, some frightening.

"Giraffe Guts?" Gordy reached for the empty bottle.

"What are they doing here?" Sasha asked.

"It was crazy!" Max's voice rose in excitement. "There I was, just taking a nap, when all of a sudden I heard a boom and a crash, and I opened my eyes to see this nut"—he pointed at Esmeralda—"cackling and wielding that wand-thing like a lightsaber. She went right after Iris, so I started throwing things. I made a mess. Then that moron"—he nodded at Yeltzin—"tried to slap the Figure Four Death Lock on me, but I still had a couple of tricks up my sleeve. Zapped him with Jackjoint Juice! It's so wicked!"

"Okay, but what about Carlisle?" None of this explained what the old man was doing there.

"I was getting to that!" Max yelled impatiently. "Right when things were about to explode, Carlisle came rushing in from out of nowhere and just laid Esmeralda out like a linebacker. And then I poured Giraffe Guts into her mouth."

Gordy read the label on the bottle, deciphering Iris's scribbled handwriting. "This says Girning Glop."

"Yeah, okay, what does that mean?" Was that actual concern in Max's voice?

Gordy wasn't sure. Maybe it was some fancy weaponized potion used by the B.R.E.W. elite. Whatever the case, Girning Glop had completely incapacitated Esmeralda.

"I've never killed anyone before," Max muttered. "I feel different already."

"And you called me the dramatic one?" Sasha asked.

Gordy stepped next to Carlisle. "You saved my friends?"

The old man kept his gaze fixed on the floor, but he held a familiar bottle in his bony fingers. It was empty except for a couple drops of dark-blue Silt. Carlisle must have been saving those final sips for an emergency, but Gordy never suspected he'd come rushing to their aid.

"Our ghost," Iris sniffled, her head bowed. "He had been hiding all this time. If only he'd have shown up just a moment earlier."

Gordy moved around to the front of Iris's chair. "What happened?"

Her eyes bloodshot, Iris had wadded tissues piled in her lap. "It's all over, child." She sobbed through wet tears. "I've been ExSponged."

Gordy sucked in a sharp breath and desperately looked at Max. "I thought you said Carlisle stopped Esmeralda."

"That was after," Max explained. "I tried to stop her,

but I . . ." He lowered his eyes, embarrassed. "I'm no good at potion chucking."

Adilene groaned. "I tried to stop her, too, but I guess I wasn't fast enough." She held out a hand, and Gordy helped her to her feet.

"What's wrong with you?" Sasha asked her.

"I jumped in front of Iris when Esmeralda attacked. She struck me with the Decocting Wand," Adilene said, stumbling for balance.

Gordy stared at her in shock. "While she was performing the ExSpongement? You could've been seriously hurt!"

Adilene winced, gingerly rotating her right shoulder. "I can already feel it starting to bruise. And my head is spinning. It's getting worse—my eyesight. Everything looks so fuzzy." She leaned into Gordy, resting her head on his shoulder.

This was bad. Adilene was lucky to have survived Esmeralda's attack, but her failing eyesight made him worry.

"I'll make you something," Gordy said. "A potion that could help."

"I just need something for my headache," she said.

Gordy nodded. "I'll start brewing some Boiler's Balm."

"Or you could just get her some aspirin," Max suggested. "There's probably some in your bathroom."

Adilene opened one eye and half smiled at Max. "That sounds like a better plan."

Max nodded and trotted out of the kitchen.

"Wait a minute," Sasha said, staring at Iris. "If Adilene stepped in front of the Decocting Wand, didn't she stop the ExSpongement?"

Iris sniffled. "She didn't stop anything."

"Then how do you know you were ExSponged?" Gordy asked. "With Adilene standing in the way, it—"

"You're a Cipher, Gordy," Iris snapped. "You can decipher ingredients, tastes, sensations." Her voice caught. "Well, I was too. I could see images in my mind of entire recipes when I inhaled. I couldn't even tell you what's in this anymore." She pointed to a bowl filled with orange cheese and soggy noodles. "My gift was taken from me."

Gordy's blood went cold. Helping Iris had been their main objective, and now everything was falling apart.

Carlisle's joints popped as he stood up. Esmeralda didn't even try to scramble away, Max's full dose of Girning Glop keeping her preoccupied.

Max returned and handed Adilene a container of pain-killers and a bottle of water. Adilene thanked him and tossed down two of the pills.

Gordy turned his attention to Carlisle. "You could have gone anywhere you wanted. No one was going to come after you. Why come back to my house?"

His lips were pursed and puckered, his breathing ragged. Carlisle didn't reply. Gordy wasn't entirely sure, but he suspected the younger Bimini had aged a few extra years since his departure from Tobias's farmhouse. He had nowhere to go, no family to speak of, unless . . .

Gordy's eyes narrowed. "You want to go home, don't you?"

Carlisle's chin dipped slightly.

"And you think we can help you," Gordy continued.

Another nod from Carlisle. Actual communication.

Sasha knelt next to Iris, grabbing the woman's knees. "How long will it take for Mezzarix to destroy the Vessel?"

"I . . . I don't know," Iris answered, sobbing. "It's not as simple as pouring out the contents. The procedure takes time and many, many steps. But it doesn't matter anymore! There's nothing standing in his way now."

"But he doesn't know that yet! Unless he's hovering over the Vessel night and day, testing it for Blood Links, he won't find out until one of his followers tells him. And we've taken down the only Scourge who knows what's happened." Sasha looked down at Esmeralda, who hiccupped and then puffed out her cheeks like a bullfrog. "We can still get to him first and stop him before he carries out his plan."

"How are we going to get there?" Gordy asked.

"Bolter!" Sasha's voice boomed. "You said he's flying here to take us to safety, right? We'll just have him take us out to the island instead. Then, once we land, Carlisle can show us how to find your grandfather."

Gordy looked at Carlisle in disbelief. The old man straightened with purpose, his posture indicating he agreed.

Gordy rocked back on his heels. "Bolter will never agree to take us to Florida," he said, remembering Bolter's determination when Mezzarix had attacked B.R.E.W. headquarters not so long ago. The wiry Elixirist had appeared out on the lawn to rescue Gordy and Max. Aunt Priss had still been inside the decimated building, but Bolter had refused to deviate from his instructions. He had been charged with an assignment and had no intention of breaking his commitment.

Sasha scrunched her nose. "Then we Blotch him. We may not even see your mom for days. She won't know about the location of Mezzarix's island."

"Bolter could call her," Gordy reasoned. "Tell her what we found."

"They're about to battle some of the deadliest people on the planet. They're not going to be able to fly down to Florida to attack your grandfather." Sasha's eyes narrowed. "And that's if she believes us. We're just kids, remember? Drams without any experience. Do your parents always listen to you? I know mine don't."

Sasha's suggestion was madness. And yet Gordy couldn't help but feel like she was right. His mom definitely considered him as more than just a child. She believed him, but she also exercised caution, which was what all parents tended to do. If his mom waited to confirm what Gordy had already discovered using the Seeking Serum, it would definitely be too late.

"Are you saying this because you want to help your mom?" Adilene asked.

Without hesitation, Sasha nodded. "Yes, I am. I want

to help my mom recover her potion-making powers. I want her back like she was before, and this is our chance. But I also want to help everyone. Our goal is still the same as it has been. Once Mezzarix finds out the last Chamber Member has been ExSponged, he will destroy the Vessel. This power outage"—she waved a hand around the room—"is just a taste of what will happen everywhere." She pressed her palms against the table, leaning forward, gaze fixed on Gordy. "And if Adilene really is losing her eyesight, there's no better cure than the Vessel."

"But how do you Blotch someone?" Max asked.

Every eye turned to Gordy.

Gordy had only seen his mom brew a Blotching potion once, but he thought he remembered the basic steps. And if he was lacking in ingredients, he had a feeling he could improvise. But trying to pull a fast one on Bolter would not be easy. He was a seasoned Elixirist, one who had seen his share of tricks.

"We're really going to Blotch Bolter?" Gordy questioned, more to himself.

Sasha smacked the table emphatically. "We're going to Blotch Bolter!"

Arhythmic pulsing churned in the distance. Gordy and Sasha had just finished putting the final touches on the potion when the kitchen chandelier flickered to life, illuminating the table. The power had returned and with it an eruption of car alarms out on the streets. Sirens blared, televisions and radios blasted at top volume from living rooms throughout the neighborhood, and above it all, deep and powerful, an unnatural thunder echoed through the sky.

Gordy rushed to the window, yanked open the blinds, and looked up as a single black cloud ballooned into the air a mile or so in the distance. It came from the direction of Kipland Middle and looked as though a giant squid had just inked into the murky gray twilight. Corded lighting crackled through the cloud like an electric eel.

Tobias wasn't messing around. That was no normal Sturmwolke Slosh.

Vibrant, fluorescent-green and purple lights flashed.

Screeching ribbons of light swooshed through the air, trailing silver sparks in their wake and impacting with a concussive din that reverberated through Gordy's chest. He could see objects catapulting through the air. Cars and trucks and severed streetlights shot up only to plummet back to earth once more.

"It's the apocalypse!" Max shouted above a wailing whirlwind that had gathered above the house. "But who's winning and who's losing?"

There was no way to know for sure, but Gordy had a feeling his mom and Aunt Priss were wreaking havoc upon the Scourges. They had messed with the wrong Elixirists.

The wind continued to howl, and the ground quaked beneath their feet. The roof seemed to groan from the pressure, the kitchen chandelier spinning on its chain as several chunks of ceiling collapsed and splattered drywall across the floor.

Adilene grabbed Gordy's hand and squeezed his fingers until his knuckles hurt. Then a beam of light shone through into the living room, catching Gordy's attention. Estelle's headlamp appeared in the window, blinking in desperation.

"I think Bolter's here!" Gordy wobbled uneasily across the trembling floor.

Sasha hurriedly shoveled her supplies into her satchel as Gordy ran from the kitchen, dragging Adilene behind.

Esmeralda, Yeltzin, and Zelda had been cocooned in Tranquility Swaths and left in the center of the living room. They would remain in that state for hours, until someone found them and woke them up. With the protective wards now devoured, there would be nothing stopping a group of Scourges from stumbling upon them. Still, what choice did Gordy have? There was no time to work up another plan.

Iris saw no point in accompanying Gordy on what she labeled a fool's mission. She sat in one of the wingback chairs, covering her ears with her hands. Standing a short distance from her chair was Carlisle, his suitcase of supplies pressed to his chest, the uncorked vial of Silt dangling from his thumb and forefinger.

Gordy pulled open the door.

Squatting on the front lawn, trying to coax a trembling Estelle from her hiding place in the bushes, was Bolter. He wore his aviator goggles and a long duster that flapped in the storm. Towering above the rooftops and producing gale-force winds from giant turbines was a monstrous flying contraption in the shape of an eagle.

"Gordy!" Bolter stood and bowed regally, whipping his hand toward the machine behind him. "Allow me to introduce you to Roseanne."

In response, the bird-shaped airplane squawked. It sounded like a jackhammer striking a gong, and Max dropped to his knees with a grunt.

"Come on, come on!" Bolter desperately waved the group toward him. "By now the entire Scourge army is aware of my unauthorized landing. Don't be afraid. She won't bite. No teeth, you see. Just mind the beak."

Roseanne had a golden beak about the size of a beach umbrella. Her aluminum wings extended from either side of her body, drooping under the weight of two enormous turbines spiraling beneath them. A tail fin made of a sleek, sparkling material rose up at the rear like a sail, and Gordy could see a rotor twenty feet in diameter perched on top, whirring at high speed. Huge chunks of sidewalk had been chewed up by Roseanne's landing gear, which was nothing more than a pair of t deep into the ground.

The cabin held controls similar to a helicopter's along with a captain's chair. There were a few other seats in line behind it but no roof. The entire machine was covered sporadically with feathers.

Max finally found his voice. "I'm not climbing aboard Mothra!" He laughed hysterically, and Gordy feared his friend might have snapped.

"Mothra?" Bolter flinched and flourished his fingerless hand in disapproval. "No, I said her name was Roseanne. And I would caution against calling her anything else." Bolter prodded Gordy toward the metallic beast with a gentle pat. "This flying wonder is perfectly safe. She is fully operational and has been infused with the essence of the triumvirate of aviary excellence: the eagle, the hawk, and the falcon." He giggled, baring his teeth, and then said, sounding like a car salesman, "She tops out at two-hundred-and-twenty-eight miles per hour, faster than the

maximum diving speeds of a peregrine falcon. She can turn on a dime, hover comfortably at fifty feet without generating a vortex, and she comes equipped with moderately working Distractor wards." His gleeful expression became slightly regretful. "Still working on those, I'm afraid. The wards have a tendency to short out from time to time. We've already been spotted by NORAD. But no matter. Once we land at the safe house, Gordy, you can take a look at my concoction and see if you can improve it."

Bolter approached Roseanne's left flank and snagged a dangling rope ladder. Battling against the gusts of wind swooshing out from the turbines, he managed to scramble up to the cockpit.

"There's plenty of room for everyone. I have buckles installed on the floor panels, so don't be shy." Bolter steadied the rope ladder with his foot and motioned for Gordy to climb aboard. "If any of you are thirsty or need a light snack, you're welcome to use the minifridge."

Gordy gripped the middle rung of the ladder, his heart pounding in his chest like a piston. He looked at the others, hoping to encourage them, but was sure he only made them feel worse. It took every ounce of courage for him to take the first step. He had to grab hold of a latch welded to the side to keep from being blasted off the ladder by the turbine.

As Gordy started to climb, he could hear Bolter grunting as though he were the one lifting Gordy a step at a time. And then Gordy was up and sliding across the floor on his belly. He found the first empty seat and immediately fastened his seat belt. Once inside the cockpit, the buffeting of the jet engines and rotor overhead magically lessened. Warm air poured out from vents, heating the temperature to a comfortable degree.

It took the others just as long to make the ascent, but soon their excited voices filled the cabin as they hurriedly took their seats, though Max detoured to the minifridge for a soda. Sasha lingered by the edge for a moment, steadying the rope ladder. Gordy watched her move aside as something invisible brushed past him. Carlisle had boarded, and the countdown had begun. Gordy had no way of knowing how much time they had before Carlisle's Silt would wear off, but he knew he had to act fast.

"Safe travels, Estelle!" Bolter called out to his scooter. "I'll meet you at the safe house! Try not to draw too much attention to yourself."

Opening his satchel made of pieced-together automotive upholstery, Bolter removed a jar of teal-colored liquid. After unscrewing the lid, he poured the potion into a hole next to the steering stick. Gordy felt a shuddering sensation beneath his seat as the two anchors began to retract into the base of the bird.

"I think I'm missing someone," Bolter said, looking over his shoulder, his goggles in place. He wore a headset with a microphone inches away from his lips. "Where's Mrs. Glass?"

"ExSponged," Gordy replied. "Esmeralda Faustus got to her about an hour ago."

Bolter's eyes widened, transforming his pupils to the size of plums through the magnified lenses.

"It's okay," Gordy said. "We know where Mezzarix is hiding. He's on an island past the Florida Keys. If you take us there, we think we can stop him before he destroys the Vessel."

Lips operating without sound as though trying to un-shell a mouthful of stubborn sunflower seeds, Bolter managed to cough in surprise. "Take you there?"

"There's no time to waste," Sasha announced from the back of the cabin. "How far can Roseanne fly without having to stop to refuel?"

Bolter guffawed boisterously. "Young lady, we have enough fuel to fly to the safe house—which is where we're going."

"We can't go there," Adilene said. "Bolter, we're B.R.E.W.'s final hope of stopping Mezzarix. Going to the safe house won't help anyone, and going to Gordy's mom will take too much time. You know we can do this. Gordy can do this!"

Bolter's eyes darted between Gordy and Adilene before landing upon Max at the rear of the cabin as though he might offer a sensible suggestion.

Max raised his can of soda. "Do you have anything other than Shasta?"

Stamping his foot, Bolter hollered out. "I am not

taking you to Mezzarix. Absolutely not! You are just children, and I am supposed to take you to safety." He shook his head at Gordy. "I'm sorry, my friend, but your mother gave me strict orders to guide you away from the danger, not toward it. And that's what I intend to do."

Gordy lowered his eyes. "Okay, maybe you're right." He glanced at Adilene, who nodded and subtly unbuckled her seat belt.

Bolter huffed, then, facing forward, flipped a switch on his control panel and the cabin lights turned off. The squeal of the turbines strengthened in volume as Roseanne rose from the ground.

"I hope you're not mad at us." Gordy leaned forward next to the pilot's chair, straining against his seat belt. "We had to try."

"It's not your battle, Gordy," Bolter said.

"But the Vessel—"

"Will be an unfortunate loss, but again, not of your concern," Bolter insisted.

"How does she fly?" Gordy asked, changing the subject.

Bolter gave Gordy a sideways look, studying him for a moment, and then his hardened gaze softened. "With lift and thrust, of course, and . . ." He pointed to the empty potion jar. "I call it Barnstorm Broth. A cocktail of albatross egg yolk; the milled fossil of the long-extinct wisdom owl, or Sophionithidae; and the crystalized plumes of a cumulus cloud." He grinned, pleased with himself. "Oh, and jet fuel and wild-cherry Pop Rocks."

"Wow!" Gordy was honestly impressed.

"My friend and I have been working on it for years," Bolter answered with a nod. "But we only recently discovered a breakthrough in the fusion compound. That's why I had to leave when I did, despite how angry I knew your mother would be."

"Kind of like us, huh?" Gordy asked, raising his eyebrows.

Puffing out his cheeks, Bolter waffled with a reply. "That's different! You're a child, a very skilled child, but what would your mother say if I—"

Gordy held up his hand, cutting him off. "It's okay."

Roseanne cleared the treetops and banked sharply to the right. Both Adilene and Sasha gasped from their seats. Then the flying contraption shot upward, the Stitsers' home shrinking to the size of a dollhouse in a matter of seconds.

"She takes a bit to get used to, but once we reach our cruising altitude, I assure you you'll enjoy the breathtaking views." Bolter spoke into his mouthpiece, his voice cascading down from a speaker in the shape of a birdhouse above his seat.

"I was hoping you could take a look at this for me," Gordy said once Roseanne's herky-jerky movements smoothed out. He showed Bolter his bracelet. "I emptied all the chambers in battle against the Scourges, and I don't know how to reload them."

"Battle with Scourges?" Bolter looked appalled, but he leaned back, glancing at the bracelet. "Ah, I'd be glad to. Once we land, I'll take a look."

"Could you do it now?" Gordy insisted.

"Now? Well, I'm sort of navigating."

"But what if we need it?" Gordy extended the weapon closer to Bolter, tempting him to take it in his hand. "What if we're attacked?"

"Up here?" Bolter laughed. "I doubt a Scourge would take to the air to bring us down." Then his smile faded, and a knowing look formed in his eyes. Peering down at the bracelet refusing to touch it, he cocked his head. "You wouldn't dare, would you?" He gave Gordy a look of disappointment. "Put that away at once and sit back in your seat!"

"What did I do?" Gordy asked, allowing his seat belt to cinch him back into place. At once, he noticed the extra body seated on the floor between Sasha and Max. Carlisle didn't have a seat belt, but he kept his balance well enough. Bolter had yet to notice the stowaway, but when he did, Gordy feared his surprise would ruin everything.

"Desperation will only get you so far," Bolter barked. "You should be ashamed of yourself. If you don't want me to tell your mother about how you tried to Blotch me, I suggest the four of you keep quiet for the duration of our flight."

Gordy looked at Adilene, and she gave him a thumbs-up.

Roseanne squawked, and the hybrid plane rocketed off in a westerly direction. As she turned, the jars in Bolter's satchel clinked together, drawing his attention. At least half a dozen containers of Barnstorm Broth were in the bag—along with one additional jar of a creamy white substance rising up above the other lids. A jar that had not been in Bolter's satchel prior to takeoff.

Delighted, Bolter unscrewed the lid and scooped a knuckle of mayonnaise into his mouth. "Yum, yum!" He slurped the condiment. "My absolute favorite." If there was one thing they could count on, it was that Bolter was powerless when it came to resisting mayonnaise.

Max made a retching noise, and Gordy promptly shushed him.

"How long until we reach the safe house?" Gordy asked as Bolter dug out more of the Tainted mayonnaise and devoured it eagerly.

"I already told you," Bolter said, shaking his head and leaning on the copter's steering stick, causing Roseanne to abruptly change directions. "This bird's headed for Florida!"

Roseanne's bulky frame dropped suddenly, and everyone, including Bolter, who had been dozing in his captain's chair, his chin digging into his chest, startled awake.

"Why did we drop?" Max grumbled, kicking his feet out and stretching.

"I'm not sure," Bolter muttered. He checked the plane's instruments, twisting knobs and tapping a few gimbals with his knuckle. "Perhaps it's the warmer temperatures. We've just passed over Miami."

Gordy rubbed his eyes and craned his neck to see over the edge. The sun was shining brilliantly, and the warm air still pumping from the vents made Gordy sweat. They had been flying for more than eight hours. Despite Roseanne's massive turbines, she only flew slightly faster than a standard single-engine airplane.

Roseanne lurched again, dropping with a clanging of metal.

"Uh, Bolter," Max called out, twisting in his seat. "Something big just fell out the back of this bird!"

Bolter nibbled on his lower lip, appearing only minorly concerned. "We have been flying almost nonstop for sixteen hours. Roseanne needed to lay some eggs."

Gordy laughed. "She lays eggs?"

"Well, she is one-eighth chicken. And it's not an actual egg. Just metal and plastic and sundry tricycle parts." Bolter glanced at Sasha's map, cross-checking it against his own instruments, and then called for Gordy to join him next to the controls. "Are you sure about these coordinates?"

"Positive," Gordy answered. "Why?"

"Because we're there." He tugged on a lever, and the turbines ground down to a low whine. The rotor whipping atop Roseanne's tail fin churned as the airship hovered in place. Pressing another button in the console produced a periscope that rose up with a pneumatic hiss. Bolter peered through it, adjusting a dial with his palm.

"But there's nothing below us." Bolter pulled back from the scope. "Have a look for yourself."

Gordy could see a few clouds drifting below Roseanne and a landscape of blue ocean filling the lens. Foamy waves lapped through the water, but there was no island of any shape or size whatsoever.

"What do you mean?" Max demanded. "Are we in the right spot?"

Bolter scoffed. "We are directly where we should be

according to these coordinates. If something's wrong, it's the fault of the directions, not the equipment."

"But there's no island," Gordy said. "Can we look somewhere else?"

"Certainly!" Bolter glanced at his control board and typed a couple of commands. "Where would you like to go? There are more than ten thousand islands off the coast of Florida." The computer chirped, and a long list of destinations with coordinates began scrolling across the monitor. "South Bimini island is ten miles from here. Perhaps that's where Mezzarix is hiding."

"Bimini," Adilene muttered. "Like Cadence." She moved next to Gordy, rubbing her elbows and shivering.

Gordy nodded, remembering something vitally important. "Carlisle, can you come here for a second?"

Climbing to his knees, Carlisle shuffled over to the captain's chair.

Bolter didn't react to Carlisle's nearness, and Gordy was glad the Blotching was still working. Gordy gestured to the periscope, and Carlisle looked through the glass for a couple seconds.

"Do you think that's the island?" Gordy asked.

Carlisle gave a subtle nod but didn't seem as confident as Gordy would have hoped.

"The island's invisible," Gordy explained to the others. "Mezzarix used Ms. Bimini's keystone to find it, so we're not going to be able to see it through the periscope."

"So what would you like me to do?" Bolter beamed at Gordy, waiting for his instruction.

"Can you land?" Max asked.

Bolter's nose twitched from side to side. "On an invisible island? Is there an airstrip? Will I be descending upon rocky terrain?"

"We don't know," Sasha replied.

"Then . . . no." Bolter gave a casual sigh. "I don't suppose I could . . . er . . . land." His eyes seemed to lose focus, and he glanced around the cockpit, suddenly suspicious.

Gordy recognized the baffled expression and grabbed the mayonnaise jar from Bolter's satchel. "Did you forget something?" He wafted the jar under Bolter's nose.

Bolter blinked and smiled, accepting the jar with a gracious bow. That was the tricky thing about this sort of rushed Blotching. Without constant interaction with a Tainted object, the Blotched individual could snap out of the trance at any moment.

"How close can you get us?" Gordy asked.

"Reasonably." Bolter licked the rim of the container. "I'll just need to be careful not to strike a mountain peak."

Returning to his seat, Gordy nodded at Sasha's satchel. "How much of your Heliudrops do you have left?" He rocked back and forth in his chair, the bolts attaching it to the floor creaking.

"We used a ton on Zelda," Sasha replied. "Why?"

40

"We're going to do what?" Max bellowed.

Gordy had already unscrewed one of the bolts beneath his chair. "We're going to use Sasha's Heliudrops on these chairs and—" He grunted, twisting Bolter's socket wrench, trying to break the seal of the second bolt. "And . . . float down, I guess." It wasn't the worst plan in the world, but by the look on his face, Max must have thought so.

"Float down?" Max repeated. "Like, how fast?"

"Pretty fast, I would think." Sasha handed Gordy a test tube of something clear and oily. "This will help." She was being cooperative, and so was Adilene, but their faces revealed their concern with dropping out of Roseanne from a distance of five thousand feet. Heliudrops weren't exactly created for this sort of thing.

Gordy uncorked Sasha's test tube and frowned. "What potion is this?"

"WD-40," Sasha replied. "I always keep some for emergencies."

Using the lubricant, Gordy made quick work of the rest of the bolts. He and Bolter strapped the seats together with the safety belts and hurriedly added a few extra nuts and bolts for good measure. When all was said and done, the contraption resembled an uncomfortable-looking couch that buckled in the middle.

Gordy tested it out, hopping up and down on one of the padded cushions, trying to see if it would break free from the others. "Seems to hold."

Max responded by shoving an entire granola bar into his mouth.

"What do you think?" Gordy asked Adilene.

"You don't want to know what I think," she said, her voice shaky.

"This will work," Gordy assured her.

"Yeah, if the Heliudrops don't malfunction," Sasha added, folding her arms.

"Weren't you the one who made them?" Max asked.

Adilene grabbed Gordy's sleeve and pulled him close. "What if there really isn't an island down there?"

Gordy had thought about that and had a prompt response. "Then we'll just land in the water, and he'll come pick us up. Right, Bolter?"

Polishing off the final ounce of Tainted mayonnaise, Bolter nodded. "Simply activate this distress signal, and I'll home in on your location." Bolter handed Gordy a small device hooked to a rabbit's-foot key chain.

Gordy tested the button, and an incandescent light began to flash from a bulb no bigger than a pencil eraser. Within seconds, an alarm rang in the cockpit, flashing in rhythm with the distress signal.

"See?" Bolter nodded at the console. "I should have no problem finding you."

After dribbling several Heliudrops onto their makeshift escape pod, which immediately lifted off the floor like a hot-air balloon, Gordy and the others hefted it over the edge. Carlisle grabbed one of the legs to keep it from flying away. Gordy steadied himself by snagging a handful of Max's shirt—he could hear his best friend's nervous breathing—and he climbed onto one of the seats. The contraption wobbled like a bobber on the end of a fishing line, but as the others took their turns clambering on and shifting their weight, the couch settled and Gordy felt his confidence increasing, if only slightly. Carlisle was the last aboard, crowding next to Sasha, hugging his suitcase as though it were a parachute.

"Don't forget about us!" Gordy shouted to Bolter, waving the distress signal. Outside the protective ward of the cockpit, the rush of gusting wind was deafening.

Bolter squinted as he shoved the couch away from the edge. As distance began to stretch between the escape pod and Roseanne, Bolter cupped a hand next to his mouth and hollered, "I'm going to land at South Bimini Island! I'll tinker with Roseanne until I hear from you."

He disappeared from the edge, and a few heartbeats later the airship began moving away. The current produced by the turbines caused the escape pod to drop, and as gravity took hold on the weighted seats, Sasha added more Heliudrops to keep them from crashing down like a meteor.

"Any minute now, Bolter's going to wake up from being Blotched," Max warned.

"Even if he does, we expected that." Gordy was impressed at how long his first Blotching had lasted without any prior instruction. Aunt Priss would have been so proud.

"Won't he leave us?" Adilene asked.

"Bolter would never leave us," Gordy answered. "He may want to strangle me when this is all over, but he'll do exactly what he promised." It was difficult to know how much Bolter would remember once the Blotching wore off, but Gordy was counting on there being enough to keep the determined Elixirist on task.

As they continued to drop farther, the wide blue beneath Gordy began to look larger, more expansive. He could make out the cresting waves and could hear the familiar ocean sounds. Each time the contraption started to pick up speed, Sasha dabbed an extra Heliudrop to slow them.

"How much is left?" Gordy asked.

Sasha cautiously leaned forward and looked down. "More than enough to get us to the bottom. But that's not the problem, is it?"

"Yeah, where is this dumb island?" Max glared at Carlisle as though it was his fault.

Gordy may have suggested landing in the ocean as a backup plan, but once Sasha's potion had run out, they would instantly sink. How long would they be able to tread water until Bolter rescued them?

"Do you think there are sharks?" Adilene squeaked.

"And whales and jellyfish and sea monsters!" Max's voice grew anxious.

"Please, be quiet, Maxwell!" Adilene buried her face in Gordy's shoulder.

And then, all at once, the ocean vanished. The blue sky, the endless expanse of water, everything was swallowed up in a haze as they passed through a mist that had not been there moments before. Sasha almost forgot to re-apply her Heliudrops as they picked up speed, heading toward the tops of palm trees less than a hundred feet below. The craggy peak of a massive mountain rose up on the eastern side of them, so close Gordy felt he could reach out and snatch a rock from the footpath.

Wind began to swirl beneath them, prickly with sand. It tore at Gordy's pant legs, stinging and sharp. The flying contraption suddenly bucked sideways, and Gordy screamed in surprise. Everyone scrambled, grabbing hold of each other, trying not to be thrown from their seats.

"Is this couch bewitched?" Max shouted.

Maybe it was just the hot wind of the island, but Gordy suspected something else was at work. The air carried with it the lacy smell of frankincense and steamed perentie fangs. A black cloud gathered just below them, snuffing out the view of the forest. It lapped at Gordy's shoes, and he immediately pulled his feet back onto his cushion.

"Don't touch it!" Gordy yelled to the others. Something was off about the cloud, something sinister.

"What happens if we touch—" Max started to reply just as a tendril of smoke extended from the mass and coiled around his ankle. Max's eyes widened, and he gasped in shock. He exhaled sharply in panic, and then he was gone, his body yanked completely out of his seat.

"Max!" Adilene screamed.

Sasha tried to grab his sleeve, but the fabric slipped right through her fingers.

Gordy leaned forward, trying to see where he had fallen, but the loss of Max's weight caused the contraption to teeter off-balance. More tendrils like phantom fingers lashed out, too many to avoid. Before Gordy could dive into his satchel for a potion, both Adilene and Sasha were pulled out of their seats and swallowed up by the cloud.

"No!" Gordy screamed as Carlisle's strong arms wrapped around his shoulders, pulling him back. "Get off me!" he demanded, tears welling in his eyes. Max and Adilene and Sasha! Where were they? How far had they dropped? Gordy had to save them, but he felt fingers of smoke around his ankle. He would be the next, but Gordy didn't care. He would let it take him.

Carlisle hurriedly raised something to Gordy's lips.

Gordy struggled against him, uncertain of what the old man was trying to do, but Carlisle's strength overpowered him, forcing a glass bottle into his mouth.

Gordy tasted Silt. He gasped and swallowed. Then he watched as his body disappeared and the tendril of smoke ripped him out of his seat and sent him tumbling, head over heels, into the abyss.

CHAPTER

41

Luckily for Gordy, he had miscalculated. The craft had only been hovering twenty feet above the forest floor when he had fallen. Though he landed in a drift of soft sand, the sheer force knocked the wind out of his lungs. Rolling on his back and gasping for air, Gordy watched as the black cloud dissolved, leaving only blue sky dappled by a canopy of leaves overhead.

Immediately, Gordy noticed how he could see straight through his translucent skin, the outline of his fingers hardly visible in the sunlight. Carlisle had given him Silt at the last minute, but why, and where had it come from?

A strange shriek startled him, and he swiveled around to see a flock of flamingoes bathing in a pond a few yards away. There were dozens of birds, legs bending at odd angles, eyes unblinking. Through the trees, Gordy could see another pond with more birds gathered: ducks, geese, cranes, storks, and pelicans. It was as though Gordy had dropped into the middle of the bird exhibit at the zoo.

Gordy heard voices murmuring above the birdsong, and he spotted Adilene less than thirty yards away. She was lying on her back next to Max and Sasha, all three of them bound with ropes. A group of ancient-looking people stood guard around them, and standing in the middle, sweaty and miserable, was Ravian McFarland.

"Try not to jostle them but hurry! My Torpor Tonic will only keep them unconscious for so long," Ravian grumbled, moving out of the way as a couple of men hoisted Adilene off the ground like a rag doll.

Gordy felt an instant rush of relief. Torpor Tonic meant his friends had survived. Instinctively slipping his hand into the unzipped pocket of his satchel, Gordy sifted through the contents and selected a potion.

"Don't just stand there like dimwits!" Ravian shouted. "Find the other boy! He's around here somewhere."

Gordy stepped forward but halted when he heard movement off to his side. Carlisle stood a few feet away amid the palm trees. His eyes scanned the ground, suddenly widening. Gordy realized his dose of Silt had worn off, leaving him exposed. Without any hesitation, Gordy leaped into the trees.

"They have my friends," Gordy whispered. He checked the clearing for any signs of Ravian or the Atramenti, but miraculously, Gordy hadn't been spotted.

Carlisle flicked his chin to where the faint etchings of a path curved through the tall grasses.

Gordy had no interest exploring the island without the

others. He pointed back toward the clearing. "We have to follow them."

In response, Carlisle turned and trudged down the path.

"Where are you going?" Gordy's hushed voice drew a shriek from a trio of macaws perched on a tree branch.

With Carlisle on his side, the two of them could fan out and attack the Atramenti from different angles. Maybe he had more Silt in his knapsack. But the old man wasn't listening, and he wasn't slowing down, either. If Gordy didn't hurry, he would lose him in the thick vegetation. Growling in frustration, Gordy made his decision and took off after him.

The path zigzagged through the jungle. The hot air was sticky with swarming mosquitoes. When he wasn't hacking his way through branches, Gordy was smacking his skin, trying to flatten the annoying pests. Eventually the path sloped downward, ending at a stream that bubbled from the base of a rock wall. Carlisle crouched next to the narrow hole.

"Can I drink this?" Gordy asked, already dropping to his knees by the water and scooping handfuls into his mouth.

The cold water tasted fresh and gritty. Gordy doused his hair, soaking his shirt collar, and then paused to scratch one of the mosquito bites. When was the last time he'd walked that far? He glanced over just as the bald patch of Carlisle's head vanished down the hole next to the stream.

"You've got to be kidding me!" Gordy groaned. First hiking, now spelunking? They were wasting time. Instead of rescuing his friends, Carlisle was taking Gordy on safari!

"Carlisle!" he called into the hole. "If I plummet to my death . . . so help me!"

Shoving his satchel down first, Gordy held his breath and slid down after it. He landed in a dark cavern, then he heard the striking sound of a match. He took in a gasping breath of air as the sudden glow of a torch ignited, illuminating an enormous cavern stretching out endlessly for what had to be miles.

CHAPTER

42

A single candle glowed in a glass-covered lamp hanging from the ceiling. Adilene sat cross-legged on the floor in a prison cell. The room—a six-foot block of stone surrounded by damp, wooden walls with no windows—felt dismal and bleak.

Lying on a cot next to her was Sasha, and though her eyes were closed, she wasn't sleeping. The tears had dried on her cheeks, but from time to time, Adilene could hear the girl sniffle. Sasha's hands had been secured by a pair of uncomfortable metal gloves designed to keep her from brewing. She couldn't even wiggle a finger. Unlike Sasha, Adilene hadn't been fitted with any sort of restraint.

Two hunks of bread and bowls of soup lay on a tray beneath the cot, growing cold and stale as the girls refused to eat anything. Adilene had wondered if the food was poisoned, while Sasha had insisted that if they took even the smallest of nibbles, they would end up Blotched.

"I'm still hungry!" Max bellowed from across the

room. "One measly roll and some broth doesn't cut it for us Pinkermans!" He had complained almost nonstop since being startled awake. Max was loud, insulting, and obnoxious, but Adilene was so grateful to hear his voice. Seeing him falling from the craft had been one of the worst moments of her life. As far as she was concerned, Max could keep shouting as long as he wanted.

Adilene had woken about an hour earlier to find herself imprisoned along with the others. After being pulled into the cloud, she couldn't remember much except for the smells. Scents of foreign chemicals and strange substances. Her nostrils burning, tongue tingling as each element seemed to trigger some sort of reaction. Then Adilene had been cradled in a blanket and drifted into unconsciousness.

They had no idea what had happened to Gordy. He wasn't in their cell, and he hadn't answered when they had called out his name. But Adilene knew he had to have survived. Gordy was more important than the rest of them combined. They were on his grandfather's island now, and that bizarre cloud had been one of his sinister concoctions. If they hadn't perished in the fall, then certainly Gordy would've made it out okay. But where was he? And where was Carlisle?

Climbing to her feet, Adilene crossed the room and jiggled the doorknob. The latch caught firmly as she twisted, refusing to budge. She took a breath and then knocked on the door. After a few seconds of waiting, she heard someone approaching.

"How may I be of assistance?" Their guardian was a boy, his voice squeaking as though it hadn't settled on a final tone.

"What's your name? And why are you holding us here?" Adilene leaned her ear against the door. She could hear the boy's feet shuffling back and forth.

"I am Gabriel," the boy replied. He possessed a slight accent, but it wasn't Spanish. At least not the Spanish she had grown up with.

Trying to imagine the owner's face, Adilene envisioned him as thin and mousy, maybe with a faint mustache sprouting beneath his nose. But the boy was also an imposter. That much Adilene knew for sure. A half hour ago, when Max had been pounding on the door, demanding a bathroom break, the boy's voice had suddenly turned from young to old. It had dribbled out like a scratchy growl, followed by a round of hacking and wheezing. Max had immediately backed away from the door in shock. The guard had tried to recover, explaining how he was under the weather, but the damage had been done. These people were just like Cadence. They were shifty and odd and capable of changing their appearance at will, but all of them, despite their disguises, were ancient.

"You are . . . our guests," the boy continued.

"Guests?" Max scoffed. "Then let us out!"

"I can't," Gabriel said. "We are keeping you in there for your own safety."

Max plopped down on the wooden cot across the room. "You're such a liar, Gabriel."

"Can you at least give us a blanket?" Adilene asked. "It's freezing in here."

Sasha sat up, staring at Adilene in confusion, sweat beading on her upper lip.

"I'm not allowed to give you anything other than your meals, I'm afraid," Gabriel explained.

"Just give her a blanket, you big dummy!" Max hollered out. Adilene could almost see the boy cringing from Max's insult.

"Very well," Gabriel said. "Do you require anything else?"

Adilene's eyes darted around the room. "May I have a glass of water?" she added. "I'm very thirsty."

Gabriel shuffled his feet some more, but then stepped away only to return a moment later. "Please take a seat as I open your door," he said, his voice pleasant but insistent.

Adilene sat next to Sasha on the cot, the wooden slats creaking under their weight.

"What are you trying to do?" Sasha asked her as Gabriel inserted a key into the lock.

The door opened, and the boy, looking almost exactly how Adilene had imagined him, stepped inside. He hurriedly laid a folded blanket on the floor as well as a glass jar filled partially with water. A ring of keys jangled at his waist as he bowed and exited the cell.

"Are you seriously freezing?" Max asked from across the room.

"No, and I'm not thirsty either," Adilene said. "But we need water to make something."

"Make what?" Max blurted.

Adilene pressed a finger to her lips, desperately trying to quiet her boisterous friend. "A potion!" she whispered.

"You're delirious," Sasha said. "They've taken my satchel. All my ingredients."

"We have water and a brewing cauldron with this glass. We can heat it up with the candle." Adilene leaped off the cot and grabbed the blanket. "We can burn some of this to add extra heat to the fire." Sasha opened her mouth to object, but Adilene cut her off. "And I have this."

She pulled a vial from her front pocket. All the rest of the potions she'd had hidden on her had been taken, along with Sasha's supplies. But whoever had frisked her when she'd been unconscious had missed the single vial.

Sasha sat up, a smirk forming on her lips. "What is that?"

"Moholi Mixture," Adilene replied.

Sasha squinted. "No, it's not. That's just some weird gunk you poured into a test tube."

"Fine, it *could* be Moholi Mixture. It just needs a little extra work."

"What does it do?" Max moved over to Sasha's cot.

Sasha sighed. "For starters, if she had actually brewed a Moholi Mixture, we could remove these awful gloves or pour it on the lock and break out of here. But that stuff will probably just give off poisonous gas and kill us."

"Keep your voice down!" Adilene snapped. The guard might have left, but he could return at any moment. "Do you know how to Philter?"

Sasha shrugged. "We need a deadening device like gold or cannonball lead to slow down the chemical reaction."

"Your earrings? Are they real or fake?" Adilene was glad she had paid such careful attention when Gordy had explained the process of Philtering during one of their brewing sessions.

Sasha rolled her eyes. "Fake? Seriously? You know where I live."

"Then if they're gold, we have a deadening device."

"It's not that simple," Sasha reasoned. "I've seen my mom do it once or twice, and I know the basic method, but . . ."

"What does it hurt to try?" Adilene pressed her fingers to her temples, a headache forming. Gordy's tonic must have worn off because her vision had begun to blur again. But that wasn't the only thing causing her head to spin. Adilene could see things. Strange things. Chemicals and ingredients. Bottles and containers. Images from Gordy's lab swirling about in a muddled mess.

Heart racing, she uncorked the vial, and a multitude of flavors and scents filled her nostrils. "Is there any way we could use the ingredients from this potion to make another Moholi Mixture?"

"If I had my hands"—Sasha rattled the metal clamps—"then maybe I could. But that's not happening."

"Then you'll just have to Project through me." Adilene had hated that term since she first learned its meaning and instantly had her hopes of becoming an Elixirist dashed to pieces. But if it helped them escape, she would gladly allow Sasha to use her as an instrument.

"I don't know how to Project," Sasha said. "It's not like you can practice that."

"But Gordy—" Adilene started to argue.

"Gordy's different, okay!" Sasha interjected. "I don't like to admit it, but he is. He's better than I am. Better than everyone."

Adilene removed the candle from the lamp and placed it on the floor. "Come on, Sasha." She held up the vial and gave her a nod of encouragement. "I know you can do this."

Sasha wiped her eyes with the back of her hand. "I don't think it will work."

"It's okay," Adilene insisted. "We just have to make the effort. Project through me and Max. Tell us what to do."

"Uh, you're on your own for this," Max grumbled, watching Adilene cautiously.

Sasha slid off the cot and knelt next to Adilene. "Can you even see?" she asked.

Adilene's temples throbbed. Her heartbeat pounded in her ears, and blurry shadows crowded the corners of her eyes. "I'm fine," she insisted. "We can do this together."

"Okay," Sasha said. "I'll try."

A shaft of sunlight crept down from the hole above, the sound of the burbling stream now distant and muted. "Where are we?" Gordy's voice echoed off the stone walls. Holding out the torch, the orange flames licking up the fuel-drenched fabric, Carlisle motioned for Gordy to follow him.

Unlike before, when they had cut through the jungle at a breakneck pace, the old man walked alongside Gordy, his gait stumbling and slow. The cavern walls were too smooth to have been hollowed out by centuries of erosion. This was an actual pathway. After several minutes of walking through darkness, Gordy caught Carlisle by his sleeve, forcing him to stop.

"No more walking until we figure this out," Gordy said. "Do you know where we're going?"

Carlisle swallowed and nodded solemnly.

"Are you showing me the way to find Mezzarix?"

Again, a slight nod, Carlisle's eyes glinting in the torchlight.

"It's a secret way," Gordy clarified to himself. This tunnel was better than trying to ambush Ravian and the Atramenti out in the jungle, where they would have most likely been captured. A secret entrance gave Gordy the upper hand. A chance to spring his trap when Mezzarix least expected it.

"Are you going to help me defeat my grandfather?" Gordy asked.

Carlisle looked ready to nod but then dropped his eyes and started walking again. Gordy hurried to catch up with him.

"He took over your island, you know? And those people are your people, right? He's Blotched them all. I can help you get them back if you help me. I just . . . I can't do this by myself." Gordy had faced off against a number of foes, but none of them frightened him as much as Mezzarix.

After another hundred yards through the tunnel, Carlisle arrived at a door. It was the same color and pattern of the stone surrounding it, and Gordy would have missed it had Carlisle not been there.

Pulling firmly on the handle, Carlisle opened the door and stepped through. Gordy peered past him into a room no bigger than a standard walk-in closet. There was a mattress shoved in the corner, but there appeared to be nothing else inside. No furniture or books. Just a bed and a few blankets covered in dust.

Reaching beneath the mattress, Carlisle felt around for a few moments before producing a box about the size of a deck of cards. He opened the box's lid, revealing a glass vial brimming with an inky substance.

"Is that Silt?" Gordy asked.

Carlisle responded by handing him the bottle.

"What do you want me to do with it?" With this much Silt, Gordy could stay invisible for more than an hour. He'd have no trouble sneaking up on Mezzarix. Is that why Carlisle had given it to him?

Staring down at the bottle, Gordy suddenly remembered Ms. Bimini's final warning that Silt could cause changes—possibly lasting changes. Like with Adilene's eyesight. Should Gordy down the whole bottle, he might be in the same boat as Adilene.

Carlisle gazed at Gordy sadly and held out a shaky finger, gesturing down the corridor. He handed over his torch and then stumbled to the mattress, where he sat down heavily. Kicking off his shoes, Carlisle slipped his feet under the sheets.

"You're not coming with me?" Gordy asked, baffled. "I don't even know where I'm supposed to go!" How could Carlisle just abandon him?

Then Gordy looked at the old man—really looked at him—and realized how old Carlisle was. He was exhausted and weak and just wanted to rest. Would his passing be like Ms. Bimini's? Would Carlisle simply fade out of existence right before Gordy's eyes?

"Are you going to . . ." Gordy swallowed, not wanting to finish the question. Something in the way Carlisle looked at him, though, seemed to answer it all the same.

Gordy felt the urge to cry. Knowing this would be the last time he ever saw Carlisle, Gordy wiped his nose with the back of his hand. He entered the room and pulled the sheets up until they covered the old man's chest, tucking him in as though he were a young child.

A few seconds slipped by of painful wheezing, and Carlisle gave a final nod.

Gordy patted his wrinkled hand in farewell, then closed the door to Carlisle's room and walked into the cavern.

44

Adilene's fingers trembled as she picked up the botched Moholi Mixture and removed the cork. Fumes wafted from the bottle, smelling like licorice and dandelions. She had already torn several pieces of stale bread into chunks. One of Sasha's gold earrings rested at the bottom of the glass. The water covering it hissed as Max stoked the candle flame with scraps of the woolly blanket.

"One or two drops at first," Sasha whispered, her eyes closed, concentrating. "Try not to get any on the edges of the glass."

Adilene wanted to close her eyes as well but knew someone needed to pay attention. Besides, brewing in the dark prison cell made her vision almost nonexistent. She wouldn't dare admit it to the others, but she feared she might miss the target. Steadying her hand, she extended the vial over the lip of the glass and dribbled out two drops of liquid. The clear water grew clouded, and the potion's fragrance increased in potency.

Sasha peeked open one eye. "More," she instructed. "Lots more. And don't breathe in the smoke. It's toxic."

Max held his breath, wafting the smoke away with his hand. Adilene poured in twelve drops, and the water began to bubble, darkening in color. Then she added the second earring. Something sparked across the surface, and Adilene jumped in surprise.

"That's normal," Sasha said, her voice calm. "The gold is causing a chemical reaction with the other ingredients. Cover it quickly!" Her eyelids scrunched, her brow furrowing; she appeared to be mulling over the next step. "Um . . . how does it feel?"

Adilene tested the side of the glass. "It's hot but not burning."

"More heat, Max." Sasha's eyes snapped open. "It needs more heat!"

"Easier said than done," Max said, feeding more of the blanket into the candle's flame. The fire began to sizzle, licking the bottom of the glass, and Adilene could hear the liquid roiling within.

A couple minutes later, Adilene tapped her finger against the glass and immediately pulled back, her fingertip reddening.

"Add the pieces of bread now," Sasha commanded. "One for each key ingredient."

"What will that do?" Max asked.

"If this actually works, the bread will absorb the ingredients," Sasha explained. "*If* it works."

It will work, Adilene told herself. *It has to work!* One by one, she dropped in each piece, and the bread floated on the surface before sinking to the bottom.

Sasha's lips pursed together in frustration. "I knew it," she muttered. "It's not like I can turn on a Projecting switch whenever I want and magically—" She fell silent.

The bread began to float again, rising to the top. Each piece sparkled with a hint of color: bronze, lavender, dark green, and a lustrous shade of silver. When the stench of putrescent beetle shells filled her nostrils, Adilene felt a tingling of excitement travel up her spine. Sasha's earrings now resembled twisted knots at the bottom of the glass.

Following Sasha's next instruction, Adilene dangled in one of her shoelaces, and the soggy bread crumbs clung to the strand. She lifted them out, laying them next to the glass, where they sizzled against the stone floor.

Sasha exhaled slowly. "We don't have a copper spoon or an Amber Wick, so this batch probably won't end up the way it should, but we have everything else we need. Maybe Zelda was right during training. Maybe the recipe doesn't have to be exact. Maybe we just need an Elixirist who knows what she's doing." Her lips pulled wide in an arrogant smile.

"And a pretty good instrument too," Max added, nodding at Adilene.

"Yeah, well, that also," Sasha said.

With Sasha hovering over her shoulder, Adilene began to rebrew the Moholi Mixture. Though her memory was foggy, Adilene could remember most of the steps. Even the part about thinking up a song to create a rhythm and possibly one that reminded her of Gordy. Upon completion, with a couple slight modifications, the potion settling in the glass was a shimmering rose color, and everyone gasped with surprised excitement.

Everyone except for Adilene. She was happy, of course, but she wasn't surprised it had come together perfectly. She had felt the potion forming with each ingredient. Sensed its power. She didn't think she could describe it—Sasha would immediately deny it had happened, and Max never took anything serious—but *Adilene* had brewed the potion. She had brewed it herself and without any help.

Gordy's torch burned out after thirty minutes, leaving him in total darkness. None of the potions in his satchel produced light, and he didn't have time to concoct something new. And though he didn't like the idea of touching the Decocting Wand, the weapon gave off a soft glow, its tip faintly illuminating the pathway.

Eventually, Gordy reached a flight of steps ascending out of the dark. The stairs led to another door, and Gordy pressed his ear against the wood, listening for sounds of movement. When he heard nothing but his own breathing, he opened the door just a crack.

Gordy peered into a large atrium surrounded by marble columns and open doorways. Beyond each opening, staircases led down to lush orchards of fruit trees and hanging floral baskets. Six thrones ringed the atrium, facing a stone table in the center. On the opposite side of the room, against the outer wall, was the Vessel.

Though it was covered by a contraption of glass tubing,

there was no mistaking it. A lid had been clamped over the Vessel's mouth, and steam spouted from one of the tubes as though pressurized. Gordy noticed a pearly liquid rising up through another tube as the chalice rattled against the countertop.

He seemed to be alone, but as Gordy pushed the door wider, unleashing a screech from the ancient hinges, he caught a glimpse of someone sitting in the center throne. Though the man faced the opposite direction, slouching to one side with his head perched upon his fist and gazing out at the picturesque landscape of palm trees, Gordy recognized the mane of white hair immediately.

Mezzarix sat directly in Gordy's path. Running to the Vessel without getting caught was no longer an option.

Slipping back into the corridor, Gordy fingered the vial of Silt. The moment had come. Knowing if he waited too long he might talk himself out of it, Gordy swallowed the contents of the bottle. His body disappeared instantly, fading into the backdrop of the stone walls. He took a breath and stepped into the room.

Mezzarix cocked his head. "Is that you, Ravian?"

Keeping his eyes on the target, pulse pounding in his ears, Gordy extended the Decocting Wand. He needed to be quick and accurate. No time to try a potion to subdue him. Mezzarix needed to be stopped immediately.

As Gordy approached, he noticed his grandfather held a flask of golden liquid. Images flashed across the glass as though he were watching a television program. Gordy tried to make sense of what he was seeing, then shook his head. The potion didn't matter!

Mezzarix made no movement, his eyes transfixed, a smile stretching across his lips as Gordy pointed the wand toward his grandfather.

"Mezzarix Rook," Gordy shouted, his voice trembling. "By the power granted me through the Vessel, I hereby declare you ExSponged!" He thrust the wand forward, the glowing tip striking his grandfather's chest, and Mezzarix's mouth dropped opened in shock.

"No!" Mezzarix screamed. "You can't!"

Gordy wanted to look away from his grandfather's horrified expression, but he couldn't.

Then Mezzarix's eyes grew dark, and his smile returned, along with a sly chuckle. "That's right, Gordy." He shook his head in disappointment. "You can't."

Invisible hands twisted Gordy's arms behind him, ripping the wand from his grasp and tearing his satchel from his shoulder. Blue light filled the room with a haunting radiance as someone forced Gordy to his knees. The atrium that had been empty a few moments before suddenly became filled with the ancient faces of the Atramenti.

46

dilene followed Max into the hallway. The Moholi Mixture had worked perfectly. She had poured the vial into the crack of the doorjamb, and the pinkish potion melted away the latch in seconds, though there wasn't enough to unlock Sasha's metal mittens. She slipped out of the room behind Adilene, hands dropping heavily at her sides.

There were three other cells along the hallway—all empty. A wooden chair rested next to a doorway at the far end, where Adilene suspected Gabriel sat to monitor his prisoners. But the boy was nowhere to be found.

"Maybe Gabriel is taking a lunch break," Max muttered, squeezing between Adilene and Sasha. "I could go for some lunch."

"We're not going to wait for him to show up," Adilene said. At any moment, Gabriel could return and their escape would be over.

The prison's main door opened easily onto a covered

walkway. Baskets of flowers buzzing with honeybees hung every few feet, and off the eastern side of the path, Adilene could see an emerald-green pond surrounded by birds. Enormous papayas dangled from trees. Max reached for one, but Sasha kicked his shin.

"Keep control of your stomach, Max!" she ordered.

The walkway sloped upward toward a domed marble structure that loomed above the treetops with arched entryways and towering white columns. It looked like a castle but without the battlements or a drawbridge.

"Not to sound like a chicken, but there's no way we can just walk right through the front door," Max said, stopping and facing the girls.

"Can we sneak in through the back door?" Adilene asked.

"How do we know there is one?" Max fired back. Then he stumbled backward, his mouth clamped shut, chin tucked down into his chest.

"Max?" Startled, Adilene ran to him. She tried grabbing his arms to calm him down, but he swung out, knocking her away. He appeared to be struggling against an unseen force, keeping him from calling out.

Suddenly Sasha lunged forward, swinging one of her clubbed fists toward the invisible adversary. Metal clanged against something solid, followed by a groan of pain. Max broke free and fell backward onto the walkway.

Gabriel blinked into existence. His eyes were closed, a reddening welt on his forehead from where Sasha had struck him. Then, just as Cadence had done back at Gordy's house after they had captured her, Gabriel transformed into a withering old man covered in wrinkles. His transformation would have shocked Adilene, but after all she had seen, this seemed par for the course.

"Who are you?" Gabriel whimpered, fingers trembling as he gingerly touched the welt on his head, which had grown to the size of a golf ball. "Why did you hit me?"

"Why do you think, creep?" Sasha hovered over Gabriel, one metal fist cocked and ready to strike again.

"I couldn't breathe!" Max exclaimed. "You were choking me!"

"I don't understand." Gabriel sat up, eyes widening with alarm. "That man who came on the boat and his two companions. Did you come with them? What do you want from us?"

"We came on our own, bucko," Max said. "On a big robot bird named Roseanne!"

"Are you talking about Mezzarix?" Adilene asked.

"I cannot recall their names." Gabriel's forehead wrinkled in confusion. "But the woman was quite short. She had green hair."

"Zelda!" Sasha said.

"That name sounds familiar." Gabriel nodded.

"Where's Mezzarix now?" Adilene demanded. "Does he have Gordy with him?"

Gabriel peered over his shoulder back up the pathway. "He has withdrawn into the portico. The stranger has, by impossible means, gained control over my people. We have had no choice but to obey."

"What's a portico?" Max asked.

Adilene followed Gabriel's gaze toward the domed structure as a blue light suddenly appeared, pouring out from the entryway.

A fter all this time, I could've sworn a bond had grown between us, Gordy," Mezzarix said, leaning forward in his throne.

Gordy's grandfather looked healthier than he had the last time Gordy had seen him, which was when he had nearly died from the side effects of the Clasping Cannikin. He was, however, still barefoot and wearing the same threadbare tuxedo.

Gordy struggled against his captors, but there were too many hands holding him down. A blue light cascaded from the top of the column where the keystone was attached, revealing all within the atrium. He was no longer invisible, and neither were the twenty or so Atramenti crowding around him.

Mezzarix's chuckle became enthusiastic laughter. "Did you actually believe I would give you the one weapon that could end my powers? My boy, how foolish of you."

"It's not real?" Gordy demanded. He hadn't used the

Decocting Wand on a single enemy, but that had been by choice, not because he believed it wouldn't work.

"Oh, it's quite real. ExSpongements from that wand are permanent and true, but you didn't think I would allow it to work against me, did you?" Mezzarix said. "And that's another thing, we need to talk about your restraint. You encountered dangerous criminals as you plotted a course to my island, and yet, not once did you use that weapon to save the ones you care about."

"How do you know that?" Gordy asked.

"I've been watching you!" Anger flashed across Mezzarix's features. He held up the flask; the image displayed was of Gordy kneeling, restrained by several ancient-looking strangers. Gordy's Decocting Wand lay on the ground a few feet away, the tip pointing in his direction, broadcasting the scene as though it were a video camera.

"I've watched you all from time to time." Mezzarix's calm demeanor returned. "I had to see how my gifts were being used, and you disappoint me, grandson. Such poor choices. Instead of a traitor like Zelda, whom you had in your clutches, you opted to ExSponge *me*. Your flesh and blood." He clicked his tongue. "I thought we shared a moment back in Greenland."

"I'm not like you!" Gordy bellowed. "I don't hurt people for fun."

"Esmeralda, on the other hand, is a different story," Gordy's grandfather continued. "Due to her own Ex-Spongement, I had to specially treat her wand to allow her to use it." Mezzarix laid the flask on the throne's armrest. "And I told her that should she succeed in capturing the final member of the Chamber, I would restore her brewing powers and revoke her parents' Banishment. You see, the Faustuses were my ace in the hole, and it would appear my gamble paid off. Who would have thought the end of B.R.E.W.'s Chamber would come at the hands of a tortured soul like Esmeralda Faustus?"

Gordy had never suspected his grandfather had been watching him, but now it made sense. It even explained the bizarre black storm that suddenly appeared above the island and snatched them at the precise moment they were landing. Mezzarix had known everything that had happened through the gift Gordy had foolishly accepted.

"Where are my friends?" Gordy asked.

"I'm a gracious host." Mezzarix pressed his fingertips together, gazing down upon his grandson disdainfully. "They are safe. But now, it's my turn for questioning. You came with a fifth stranger. An older gentleman. Who was he?"

"His name's Carlisle," Gordy said.

The name caused a rumble of whispering through the crowd of Atramenti, and Mezzarix raised an eyebrow. "Ah, the prodigal son of Ms. Bimini has returned? Where is he now?"

"You didn't see?" Gordy jutted his chin toward his grandfather's flask.

"I haven't been watching every step you've made,"

Mezzarix reasoned. "It's not a television I can simply turn on with a remote."

"Carlisle's no concern of yours." Gordy looked at one of the Atramenti. The man's sunken eyes had burrowed deep in their sockets, and most of his teeth had rotted away. How old was he? A century? Two?

Mezzarix nodded to a couple of the others. "Find him and bring him here."

A man and a woman, equally as decrepit as Gordy's guards, hurried toward the door from which Gordy had entered the atrium.

"Did you Blotch all of them?" Gordy asked.

"I needed total cooperation," Mezzarix snapped. "Care to hear a secret?" He continued before Gordy could reply. "Did you know I've been Blotched dozens of times? But each time, I was able to break the trance long before the Blotching effects wore off. Want to know how?"

Gordy stared back at his grandfather defiantly.

"I simply plan ahead by asking myself a question only I know the answer to." Mezzarix continued. "A complete secret from everyone. And I keep this question in my mind always. Then, at the moment I suspect I've been placed under a spell, I simply ask the question to whomever I feel may be the perpetrator in my Blotching."

"That's it?" Gordy asked, unimpressed.

Mezzarix nodded. "If they answer incorrectly, I can rest assured that my thoughts are indeed mine alone. But if they give the right answer, then I know they are my enemy."

"But how could they give you the right answer?"

"Precisely!" Mezzarix smacked his knee emphatically. "They cannot know the right answer, and yet somehow they do. That's how I know I've been duped. The Tainted item confusing me has changed the answer to my question, and I no longer know the truth of it. I'm being fed a falsehood, but since it's coming from my own thoughts, I accept it as fact."

Gordy leaned back against his captors. His grandfather's trick actually made some sense.

Cocking his head, Mezzarix studied Gordy. "I have never shared this before. The moment anyone realizes how easy it is to break a Blotching, it will no longer be a practical method of control."

"What's going to happen now?" Gordy asked. "To me and my friends?"

"Now?" Mezzarix inquired. "We wait for the Dissolvement Draught to run its course on the Vessel."

"And then the power will go out everywhere," Gordy said flatly. He had witnessed firsthand what had happened in his town, and that had been on the tiniest of scales.

"My dear grandson, you are looking at this the wrong way. Yes, the power will go out for a time, but then we will usher in a new age. New developments. Ones not linked to B.R.E.W." Mezzarix exhaled blissfully. "And in the interim, there will be no more cell phones or automobiles or toaster ovens. No more distractions. Within a week, millions of people will be in dire need."

"Why are you doing this?" Everything ran on power. Gordy thought about hospitals unable to tend to the sick and wounded, about people unable to heat their homes. It wouldn't take long before the number of people suffering would be too high to count.

Mezzarix sighed impatiently. "Their need will turn them to us. To me and to you. *We* will provide their aid. Not B.R.E.W. and certainly not the oppressive governments of the world. We will show them the true power of the Elixirists. With the Vessel destroyed, the world will turn to us for mercy. Before B.R.E.W.'s establishment, there lived a different breed of Elixirists. Restrictions and punishments ended all that, and technology buried their existence even deeper beneath endless layers of distraction. I'm simply restoring an older way—a better way."

Gordy's eyes drifted across the room to where the Vessel vibrated beneath the twisted maze of glass equipment. He had no idea how much of the original potion remained, but even if he could reverse the Dissolvement Draught, Gordy could never make it across the room through more than two dozen Atramenti.

Mezzarix's servants returned to report how they had searched the corridors but hadn't been able to find Carlisle anywhere. Maybe Carlisle had gotten away, or maybe the old man had vanished, just like his mother.

The news of Carlisle's vanishing troubled Gordy, and

then he caught a whiff of something strange in the air. Though nearly masked by the countless other smells saturating the room, Gordy detected the faintest scent of black cohosh. The feathery herb had a fetid, bitter tang to it, like raw sewage.

Black cohosh, otherwise known as snakeroot, was the primary ingredient in Blotching potions. That meant the object placing the Atramenti under Mezzarix's control was in the atrium, and it was close by.

"Show me where you looked," Mezzarix commanded. Taking the flask with him, he followed the servants back toward the corridor. "Keep your hands on my grandson," he ordered the remaining Atramenti, "but don't bruise him. I'll be back shortly."

Once Mezzarix had left, the Atramenti remained silent, hopelessly entranced. They paid Gordy no attention as he frantically scanned the room, sniffing the air. Gordy smelled passionflower and ant pheromones, tungsten shavings, and sulphured molasses. All the scents mixed together in his nostrils, distorting the air like heat waves.

Gordy saw an opal-colored container resting on the stone table in the center of the room and knew he had found the Tainted object. That bowl was the source of their Blotching. If he could somehow get to it and snap the spell with a disruption potion, he could set the Atramenti free. But without his satchel, he'd need something else—some kind of distraction.

Luckily, Gordy's best friend was somewhat known for his legendary distractions.

A sudden shattering from across the atrium, followed by liquid hissing as it struck the floor, caused all eyes in the room to whip around.

Gordy grinned to see Maxwell Pinkerman ripping the Vessel free from the glass tubing and hefting it off the table.

ax nearly tripped, but Adilene and Sasha steadied him from behind. A variety of cauldrons and mixing utensils—copper spoons and pewter ladles—clattered to the floor. The Vessel still had the pressurized lid on it, which was good, otherwise the potion would have ended up everywhere.

"Zombie horde!" Max screamed, stumbling away from the table as the Atramenti sucked in a collective breath and took off after him. "Zombie horde!"

Max took off for one of the openings. Sasha's eyes widened, and she followed after him. Then, as some of the Atramenti drew closer, she started pummeling them with . . . with . . .

What on earth? Gordy wondered in disbelief.

Sasha's hands had turned into medicine balls, and she walloped an old woman in the chest, sending her sprawling. Gordy couldn't figure out what potion she had ingested to make her hands so solid, but that wasn't important. The

Atramenti were too old to be bashed around, and it wasn't their fault anyway.

"Don't hurt them!" Gordy called out quickly. "They can't help themselves!"

Rolling her eyes, Sasha held back from slugging another assailant, opting instead to knock more of Mezzarix's diffusing equipment onto the floor.

"Well, come on!" Sasha shouted. "We're getting out of here!"

Adilene ducked as a man with a crooked back made a grab for her. Narrowly avoiding capture, she ran across the room, sliding on the floor and up next to Gordy.

"Where is your grandfather?" Adilene asked breathlessly.

But Gordy barely heard the question. His thoughts were elsewhere. Max had the Vessel, which meant he had stalled the Dissolvement Draught. If he and Adilene ran after Max and Sasha to the beach, they might even make it off the island without getting caught. There was a chance that with his mom's help and other members of B.R.E.W., they could restore what had been destroyed.

But Mezzarix would still be free. He would find Carlisle's stash of Silt, and with the Atramenti at his disposal, he would eventually attack again.

Scrambling to his feet, Gordy snatched up the Decocting Wand and handed it to Adilene. "Careful," he warned. "It doesn't work against Mezzarix."

"Why not?" she asked, staring down at the rod, which hummed with energy.

Gordy grabbed his satchel and pulled out a handful of vials on his way to the stone table. Some of the Atramenti had turned back, hobbling toward them with a distant but determined gleam in their eyes. They *were* like a zombie horde, and Gordy's arm hair stood on end. With no time to brew a proper potion, Gordy had to improvise, but that had always been what he did best.

Careful not to touch any part of the Tainted object, Gordy uncorked vials and poured both a Fire Rocket and a Dunka Draught directly onto the bowl. He shielded his eyes as the volatile potions immediately ignited into flame in the opal bowl. The corrosive smells of black cohosh, tungsten, and burning molasses filled the room, and as the bowl melted into a molten puddle, the throng of Atramenti, including the ones closing in on Gordy and Adilene, came to an abrupt stop.

Gazing around the atrium in a stupor, some of the Atramenti mumbled incoherently to each other. Their trance broken, they dispersed, wandering away in different directions.

Gordy heard footsteps from the corridor as the door burst open and Mezzarix emerged. Though slightly annoyed, his grandfather appeared unfazed. He called out for his servants to return, but they paid him no attention. Still Mezzarix smiled, until his focus fell upon the table and the missing centerpiece.

He gave an aggravated sigh. "That Dissolvement Draught took me a week and a half to concoct. Why do you insist on causing me grief?"

Stepping in front of Adilene, Gordy fished a Torpor Tonic from his satchel and heaved it toward Mezzarix. The bottle struck him directly in the thigh, the aquamarine liquid dousing his tuxedo. But instead of toppling to the floor, unconscious, the Scourge of Nations merely looked down at his damp clothing and sneered.

"I could train you how to resist Torpor Tonics," he said, stepping forward. "It takes practice and tight-jawed determination, but you could learn. I have so many secrets I could share with you."

Gordy fired a Vintreet Trap next.

Vines enveloped his grandfather, constricting like coiling pythons around his chest. But within seconds the vibrant-green vines withered, disintegrating like ash.

"Those too." Mezzarix brushed away the flakes of crumpled vines from his sleeves. "And Dunka Draughts and Fire Rockets and Booming Balls and Ragaszto Ragouts. I've spent my years in captivity developing an immunity to a plethora of standard concoctions, and my access to the Vessel these precious few weeks has enhanced my abilities. Unless you've stashed away a Mangle potion deep within your satchel—something I highly doubt— there's nothing you can throw at me that will—"

Gordy struck Mezzarix with another potion, but this

time his grandfather stumbled back a step, blinking in surprise as he found himself suddenly encased in glass.

"That's a new one," Gordy said. "It's called the Aladdiner." At least until he could think of a better name.

Max's screams rose up from outside as he came charging back up the stairs, still holding the Vessel, though it was tipped precariously to one side. "Birds!" he gasped, his face shiny with sweat. "The whole beach is covered in birds. And some lunatic has captured Sasha!"

The sky turned black behind Max as Gordy and Adilene ran to him, relieving him of the Vessel. The potion sloshed beneath the lid, but the Vessel seemed to still be filled to the brim, giving Gordy hope.

Wind began to thrash against the building as a flock of fifty warbling pigeons careened into the room. They swarmed clumsily, hovering above Gordy's head, and then dove all at once, striking with sharp beaks. All three friends hit the deck, covering their heads as the pigeons swooped away and regrouped near the ceiling, readying for a second pass.

When they attacked again, Gordy tossed an Ice Ball into the center of the swarm. Almost all the pigeons dropped to the ground, encapsulated in a block of blue ice.

"Impressive," Mezzarix called out from within his bottle. "You are full of tricks, aren't you? Just like a Rook." He rapped on the glass with his knuckles. "I like this one, Gordy. It feels poetic. As though you consider me an explosive potion worthy of bottling."

Slipping his hand into his pocket, Mezzarix pulled out a tiny ampoule of opaque liquid and poured the contents down his throat. Slender, bladelike claws began to grow from his fingertips. Gordy watched in horror as his grandfather tapped the glass and then cut through the side of the bottle with his sharpened fingers.

"What else can you show me?" Stepping through the hole, Mezzarix dragged a Wolverine-like claw through his thick hair.

Gordy checked the contents of his satchel. He had six or seven other concoctions ready to go. Ones that could cause Mezzarix to violently throw up or sink into the floor. Gordy had Blind Batched a potion that could make a target sprout an enormous beaver tail, though he hadn't tested it out yet. But he feared none of them would truly work. His grandfather always seemed to be several steps ahead.

The atrium filled with the cawing of more birds, much bigger ones than the pigeons, by the sound of them. The blackened sky seemed to bulge and billow overhead, the beginnings of a funnel cloud peeking out from a gaping eye in the clouds. Ravian McFarland was having too much fun.

Looking at Max and Adilene, Gordy made a decision. "I need you to distract him." He plopped his satchel in Max's arms and patted him on the shoulder.

"Who?" Max gaped down at the leather bag in shock.

"Mezzarix."

"With what?"

"Anything you want." Gordy unzipped the inside pockets where more bottles clinked together. "Take your pick. Go nuts."

One corner of Max's mouth poked up in a half smile. He looked both terrified and delighted.

"How can I help?" Adilene asked.

Gordy pried the lid from the Vessel, revealing the lustrous liquid swirling within. "Just make sure Mezzarix stays occupied and Max doesn't get killed." He swallowed. "And . . . um . . . try not to freak out."

"Freak out?" Adilene sucked in a breath as Gordy plunged his hands into the Vessel and his eyes rolled to the back of his head.

The potion shivered beneath his touch, recoiling as though threatened by an intruder's presence. Gordy could feel it shifting to the sides of the chalice, trying to avoid his fingers. After a moment, it surged back, lashing out with a stinging sensation that traveled through Gordy's fingertips. He could feel a hundred different ingredients eddying up beneath his skin. Antarctic dragon-skin ice. Purwaceng milk. Edelweiss flower. Black rhinoceros tongue. He tasted wolf-spider venom and foxglove seeds. Countless other ingredients without names and scents swirled about in a liquid that alternated between scorching heat and subzero temperatures.

When Gordy thought he could handle no more, something warm and soft pressed against him. His eyesight cleared, and he glanced down to see Adilene's hand squeezing his forearm. She still held the Decocting Wand in her free hand, but she had never left his side.

"What can I do?" Adilene whispered. How could she sound so calm when the island seemed to be primed to explode?

Gordy saw more pelicans and cranes circling above. Their beaks looked capable of skewering any one of them. Ravian McFarland stood on the stairs, shouting commands into the rising steam from a golden cauldron. Max was desperately trying to evade a flock of storks, flinging bottle after bottle over his shoulder. A Torpor Tonic shattered against the lead bird; it crashed headlong into a wall, and Max's Vintreet Trap tied up the rest of the birds in a net. He was surprisingly accurate with his tossing when he wasn't looking. He also seemed to have grown a beaver tail at some point during the battle.

Mezzarix, stuck halfway in the floor from a Trapper Keeper potion, sliced at the marble with his razor claws, trying to get closer to Gordy.

Withdrawing his hands from the chalice, Gordy took the Decocting Wand from Adilene. Fingers soaked with the primordial goop of the Vessel, he could feel the wand pulsing as though alive.

Mezzarix managed to break free from the floor, and he clambered out of the hole.

Max had another potion ready to toss, but the Scourge of Nations struck first, smashing a tube of salmon-colored cream at Max's feet. A gargantuan chewing-gum bubble formed around Max. It lifted him off the ground and sent him flying to the top of the marbled ceiling.

Mezzarix immediately poured the contents of another bottle into his opened palms. Rubbing his hands together, he slathered the liquid over his elongated fingers.

The screeching birds fell silent. They bolted through the entryways with the sound of flapping wings.

Mezzarix shot his hand upward, and a bolt of lightning struck the domed ceiling, shattering the marble into huge chunks that crashed against the floor. Ravian's own storm dimmed as the electricity from Mezzarix's lightning gathered into a glowing orb. His potion-coated hand began to shimmer as the lightning illuminated his face, his eyes wide with fury.

"Enough!" Mezzarix bellowed. He whirled on Gordy. "Bonus points for effort, my boy, but this has got to stop. I don't wish ill on any of you, especially my own grandson, but you will surrender the Vessel to me at once, or I shall not stay my hand!"

Gordy gaped at his grandfather, watching the ball of lightning pulsing above his fingertips.

Ravian dropped his cauldron, the contents spilling on the floor, and limped to Mezzarix's side, his left leg dragging behind him.

"What happened to you?" Mezzarix asked, hardly sounding concerned.

"Could've warned me about the Brexil brat's metal hands, you know?" Ravian grimaced.

"Where is she now?" Mezzarix asked.

"Neck-deep in sand," Ravian replied, picking at his teeth with his thumbnail. "And I do believe the tide is coming in."

"This will not end well for your friends," Mezzarix said to Gordy. "It is up to you how this plays out."

Bowing his head in defeat, Gordy gazed down upon the Decocting Wand. The glowing tip had gone dark and no longer hummed with energy. "Just come and take it from me," he muttered.

"What was that?" Ravian held a hand up to his ear.

"You heard me." Gordy's eyes burned with tears.

"We can't give it to him," Adilene whispered.

"It doesn't matter," Gordy said. "They won't stop. Max and Sasha—we have to think about them too."

Max, still encased in his bubble, hovered near the ceiling as his balloon drifted toward the hole in the roof. Should it reach the opening, Gordy feared his friend might float away. And somewhere down on the beach, Sasha was buried in the sand. Gordy didn't know how much time she had left before the waves drowned her, but he couldn't risk waiting any longer.

Raising it up by its base, Gordy held the Vessel toward his grandfather. "Take it."

The lightning continued to radiate energy from Mezzarix's fingers. It swirled and sparked, primed to launch across the room upon his command. Then he lowered his hand, the lightning sparking out, and nodded at Ravian.

Ravian looked reluctant to comply. "If he hurts my good leg . . ."

"He won't," Mezzarix insisted. "Bring it to me, and we will put an end to this."

Ravian's eyes darted everywhere, watching for a surprise attack, as he moved closer to Gordy and Adilene. He reached out for the Vessel. Gordy didn't fight it and allowed Ravian to take it.

"Well, that seemed anticlimactic, didn't it?" Ravian chuckled as he cautiously backed away. He raised the Vessel, and Mezzarix took hold of the handles.

"This was not a defeat, Gordy," Mezzarix said. "More like a test. And you passed brilliantly." He nodded at Ravian. "Bring down Max and then rescue that poor girl from the beach."

But Ravian wasn't listening. The feathery-haired McFarland stared at his fingers, eyes widening. His chest began to heave great breaths of air as though he might collapse from a heart attack.

"What's gotten into you?" Mezzarix demanded. But then his expression contorted into one of shock. He gasped for air, letting go of the Vessel, as the color drained from his face. The metal chalice thudded against the floor, but the potion remained within, not a single drop spilling over the edge.

Looking desperately at Gordy, Mezzarix shook his head as his grandson rose unsteadily to his feet and wiped his nose with the back of his hand.

"This cannot be," Mezzarix said. "It cannot!"

Of all the terrible things Gordy had ever witnessed, this was the worst. He had dreaded this moment but knew it was the only way to save the world from chaos, to save it from an evil so great as Mezzarix. But it didn't make it any easier to do.

"I'm sorry, Grandpa," Gordy sniffled, gazing upon the man once known as the Scourge of Nations. "But you've been ExSponged."

49

Roseanne's thunderous cries filled the air as she banked west, turbines revving to full strength. The island of the Atramenti had vanished the moment the gargantuan flying machine cleared the treetops. Now, only dark ocean shimmering in the moonlight stirred beneath her.

Gordy sat on the floor next to his friends while Bolter fussed over the controls. No one spoke, not even Max. For once, Gordy's best friend appeared to understand the gravity of what had happened, at least for the time being. Even Bolter had hardly said a word to anyone after his impressive landing on the beach. Gordy wasn't sure if he was still discombobulated from having eaten an entire jar of Tainted mayonnaise, or maybe he was just in awe from the presence of the Vessel cradled in Gordy's lap.

A believer from the beginning, Bolter had often said that Gordy would one day do great things. Still, defeating

Mezzarix and rescuing the Vessel was a tall order for any-one to digest. Even for someone as faithful as Bolter.

Gordy had ExSponged both Mezzarix and Ravian McFarland. He hadn't told any of his friends how he had done it. Honestly, there wasn't a clear way to explain it, and Gordy knew it would be too difficult to discuss.

When he had plunged his hands into the Vessel, the Eternity Elixir still churning through Gordy's veins had filled in the gaps of what was missing. All at once, he understood how to manipulate the Vessel and use its power. A world of possibilities expanded within his mind. Mezzarix had learned much about the three-hundred-year-old chalice's capabilities during his life. Gordy, with his fingers acting as a conduit, had gained the same knowledge in a matter of seconds. After that, he just needed to be one step ahead of his grandfather.

When the idea struck him to turn the Vessel into a temporary Decocting Wand, the necessary elements were already there. Gordy simply had to transfer them to his de-sired location. As soon as he took hold of both the wand and the Vessel, the transfer was completed. With no need for ceremony or special words, Ravian and Mezzarix were in-stantly ExSponged when they touched the chalice's handles.

Mezzarix had crumpled in a heap, and Gordy had rushed to his side. Nothing was said, but Gordy's grand-father gave him a look of what might have been under-standing. Ravian, a blubbering mess, had wandered to the edge of the atrium. He called out to his birds, begging them to obey, but without any magic inside him anymore, no birds heeded his call.

The next events transpired in a blur.

A boy named Gabriel, the leader of the Atramenti, had entered the atrium and taken Mezzarix and Ravian prisoner. Somehow the hidden island felt like the right place for his grandfather's Banishment. Gabriel promised mercy, but the Scourges would never step off the island again.

When Gordy said goodbye, his grandfather looked so much older now, and weaker. The removal of his potion-making ability seemed to have added years to his age.

After almost an hour of flying, as Roseanne soared over Florida, Max finally broke the silence.

"Nobody look, okay?" he said, getting to his feet.

"Look at what?" Sasha still had sand caked beneath her ears from where she had been buried, but Gabriel had found a key in one of Ravian's pockets and had freed her from the metal clamps.

Max glared at Sasha. "I need some snacks, and I don't want anyone staring at me when I turn around." The beaver tail had finally dissolved, leaving a gaping hole in the back of Max's jeans.

"I've been wanting to ask you," Gordy said, leaning toward Adilene and Sasha. "How did you guys break out of your cell?" With Sasha's hands covered in metal and no potions to speak of, that had been quite the mystery. If his friends hadn't shown up when they had, things most certainly would have ended differently.

Adilene fidgeted with an empty glass bottle. She had been holding the same vial for most of the evening while they waited for Bolter to return. "I mixed a Moholi Mixture and melted the latch," she said.

"You did?" Gordy wasn't trying to sound surprised, but it caught him off guard.

"I Projected through her," Sasha explained. "We Philtered out the ingredients of Adilene's first attempt and then rebrewed another one together."

"Yeah," Adilene agreed, looking down at the floor. "Maybe, but I think it was more than that."

"What do you mean 'more'?" Gordy asked.

Adilene made eye contact with Gordy but then looked at Sasha, who appeared to be biting her lip. "I know what you think, Sasha. That you used me as an instrument, but I think it was more. I felt like it was working, not just from what I could see, but inside me as well."

"But you're too—" Sasha started to say.

"I know, I'm too old," Adilene hurriedly answered. "And you probably did just Project through me, but . . . I don't know." Her shoulders slumped.

"Maybe we can talk to somebody when we get back," Gordy suggested. "Someone who could test you."

"Yeah, maybe," Adilene said.

"She was great, though," Sasha added. "I couldn't have done it without her. I know I give you a hard time"—she caught Adilene's eyes—"but you really are a great lab partner. Gordy's lucky to have you."

"Thanks, Sasha," Adilene said, her cheeks turning a slight shade of pink. "He's lucky to have you too."

~

As Roseanne began her descent onto the football field behind Kipland Middle, Gordy gaped at the destruction. Buildings had been set ablaze, black smoke curling into the sky. Downed power lines sent crackles of sparks along the roads. The center building of Kipland, which housed the main offices, had been demolished by a block of ice easily the size of a school bus.

"What is that?" Max asked, pointing to an enormous mound of spindly limbs and claws lying on its back across three rows of bleachers.

Bolter squinted. "Probably some sort of prop or a balloon or a—"

"It's a centipede," Gordy said.

The creature, significantly larger than the one Gordy had fought on Tobias's property, looked dead, its legs shriveled, its head pitched back at an odd angle. The centipede meant the Scourges had dug deep into their arsenal of deadly weapons. What other nasty insects had been enlarged for battle? And were they still scurrying around somewhere in the shadows?

The field had been torn to pieces at the fifty-yard line. Fountains of water spewing from busted pipes gave Roseanne an uneven landing. A group of people congregated near the concession stand, and Gordy spotted his

Aunt Priss at once. Dressed in military fatigues and bending over a table, Priss barked orders to those surrounding her. Swinging down from the rope ladder, Gordy hit the ground almost at a run.

"Where's my mom?" Gordy shouted, racing up to his aunt.

Several Elixirists whirled around, potions in hand.

"Stand down!" Priss commanded, pushing her way through. "What are you doing here, Gordy?" Gawking at Gordy momentarily in shock, she pulled him into a tight squeeze. "Where's Bolter? Why did he bring you here?"

"What do you mean? Bolter is right there." How had his aunt missed the giant bird-machine parked on the football field? But when Gordy pointed to the spot where Roseanne had landed, he could see Max, Adilene, and Sasha running toward him but no flying contraption looming behind. Roseanne had vanished.

"Where did he go?" Gordy blinked in confusion.

"Where did who go?" Max asked, panting as he ran up to Gordy. Max turned and appeared equally flummoxed by Roseanne's disappearance.

"Bolter hasn't removed the cloaking potion," Sasha explained when she and Adilene arrived at the concession stand. "He wasn't sure if it was safe to reveal her just yet. But he's powering Roseanne down now."

"You should be in Colorado with your dad," Priss grumbled to Gordy. Laid out on the table behind her was a large map with pushpins marking several areas. "There are still Scourges hiding everywhere."

"The safe house is in Colorado?" Max asked. "That's lame."

Priss's eyes flashed with rage. "When I get my hands on Bolter, I swear I'll—"

"It's not his fault," Gordy chimed in, interrupting her rant. "You can't get mad at him. He did what he was supposed to do, but I Blotched him."

"You did what?" Priss recoiled.

"*We* Blotched him," Sasha corrected. "It was my idea."

Gordy wasn't sure if Sasha was actually coming to his aid or just trying to take credit. "Yeah, but I laid the trap," Gordy said.

"Technically, Adilene had planted the mayonnaise in Bolter's satchel," Max added, shoving Adilene in the arm.

Adilene scowled in embarrassment.

"You . . . you what?" Priss shook her head. "Why would you do that? Bolter was given specific instructions for your safety."

"Yeah, well, we had no choice," Max said, folding his arms. "We held the fate of the world in our hands. Someone had to step up to the plate."

"Fate of the world," Priss mocked, exasperated. "And I suppose you were in on this as well, weren't you, Max? What did you do?"

Max opened his mouth, but his eyes suddenly widened. "I feel a draft." Throwing his hands behind his back, he covered the rip in his pants now exposed to at least a dozen Elixirists nearby.

"Where's my mom, Priss?" Gordy demanded.

"Your mother's fine," Priss said. "A few bumps and bruises, but nothing to lose sleep over. She's in the gymnasium, but you can't go in there right now." Priss snagged Gordy's sleeve as he turned to run, pulling him back. "She's tending to the fallen."

"What does that mean?" Adilene asked.

Priss lowered her eyes. "This was unlike any battle we've ever fought. We were unprepared for the Scourges' weapons, and a lot of good Elixirists were ExSponged."

"Tobias?" Gordy blurted, his panic rising. "Was he—"

Squeezing Gordy's shoulder, Priss smiled. "Tobias survived. He's the one responsible for that monstrosity." She flicked her chin toward the main school building and the enormous block of ice protruding from the roof.

"It's an Ice Ball on steroids!" Max squealed.

"More like an unplanned hailstone from a Sturmwolke Slosh," Priss explained. "Those Scourges picked the wrong person's garden to destroy." A murmur rose up behind her as several Elixirists urgently gestured to the map. "Anyway, I have work to do and Scourges to hunt," Priss said. "I'll find someone to take you four out of the city. This is no place for children."

"I don't know that we can address them as children anymore," Bolter announced, suddenly appearing from the football field.

"You wait your turn, Bolter!" Priss gave the man a fleeting glance, then did a double take. "Where did you get that?" She stepped forward, drawing the attention of the other Elixirists, who immediately stopped what they were doing and stared at Bolter, mesmerized by what he held cradled in his arms.

"You should ask Gordy," Bolter said. "And then perhaps give him and his companions medals. They deserve our respect." Bolter held up the Vessel. "Thanks to them, we just won the war."

The Kipland Middle gymnasium had never smelled so strange, and that was saying something. Each bleacher seat was occupied by a satchel-toting Elixirist, their vials and ampoules filled with every color of the rainbow and giving off a variety of scents. Many in attendance represented the recently dissolved B.R.E.W., while more than half earned their livelihood in the Swigs.

Yosuke Nakamura stood behind a podium at center court, tapping the microphone with his finger, trying to bring the mass of chattering Elixirists to order. "Can we get started, please?" he asked, clearing his throat.

Behind Yosuke, seated in more than a dozen folding metal chairs, was an odd assortment of faces. Wanda Stitser and Aunt Priss sat next to each other. Tobias, on the far end, fed potato chips to the potted Venus flytrap balanced on his knee. Next to him was a muscular-looking fellow with coarse arm hair—the real Scheel Abboud.

Finally home from a covert operation in Egypt, Scheel seemed particularly grumpy.

Paulina Hasselbeck of the Stained Squad sat between Bolter and a man named Nestor Wax. There was one more representative of B.R.E.W.—a woman named Goldie Greta, who had been promoted to Lead Investigator directly following Wanda's termination. Due to their recent ExSpongements, none of the current Chamber Members sat in attendance. Rounding out the row in the four folding chairs closest to the podium were Gordy, Adilene, Max, and Sasha.

Only one week had passed since Mezzarix's defeat, but the world had already changed drastically. For starters, entire neighborhoods had been demolished in the battle against the Scourges, houses and businesses razed to the earth in rubble. Gordy's mom and the Stained Squad had managed to apprehend many of their enemies, but quite a few were still on the loose. Though the Decocting Wands in their possession could no longer ExSponge victims, thanks to Gordy reclaiming the Vessel, there were still violent Scourges, and something needed to be done to handle them.

When Mrs. Stitser learned what Gordy and his friends had done, she'd been angry. Gordy had expected to be grounded for life, issued a Sequester Strap, and never allowed to step foot in a potion laboratory again. But when Gordy burst into tears explaining what he had been forced to do to his Grandpa Rook, her anger fizzled away. She had hugged him nonstop for an hour, which could have been awkward for his friends, but they didn't seem to mind.

In the end, Gordy avoiding grounding. After all, he had defeated the greatest enemy the Potion Community had ever known and prevented a global meltdown by rescuing the Vessel. Sometimes taking risks was necessary for the greater good.

When Mr. Stitser, Isaac, and Jessica had returned from their surprise vacation the next afternoon, things almost started to feel normal again. The family spent several days in a hotel while repairs were made to their home following the catastrophic wind damage Roseanne had caused when she had landed in the yard, but events like that had become almost regular occurrences with the Stitsers.

"We have many things to discuss and vote upon, and our first order of business—" Yosuke began but was immediately interrupted.

"Who put you in charge?" one Elixirist demanded from the bleachers. Gordy wasn't sure of his name, but knew he had worked for B.R.E.W. Burly and imposing, the man towered over those seated around him, with a square jaw and a furrowed forehead.

"I am not in charge," Yosuke reasoned, pressing a hand against his chest. "I am simply conducting a meeting. I think you will find not one of us here has any desire to take the lead during this very tense time."

The man gave a sarcastic smirk, and several people seated around him grumbled in support of his complaint.

Mrs. Stitser had warned Gordy how this meeting would proceed. Combining that many Elixirists together, all with varying beliefs on what was right and wrong for the Community, was like trying to stir a discomfited batch of Pele Punch with a nickel-plated spoon.

"However!" Yosuke's voice grew distorted through the microphone, and he raised a finger to regain order. Other Elixirists in the audience began to stand, shouting accusations. They were ill-tempered and loud, but Yosuke's microphone was louder. "However, if anyone should be in charge, it would be Gordy Stitser. I am certain you have heard by now how he has taken control of the Vessel and defeated the Scourge of Nations." He gestured to the small table in front of the podium where the silver chalice sat, its pearly liquid producing a haunting glow. "Therefore, it is through his permission I conduct this meeting."

Gordy didn't feel in charge of anything, and Yosuke needing his permission to conduct a meeting sounded ridiculous. But when asked who should handle the proceedings of the gathering, Gordy's mom had suggested Yosuke. It was no secret Mrs. Stitser felt betrayed by her former mentor's departure from B.R.E.W., but Yosuke had fought bravely by her side during the Potion War, and without him, the town may still be under Scourge rule.

"Let us not forget why we are here," Yosuke continued. "We need reasonable minds to mend the wounds of our Community. You have all been invited because your voices need to be heard. And those seated behind me on this panel were selected by you to represent your best interests. Please keep that in mind."

"Who agreed to allow children on the panel?" asked a frail woman with pinkish skin and blue hair. More murmuring rose from the bleachers.

"They are here because Gordy requested it," Yosuke replied. "Beyond that, they earned their right to be seated behind me; they are heroes."

Max puffed out his chest, and to Gordy's amazement, Yosuke's statement seemed to settle the crowd. But now all eyes homed in on Gordy. He nervously fiddled with the zipper of his satchel.

Priss leaned over. "Don't make it obvious, but take a hard look at that woman," she whispered in his ear. "Seem familiar to you?"

Trying his best to be inconspicuous, Gordy casually glanced toward the woman, who was squeezing back into her seat. She did seem somewhat recognizable, but she was wearing a distracting fur stole draped over her shoulders that appeared to be breathing.

"Ingrid Morphata," Priss said under her breath. "Zelda's oldest sister."

"You've got to be kidding me." Gordy felt a chill run down his spine. "Whose side is she on?"

"Zelda's," Priss replied. "Ingrid's here to make sure her sister receives a fair trial, and she's heard all about you."

"Just what I need!" Gordy groaned. "Another enemy."

Did Ingrid Morphata work exclusively in explosives like her sister?

Priss smirked. "You worry too much. Ingrid's a subpar Elixirist at best. She would never dare square off with the great Gordy Stitser."

With no further interruptions, Yosuke stated the first order of business. The town needed to be memory-wiped. Almost half the neighborhoods surrounding the middle school were filled with Blotched citizens, and some were beginning to remember bits and pieces of how they had been abducted by strange, bottle-throwing criminals. After some deliberation, it was agreed that Scheel Abboud and Nestor Wax would jointly head up the Purging Committee. Many Elixirists volunteered to assist, and the De-Blotching and subsequent Memory-Erasing of all citizens would commence directly after the meeting.

Gordy glanced at Max. His best friend had brought snacks and passed Gordy a package of red licorice.

"When's lunch?" Max asked, leaning across Adilene.

Gordy checked his phone. "Since we just started, I think it might be awhile."

"Lame," Max grumbled. "I hope I make it on the Hunting Down Committee."

"The what?" Adilene glanced up and adjusted her new pair of prescription-strength eyeglasses.

After they left the football stadium, Gordy and his mother, along with the help of a few others, had harnessed the power of the Vessel to reverse some of the effects of

Adilene's waning eyesight. It didn't cure everything, but the improvement was immediate. After that, Adilene's parents took her to a regular optometrist. She said she was having a hard time getting used to wearing glasses, but Gordy thought they made her look older.

"What committee are you talking about?" Adilene asked.

Max ripped off a hunk of taffy with his teeth. "The one that scours the countryside, bringing Scourges to justice," he said in his best movie-announcer voice.

"There's no way you'll be allowed to join that," Sasha chimed in.

"Why not?" Max chomped noisily. "I'm pretty sure I've taken down more Scourges than most Elixirists in this audience combined."

Adilene scoffed.

Gordy shrugged. "He has a point." His best friend had seen his fair share of action in the past year.

"Don't encourage him," Adilene said.

Max gave Gordy a confident nod and extended his hand for a fist bump.

The rest of the morning progressed slowly as the gathering had many issues to discuss.

How to remove evidences of the Potion War?

What location should become the Vessel's permanent residence?

How to handle the captured prisoners?

To no one's surprise, the issue of what to do with those

Elixirists recently ExSponged caused the greatest outburst from the audience. Those from B.R.E.W. demanded a restoration of powers for their fallen associates, while most from the Swigs believed the punishment seemed justified on account of the Chamber Members' previous behavior.

In the end, the decision was made that each ExSponged Elixirist would be presented at a future date in front of a jury of their peers to determine their fate. This news did not sit well with Sasha, who desperately wanted her mother's powers restored. She almost stormed out of the gymnasium, but Gordy convinced her to stay.

"She was the Chamber President!" Sasha hissed, choking back tears. "And now she'll stand trial? A trial for what?"

"I made you a promise," Gordy said. "We'll make it right for your mom."

"The final order of business!" Yosuke's voice boomed, snapping Gordy's attention to the podium. "A decision must be made on what to do with B.R.E.W."

This was why most of the Elixirists had come to the meeting. Yosuke and the others seated beside Gordy had all agreed that morning that no matter the outcome of the other topics, the issue of B.R.E.W. would have to be settled before the meeting was adjourned. It was too important to postpone. The future of B.R.E.W. impacted every Elixirist for better or for worse. But with the audience teeming with equal numbers of both supporters and opposers, Gordy had no idea how that would work.

"It is proposed by this committee that B.R.E.W., from this day forward, be dissolved," Yosuke stated.

A collective gasp echoed through the crowd. A few Elixirists applauded, but that petered out almost at once. No one knew how to respond to Yosuke's statement.

"Dissolved?" The tall, imposing Elixirist from B.R.E.W. sprang from his seat. "Meaning?"

"Meaning it will be no more," Yosuke replied calmly.

Several representatives from the Swigs began nodding in agreement. Gordy watched as they shook hands with each other, pleased with this latest development.

"That is preposterous!" exclaimed a fair-skinned woman with blonde hair and wearing a white pantsuit. She appeared ready to leap from the top bleacher all the way down to the gymnasium floor. "You've Blotched the committee members!"

"I have done no such thing, and I am not finished speaking!" For the first time, Yosuke appeared angered by the outbursts. "As of this day forward, the Swigs will also be terminated. The entrances sealed, the storefronts closed, and the memberships revoked."

Those previously celebrating had their gleeful expressions instantly erased. Many more rose to their feet, pointing and accusing.

Gordy felt certain that vials of volatile chemicals would soon be flung from the stands. Things had gotten ugly in a hurry. He looked desperately up at Yosuke, who remained composed, his mustache twitching as he itched his nostril.

Then, with a flick of his finger, Yosuke signaled to Tobias seated at the end of the row, and thunder crackled in the gymnasium.

The arguments were stifled as all eyes peered up at the ceiling at the dense storm cloud forming near the rafters. Gordy could smell rain, and the hairs on his arms began to prickle with electricity.

Pooling upon a long, pewter tray at Tobias's feet was a mixture of green-and-gold sludge, bubbling with agitation.

"If you don't want to be soaked, I suggest you sit down and listen, friends," Tobias shouted. He sprinkled a few unrecognizable herbs into his concoction, and the overhead cloud rumbled.

"Thank you, Tobias." Yosuke smiled curtly at the Irishman as pattering raindrops began to fall, clinking against the metal guardrails of the bleachers. He turned to address the crowd.

"There will be no more need for underground trading. With the dissolvement of B.R.E.W. and the Swigs, we usher in a new union! Without structure, our Community will fall into chaos. That was Mezzarix's way, but it is not our way." Yosuke gave Gordy a sidelong glance and winked. "For that reason, we have decided to share all decisions involving the Vessel equally. The new leadership announced today will be Paulina Hasselbeck, Goldie Greta, Tobias McFarland, and Bolter Farina."

Though still unsettled by Tobias's storm potion, a few dissenters in the crowd voiced their opposition of the new leadership, but most of the Elixirists seemed satisfied by the decision. Bolter and Goldie both had been loyal to B.R.E.W., while Tobias and Paulina had held the Swigs as their top priority. It was the perfect match. An equal pairing.

Yosuke's middle ground.

Gordy smiled at Bolter. Despite having learned of the committee's decision the previous evening to make him a leader, Bolter looked uncomfortable as he eyed the massive throng of his peers.

"Before we conclude, I would like to propose a slight change to our decision." Yosuke's voice hushed the crowd, punctuated by a blinding flash of lightning. "Ah, Tobias, I think it is safe to put an end to your potion for the moment. Please."

Tobias's cheeks reddened as he dropped a damp dishcloth over the platter, bringing the storm to a simmer. The cloud dispersed, and a faint rainbow appeared, dipping behind the basketball standard.

"Nice touch," Yosuke said, smiling.

Tobias offered a slight shrug.

"As I was saying," Yosuke continued. "While the four selected are certainly qualified to govern, not all verdicts will be easy. Some decisions may seem impossible to determine, resulting in a tie."

Gordy's brow furrowed. He had been present during the voting for the members, but this was a new development.

"Therefore, I would like to nominate Gordy Stitser as the fifth member of the leadership."

Silence engulfed the gymnasium.

Then Max suddenly erupted, whooping and waving his fist in the air as though he had just won the lottery. Adilene leaped up and wrestled Max back into his seat.

"I have already received his parents' permission," Yosuke said. "Though he is highly qualified due to his extensive skill demonstrated in the field, because of his age and lack of formal experience in governing, perhaps it would be best if this nomination be voted upon by everyone in attendance."

Gordy wanted to protest, but he didn't have the voice to put a stop to Yosuke's madness. Looking at his mother in desperation, he was shocked to see her smiling at him, nodding reassuringly. Eagerly leaning forward in the seat next to Wanda, Aunt Priss appeared ready to burst with excitement. Before Gordy knew it, Elixirists distributed ballots into the audience, and the vote was cast.

51

Adilene stepped around a crowd that was arguing over the final announcements. She ducked to avoid a clobbering from a tall, dark-skinned man wearing tiny basketball shorts who was waving his arms and gesturing wildly. Adilene wasn't sure which side the man represented, but he wasn't happy. Most in the group weren't. She wasn't certain whether they were upset about the dissolvement of B.R.E.W. and the Swigs or by the newly called members of the leadership. Whatever the case, Adilene couldn't believe what Yosuke had just said. Gordy might end up as one of the main Elixirists in charge. She was excited for her friend, but Gordy looked positively ill.

Right after Yosuke had opened the floor for voting, Wanda and Priscilla ushered Gordy to a corner for a private conversation. Adilene would have loved to hear what they were talking about, and she couldn't wait to smother Gordy with a massive hug, but for now, she would have to wait.

Plugging her nose and gasping for breath, Adilene

pressed through the crowd, trying not to gag from the overwhelming scents of spices and herbs permeating the air. Max didn't seem affected by the smells. With half a strand of red licorice protruding from his mouth, he elbowed his way into the center of a conversation between Paulina Hasselbeck and the grisly-looking Scheel.

Sasha had vanished. Adilene suspected she had gone home, and she felt horrible about how things had turned out. Still, Adilene had her own issues to address. Politely brushing past elbows, Adilene made eye contact with her target and picked up her pace.

Yosuke lingered behind the podium, engaged in a one-sided conversation with the argumentative woman wearing the fur stole. She brandished her crinkled ballot under Yosuke's nose as though trying to sell him an expensive bottle of perfume. When he noticed Adilene closing in, Yosuke politely excused himself from his discussion and smiled warmly at her.

"Hello there," Yosuke said, bowing to Adilene.

"Mr. Nakamura?" Adilene's heart raced. "May I speak with you for a moment?"

"Please!" He motioned toward a pair of folding chairs and turned his back on the woman. Though she harrumphed with annoyance, she immediately stormed away to argue with someone else. "My name is not Mr. Nakamura, by the way," Yosuke insisted. "Certainly not to my friends. You may call me Yosuke. It is Ms. Adilene Rivera, am I correct?"

"That's right." Adilene took her seat and adjusted her glasses. They felt like a pesky horsefly permanently perched on the bridge of her nose, but at least she could read again without every word blurring together in a garbled mess. Though she had been allowed to join Gordy with Max and Sasha on the committee, she and Max hadn't been present during the secret meetings throughout the week. This was the first time Adilene had been able to speak with Yosuke. The old man seemed kind but incredibly intimidating. "I'm Gordy's friend."

"Oh, of course! But you are more than just a friend, from what I hear." His eyes twinkled. "You are Gordy's trusted lab partner and faithful companion. It is an honor to officially meet you. Now, what do you wish to discuss?"

Adilene felt as though every pair of eyes had suddenly whirled to stare at her. Now that she had Yosuke's ear, she was terrified to ask her questions.

"I assure you, I will not snap your head off," Yosuke said, crossing his legs and steepling his fingers at his chest. "Please do not be nervous. Let us talk. I sense you have many urgent concerns."

Adilene swallowed. "I do. Back at Gordy's, when we were attacked by Esmeralda Faustus, something happened."

Yosuke nodded. "You are referring to when Ms. Faustus ExSponged Iris Glass?"

"Well, when she swung her wand, I . . ." Adilene cast a wary eye at a group of nearby Elixirists, making sure they were minding their own business. "It hit me first." She rubbed her shoulder, indicating the spot struck by Esmeralda's weapon. "And I felt something change inside me."

Yosuke raised an eyebrow. "How so?"

"Is it possible that when Esmeralda ExSponged Iris, some of her potion-making ability transferred to me?" The question had been plaguing Adilene all week, and now that she had finally asked it, she felt exhausted. She wanted so desperately for it to be true.

"Hmm . . . a transfer? Interesting." He stroked his chin with his long fingers, eyes closing in thought.

Adilene held her breath, her pulse quickening.

Yosuke bowed his head solemnly, and her spirits plummeted. "It is not possible," he said with a deep sigh. "No one has ever transferred their ability by ExSpongement or any other means. It cannot happen."

"It can't?" Choking back tears, Adilene willed herself to keep control in front of the master Elixirist. "Are you sure?"

"I am. When Esmeralda performed the ExSpongement on Iris, she lost her powers. It is not as though the Decocting Wand absorbed her ability, so to speak. It was simply blocked. This is the method behind an ExSpongement. If our leadership deems Iris worthy of restoration, the block will be lifted, and her ability will return."

"I see," Adilene said, her throat dry.

"Why is this a concern of yours?" Yosuke asked.

Adilene shook her head. "It . . . It's nothing. I just thought maybe I could do more now." She looked across the gymnasium to where Gordy sat, head in his hands, waiting to learn his fate, as his mother rubbed his shoulders.

Adilene knew most of the votes had already been tallied, which meant Gordy might become even more powerful, while she would remain as plain as always. She didn't want to be jealous. Adilene wanted to be happy for him, but it was hard now that she knew the truth.

"I do not understand. What do you mean by this 'more'?" Yosuke tapped Adilene's hand with his finger.

"I mean, I wish I wasn't so . . . normal. Just some tool that Gordy and Sasha are able to Project through."

Yosuke's eyes narrowed with skepticism. "Project?"

"Yeah, you know when an Elixirist uses another—"

"I am aware of what it means," he replied. "Almost every Elixirist has heard about that myth."

"Right, exactly. That's what . . ." Adilene blinked, suddenly confused. "Did you just say 'myth'?"

"I did." Yosuke nodded. "Because that is what it is."

Adilene frowned. "I don't understand."

"It is a myth. Projecting was disproved years ago by B.R.E.W. The practice does not work, has never worked, and I cannot see how it would ever work."

"But Sasha told me that Gordy Projected through me like I was some sort of Bunsen burner!" Adilene raised her voice. How could it be a myth? She had seen potions working by her hand because of someone Projecting through her.

"We are talking about Sasha Brexil, correct?" Yosuke raised another eyebrow. "Interesting girl, but not the brightest, I suppose. And I just told you that no one's potion-making ability can be transferred to another by any means. Either you are the instrument, or you are not. There is no in between."

Adilene covered her mouth, catching her breath. "I brewed a potion on the island all by myself," she said, squeezing her fingers together into fists and speaking rapidly. "Sasha didn't help me, because she couldn't. Her hands were clamped in these metal gloves, so I added all the ingredients and performed all the steps and made a Moholi Mixture that broke us out of prison."

Yosuke clapped his hands softly. "Well done! That's a basic potion for first-year Drams but still tricky to master. I assumed you were limited in your ingredients because there are dozens of other draughts you could have used as a more effective means of escape."

"Are you saying I actually brewed the potion all on my own?" Adilene stood abruptly.

"*You* just said that!" Yosuke answered, chuckling in confusion.

"I know, I know! But are you confirming that I'm an actual Dram?"

Yosuke's nose crinkled as he half scowled, half smiled. "Was there any question that you weren't?"

"I'm too old!" Adilene shouted, and several Elixirists turned, noticing her excitement. "I thought you couldn't become a Dram once you became a teenager."

Yosuke puffed out his cheeks, scratching the back of his head and ruffling his long black hair. "It is rare, but it happens from time to time. I apologize. I assumed since you were Gordy's lab partner, you were already considered a Dram. There are tests that will confirm it, but—"

Before she could stop herself, Adilene threw her arms around Yosuke's neck. She heard his muffled laughter and the appalled murmur from several Elixirists close by, but Adilene didn't care. Not one bit.

CHAPTER

52

I can't do this!" Gordy exclaimed, cornering Yosuke as the gathering dispersed for lunch. "There's no way I can be a leader!"

"Seventy-two percent of the vote disagrees with you," Yosuke replied, eyes beaming with delight.

"But I can't. I . . . I have school!"

"Which you should continue to attend, though I do believe you'll finish the eighth grade in another building." The old man's eyes drifted toward the crumbling ceiling. "The reconstruction plans for Kipland Middle will be quite extensive."

"How can I be in charge and still be a kid?" Gordy had been looking forward to spending his weekends playing video games with Max and brewing in his lab with Adilene. Not governing and lawmaking and Banishing. Those were adult decisions.

Yosuke clicked his tongue. "You are the fifth member, only called upon when necessity demands it. That may not happen for many, many months. Maybe never." He raised his eyebrows encouragingly, but his tone suggested otherwise.

Gordy felt as though he had just swallowed a Funnel Formula and his insides were being spun into a knot.

Yosuke snickered. "You and your friends—always so grim. Gordy, your days will not be spent in lawmaking unless you choose them to be. You can have a normal life. Well, as normal as one can having been so involved with the Vessel. There is no denying your impact on our Community already."

"But why not you or my mom or . . . or even Sasha?" If they had to pick a kid to sit on this new Board of Directors or Chamber or whatever they were going to call it, Sasha seemed like the most willing.

"I cannot return to my old position, and I believe Wanda feels the same way." Yosuke gazed piercingly into Gordy's eyes. "Our ways are not the ways of today. We represent the old B.R.E.W. and the old Swigs. You represent the future. And are we talking about Sasha Brexil?" His tone lightened. "I am sure she is a lovely friend, but previous conversations have led me to believe granting her legislative rights would be a decision most unwise."

The last of the Elixirists filed through the door, and the tantalizing scents of lunch filled the room, but Gordy wasn't ready to mingle just yet.

Yosuke noticed Gordy's hesitation. "I see that you will not be consoled so easily. But perhaps this will help. There are four essential elements to a potion—liquid, mineral, chemical, and herb—and in order to brew anything of merit, each must be present. This new organization is just another potion that requires specific ingredients. That is why four were chosen to represent those elements. This was not by mere happenstance. You understand this, right?"

Gordy nodded somberly, remembering all that Zelda had taught him not so long ago.

"But what if I told you that way of thinking was incomplete?" Yosuke asked. "That in order to truly brew, an additional element is not only required but paramount to the successful completion of that potion?"

Gordy glanced up, puzzled. "What additional element?"

Yosuke chuckled, his laughter pouring out soothingly. "The Elixirist, my boy. That is the missing piece. The one combining all the other elements into an intricate concoction. The one whose wisdom brings balance to every potion." Yosuke squeezed Gordy's shoulder warmly. "You are that final element, Gordy Stitser. *You* are the Elixirist!"

EPILOGUE

Frothy liquid effervesced within a brass cauldron as indigo smoke drifted away from the bowl and gathered around the light fixture in Adilene's bedroom, casting wispy shadows upon the floor. Referring to the recipe printed in Gordy's handwriting, Adilene reduced the heat of her Bunsen burner and sprinkled a handful of ginger wax pieces into the turbulent mixture. The inside of the cauldron had turned the color of raspberry syrup.

Adilene's walkie-talkie squawked.

"How's it going?" Gordy's voice came through the static.

She clenched her fists, jaw tightening. "I think it's going great, but you seriously just scared me to death."

"Sorry!" Gordy apologized. "I'm curious, that's all."

"I know, but I'm a little tense right now." Adilene peered into the cauldron as a purple bubble filled with air, then popped. She checked the recipe once more.

One ingredient remained. One final step. And then she would know without a doubt.

"Are you done yet, Rivera?" Max's voice bellowed from the walkie-talkie, and Adilene's guinea pig, Irene, chittered angrily inside her cage.

"No, I am not done, Maxwell." Adilene squeezed the radio hard enough to make the plastic receiver crinkle. "But I'm close."

So close!

Closing her eyes, Adilene peeled off the lid of the small container of timbo snake scales and made one final pass over the recipe, making sure she hadn't missed any steps.

"I'm signing off," she said, gripping the walkie-talkie. "I have to know what I'm doing is on my own and that Gordy isn't somehow Projecting through the radio."

"Yosuke told you that was a myth," Gordy said.

"And I want to believe him," she muttered. "But this way I'll know for sure. Okay?"

"Got it," Gordy replied.

"Yeah, whatever," Max grumbled.

The walkie-talkie fell silent.

Adilene waited for a moment, then dashed the pinch of scales across the surface of the mixture. Holding her breath, she leaned across the rim. The rising smoke dispersed.

The potion, no longer a frothy violet, had settled within the cauldron. Thick and glossy, shimmering like an antique mirror, the concoction now possessed a faint emerald hue.

Adilene released a long, satisfied breath.

Then she smiled.

ACKNOWLEDGMENTS

It's hard to believe this story is already coming to an end, and I'm so thankful for the family, friends, and publishing professionals who made this trilogy a reality. It has been a dream of mine, many years in the making, to work with Chris Schoebinger, and I've loved every minute of it. There's not a creative team in the industry that rallies behind an author quite like the Shadow Mountain crew. A huge thank you to Lisa Mangum, my editor, and Heidi Taylor Gordon. Our brainstorming sessions for Potion Masters were the stuff of legends. Gordy Stitser owes a massive chunk of his story to both of you!

To Owen Richardson, my illustrator. I don't think you understand how high up on the awesomeness pedestal I've placed you. Your illustrations of my Potion Masters novels are simply the best. I hope we get many more opportunities to work together on future projects.

I'm so grateful for my agent, Shannon Hassan, for having such enthusiasm about my work, pushing me to be a better writer, and just making good things happen for my books.

To Laurel Day, Jill Schaugaard, Callie Hansen, and Roberta Stout—thank you for your help in sending me on my author tour. Being able to chat with readers at schools and feed off their enthusiasm has fueled my writing fire, and it wouldn't have been possible without you.

I would be nothing at all without my wife, Heidi, and my amazing children, Jackson, Gavin, and Camberlyn. You guys put up with a lot, especially when I'm elbow-deep in a writing project. You're the best, and I love you!

Thank you to Amanda Sowards, Michelle Wilson, Tyler Minson, and Jaric Minson for helping me come up with some really awesome potion ideas for this book!

Lastly, to all the readers who started this journey with Gordy when he was nothing more than a slug monster in his living room. I hope you've enjoyed being part of this adventure as much as I have enjoyed writing it. There will be more books for sure, so stay tuned. I can't wait for you to read the next one!

GLOSSARY OF POTIONS

A compendium of both approved and unapproved potions and ingredients, as well as common terms used throughout the potion-making community. Locations in italics pinpoint the exact source of where, B.R.E.W.'s most-elite Elixirists have worked tirelessly to discover key ingredients to their respective potions.

Barnstorm Broth—*United States of America, Michigan.* A complicated fusion potion that melds the essence of multiple birds with complex machinery. There have been only three successful attempts to concoct a successful Barnstorm Broth in B.R.E.W.'s history. (Key ingredients: albatross egg yolk; jet fuel; wild-cherry Pop Rocks.)

Blitzen Beads—*Germany.* When thrown, these marble-sized pellets cause disorientation and temporary blindness without permanently damaging the target's eyes. (Key ingredients: cuckoo talons; glass from a busted lighthouse bulb.)

Cepha Slop—*Georgia.* A favorite among uncivilized Scourges, this mixture, combined with Essence of Ampliar, produces a fully-functioning, albeit ill-tempered, cephalopod-type creature that will instantly attack any foe. (Key ingredients: blowhole of a bottlenose dolphin; lion's mane mushroom caps; fossilized trilobite.)

Choresine—*New Guinea.* Toxic chemical harvested from the shells of melyrid beetles. Primary ingredient in concocting powerful home Distractor wards.

Decocting Wand—*Origin varies.* Outlawed by B.R.E.W., this weapon, etched with chemically enhanced runes, is used to ExSponge an Elixirist. Though the effects are reversible, often the ExSponged are never able to brew quite the same. Any Elixirist caught in possession of a Decocting Wand faces immediate Banishment to a Forbidden Zone. (Key ingredients: papaya pulp; trigger hairs of a Venus flytrap.)

Dissolvement Draught—*Chile*. Also known as a Borrar Bomb, this corrosive goop is used to break down substances believed to be indestructible. (Key ingredients: cobra hoods; epizootic egg.)

Essence of Ampliar—*Spain*. An enlargement tonic used to increase the size of small creatures—mostly bugs, amphibians, and some rodents. Overall growth may vary and is not permanent, but creatures typically react violently to the sudden change. (Key ingredients: processionary caterpillar pupa; baskian viper hearts.)

Forbidden Zones—Term used throughout the Elixirist Community to describe areas of Exile and Banishment. Though arctic tundra regions are the most common due to the bleak nature of their locations, barren deserts, remote islands, and arid wastelands have also been utilized when sending condemned Scourges to live out the remaining years of their existence.

Girning Glop—*United Kingdom*. An unusual concoction once used ages ago during playful competitions in rural England. The glop causes a ridiculous expression to instantly appear on the consumer's face. The potion is mostly harmless but has been known to result in permanent, undesired facial expressions when administered in heavy doses. (Key ingredients: Japanese plum pits; melted latex mask.)

Glowworm oil—*Australia*. An odorless and tasteless substance produced by fungus gnats and used to unmask those who have ingested Disfarcar Gels or other brewed disguises.

Iskry powder—*Ukraine*. A tiny pinch of this fire-starting substance will ignite dry timber into an impressive flame. (Key ingredients: vanilla bean; horse whiskers.)

Jackjoint Juice—*United States of America, California*. Opalescent substance used by Elixirist spies to easily slip through tight, inaccessible spaces by temporarily turning their joints into rubbery pulp. (Key ingredients: recently-deflated balloon animal; chimpanzee hairs.)

Joslat Juice—*Hungary*. Dream-inducing potion believed by many within the Swigs to fortell the future. Most predictions, however, have not been substantially proven to be true. Frowned upon by B.R.E.W.'s Chamber of Directors. (Key ingredients: sandalwood; warped forint coin.)

Konfizyon Cream—*Haiti.* A milder technique than Tainting, this cream places the target into a blissful hypnotic state. (Key ingredients: pungi reed pipe; Caribbean reef squid tentacle; limestone granules.)

Luminescent Lamps—*Origin varies.* Typically pink or fluorescent yellow in color, these clever concoctions, once agitated, can glow for several hours, lighting up hallways, caverns, and broom closets. Also known as Jarqil Candles or Vofa Votives depending on the region. (Key ingredients: swallowtail butterfly scales; firefly thorax; star-fruit juice.)

Mezzarix's Manifesto—*No More Prisons. No More Governments. No More Secrets.* Printed on pamphlets and widely distributed during Mezzarix Rook's first attempt to overthrow B.R.E.W., his Manifesto rallied many Elixirists to his cause.

Moholi Mixture—*South Africa.* Basic melting potion used to reduce metal to vapor. Also an excellent Scruting substitute when Quicksilver is unavailable. All first-year Drams must master a Moholi Mixture before continuing on with the program. (Key ingredients: bronze fennel; flower chafer beetles; proteas flower petals.)

Mureta Mush—*Finland.* Pulverizing potion that effectively reduces lumber into sawdust. The perfect tool for boring a quick getaway through solid-wood walls or flooring. (Key ingredients: black woodpecker bills; heated vulcanite sauna stones.)

Perplexity Projectile—*United States of America, Ohio.* This explosive, crowd-controlling potion will place large groups of people in a hypnotic stupor. B.R.E.W. typically uses these projectiles whenever Rule #1 of the Five Rules of Potion Making has been broken and a gathering of non-Elixirists start asking questions. (Key ingredients: black-eyed susan stalks; muskellunge gills.)

Potable Penyiram—*Indonesia.* When tossed upon fertile soil, this egg-shaped tablet will form a pair of functioning watering cans from which a seemingly endless deluge of water will pour. (Key ingredients: hole-in-the-head frog tongue; powdered pumice; stem of a titan arum plant.)

Seeking Serum—*Origin unknown.* Better than GPS, this ultimate tracking potion, when brewed to perfection, can pinpoint the location of any desired target no matter how far away the location. (Key ingredients: dousing rod; pickled piranha scales.)

Smoke of Unmocita Kara—*Bangladesh*. Revelatory incense that will reflect the true identity of an intruder through a specially treated mirror. The smoke is dangerous if burned for prolonged periods of time and banned by B.R.E.W. (Key ingredients: sputtered aluminum; Bengal tiger dander.)

Society of Canadian Agro-Healers—A well-respected organization made up of multiple high-ranking B.R.E.W. officials, SCAH has made it their sole aim to educate non-Elixirist doctors and medical practitioners about herbal remedies and ingredients available in every region of the world.

Sturmwolke Slosh—*Germany*. A highly illegal storm-creating potion able to be launched directly into the atmosphere. It is almost impossible to know what sort of catastrophes the slosh will produce, though certain Elixirists have developed a knack for predicting the weather. (Key ingredients: shrew whiskers; badger fangs; Bavarian orchid roots.)

Sumi Sauce—*Macedonia*. An effective weapon to eliminate a target without causing bodily harm. This concoction catapults an enemy toward the nearest growth of vegetation. (Key ingredients: Ajvarski pepper zest; Eurasian lynx bladder.)

Tainting—The process of tampering or coating an object with Stained ingredients in order to Blotch an unsuspecting Elixirist. (Key ingredients: passionflower; ant pheromones; tungsten shavings; sulphured molasses.)

Terramoto Tonic—*Mexico*. This volatile potion can cause catastrophic damage as it simulates earthquakes through seismic vibrations. (Key ingredients: Kadupul seeds; tectonic silicon; mountain-quail beak.)

Tickling Tinik—*Philippines*. Horribly deceptive, this substance starts off as a harmless itch but rapidly transforms into one of the world's most uncomfortable irritants. The only known remedy is a dose of ampalaya rind. (Key ingredients: ulupong venom; hogweed pollen.)